MOON SHADOW

/ / / /

J.R. RAIN

THE VAMPIRE FOR HIRE SERIES

Published by
Crop Circle Books
212 Third Crater, Moon

Printed in the United States of America.

ISBN: 978-1548800765

Dedication
To Jason and Alberto.
You two clowns make life interesting.

Acknowledgment
A special thank you to Mariah! Welcome aboard!

1.

I was missing *Judge Judy*, and I wasn't happy about it.

Instead, I was being treated to a ninety-nine-cent cup of coffee at a McDonald's in a city called Lake Elsinore, which boasts the biggest natural lake in Southern California. The problem with Lake Elsinore is that it's in Lake Elsinore. One has to drive out of Orange County (where I happily live) through 60 miles of desert (where I had no business living), and there, shimmering like a mirage, is an honest-to-God lake. It sits at the foot of a mountain chain called, inexplicably, the Cleveland National Forest.

The city of Lake Elsinore is rough around the edges. It sports a downtown that feels forgotten and dismal. It also sports a lot of homes that have beautiful views of the lake, homes that look just as dismal and forgotten. Which is strange. In Southern California, any home with any sort of water view, be it a beach, lake, pond, inlet, outlet, river, stream or reservoir, is worth, exactly, ten million dollars. Give or take.

But not here. In Lake Elsinore, homes with a lake view seem to be an afterthought. In fact, one gets the impression that the residents of Lake Elsinore don't fully appreciate the beauty of the lake—or the sheer unlikeliness that such a body of water would be out here anyway. Had this lake been in, say, Orange County, lakeside restaurants with shaded patios would abound, and so would storefronts boasting designer doggie treats. In no time flat, had this lake been in Orange County, few people would actually have access to the lake... unless they paid for it.

The man sitting across from me was Roy Azul. He was the owner and operator of a group of vacation cabins along the west side of the lake. He was also friends with Detective Sherbet. When I asked how he knew Sherbet, Roy explained that he and the detective were part of a model aircraft flying club. I made a mental note to ridicule Sherbet about that. Then added a follow-up note to make sure I did so to no end.

"Sherbet said you could help me."

"Sherbet is paid to say that—in greasy pink donuts, no less."

"He also said you could be sassy, and that you would mention the pink donuts."

"Maybe Sherbet is a mentalist," I said. "Whatever that is."

Roy was dressed in cargo shorts and a black t-shirt, wearing one of those old-school paperboy, duck-billed caps that I think are actually cute. Roy looked good in the hat. Then again, most everyone did. In particular, Roy looked relaxed, calm, and excited to talk about whatever was on his mind. Sherbet wouldn't tell me details. Sherbet had called yesterday and said he had a job for me, if I wanted it. He only told me that it wasn't another cheating spouse case and that I should get a kick out of it. Sure, I could have plumbed Sherbet's mind—even through a phone line—but I let him have his fun and his little secret.

So here I was, in the back of beyond, sitting across from a lake no one seemed to care about. His "fun" had cost me my afternoon and a half-tank of gas. Not to mention, I had to make arrangements with Mary Lou to pick up my kids. That is, if Tammy even finished school today. These days, she missed more classes than she attended, and was proving to be a major pain in my ass.

"Thank you for meeting me," he said. "I know you came from Orange County, but Sherbet thought it would be important for you to see the scene of the crime, so to speak."

"Sherbet seems to have this all figured out."

"Not exactly. When I told him about it, he only laughed. Most people laugh, which is why I quit talking about it. Except now, I've seen it twice—

and both times after I'd seen it, someone in town went missing."

"Okay," I said. "This just got a little more interesting."

"Sherbet says that you sort of specialize in the strange and the unusual. The Queen of Strange, he called you, actually."

"Did he now?"

"I don't think he meant any harm by it. He said it sort of, I dunno, endearingly."

"Well, as long as it was said endearingly. So how can I help you, Mr. Azul?"

"Please, call me Roy."

Yes, I could have dipped into his mind, but I decided not to. At least, not yet. These days, I dip into minds when needed, and, in turn, kept mine mostly locked up. No more accidental telepathy for me, thank you very much. In fact, the less often I used my powers, and the more often I embraced my humanity, the more the demon within me lay dormant. No, she wasn't really a demon—more of a highly evolved dark master who'd been banished from Earth by forces much greater than her. Or me. Except she—and others like her—had figured out a loophole back into Earth. The loophole? The possession of others. And possession by such powerful forces led to vampirism, lycanthropy, and other supernatural oddities.

And, yes, I was a supernatural oddity.

Anyway, she liked for me to read the thoughts of others; she liked for me to control others, to use my great strength, to hurt and kill and destroy. Mostly, she liked when I fed on others. Oh, yes. She really, really liked when I fed on others. Human blood gave her strength and boldness. It gave her, in fact, the ability to control me, too. But no more. Now, I'd learned to use my powers sparingly. To fly sparingly. To use my telepathy sparingly.

But most of all—which frustrated her to no end —I quit feeding on humans. Live humans, dead humans. Any human.

All of which had weakened her and reduced her to nothing more than a very bad memory. But she was still there, waiting in the shadows of my mind, waiting for me to screw things up, waiting for me to let her in through that cracked door. What happened once she got in, I didn't know. But Samantha Moon, as I know her to be, as I know myself to be, might just cease to exist altogether.

"How can I help you, Roy?"

He looked at me. I looked at him. He seemed about to speak, thought better of it, then shut his mouth. I nearly gave him a telepathic prompt to start speaking, but I waited. Patience was good for the soul.

He nodded to himself, clearly conflicted, then steeled himself, looked at me, and said, "Do you believe in monsters, Ms. Moon?"

2.

"Call me Sam, and why do you ask?"

His hesitancy returned. I might have shot him a "Go on" prompt, but I'd never admit to it. Finally, he said, "Well, if you laugh at me, you wouldn't be the first. Even Sherbet had a chuckle or two. Or five."

I waited. McDonald's smelled like McDonald's: grease and potatoes and frying meat, coffee and recently mopped floors. Two kids were running in circles around their mother. One of the kids stopped and stared at me, then continued running, although flashing me furtive glances. I get that sometimes: kids who just somehow *know*.

"Okay, here goes," said Roy.

"The anticipation is killing me," I said.

"Really?"

"No. Spill the beans, unless you want me to

wrestle it out of you. Be warned, I give wicked noogies."

He chuckled. "You're right. I'm making it bigger than it is, I guess. Weirder than it has to be. Okay, here goes: I'm pretty sure—no, damn sure—that I saw a lake monster. Twice."

"Now," I said, "that is pretty big and weird."

"I knew it!"

"So to clarify, you did say *lake monster* and not *late mobster*. As in the ghost of Al Capone?"

"Correct, *lake monsters*. As in Loch Ness, I guess."

"I think I would have preferred you'd seen Al Capone."

"Honestly? Me, too. This thing has really rocked my world."

"Okay," I said. "I guess we're really doing this. Tell me about the lake monster."

And so he did, and somehow, kept a straight face while doing so. The first sighting had been two weeks ago, when the first young boy had disappeared. Yes, I'd heard about the missing boys. They had disappeared a week apart—and each was still missing. In fact, a part of me was not very surprised when Sherbet had sent me out to Lake Elsinore. The city had been in the news, and I would have bet good money that the case would have been tied to the missing boys. Not lake monsters.

Moving on. Roy told me that he had just finished giving his cabin guests a tour of the lake— Roy, in fact, ran the only lake tour in town. Roy was busy tying up the boat for the evening... when the hair on the back of his neck stood on end... followed by a feeling of being watched. He turned, and spotted a strange ripple in the water. And there, just beneath the surface, was a dark shape. A shadow, he called it. A very, very long shadow. It circled around the prow of his boat, then went under the dock itself. He didn't know for sure, but then he watched it turn to starboard. Then the shadow headed out for deeper water... and that was it.

I studied his aura: bluish with splashes of yellow. He was telling the truth. Or, at least, what he believed was the truth.

"How long?"

"Longer than my boat. Maybe thirty feet."

"What time of day was this?"

"Evening. It was the last tour. It was getting dark, but there was still enough light to see."

"How long would you say you saw it?"

"Twenty... thirty seconds."

"And you've never seen anything like that before?"

"Hell, no. And I've lived in Elsinore all my life. Been boating on it all my life, too. Seen nothing like it."

I nodded, picked up the McCup and took another McSip of the McCoffee. It tasted McHeavenly. I said, "Is that about when the first boy went missing?"

He nodded, looking scared and foolish and desperate. "Disappeared that night."

I nodded. "Tell me about the second incident."

He did. The incident took place about the same time, early evening. This time Roy was out fishing with a longtime customer. The lake had been flat, like smoky glass, as he recalled. His customer had been digging around in the cooler for a beer when the entire boat suddenly lurched, Roy nearly dropping his pole. He leaned forward, looking over the rail, just as the massive shadow rushed underneath. His guess: the thing was going about sixty knots.

"I assume that's fast?" I said.

"Almost seventy miles an hour."

And I almost said he could have omitted the 'almost' and just said seventy miles an hour, but I kept my mouth shut. "And your friend didn't see it?" I asked.

"You blink and you miss it."

"Because it was going seventy knots."

"Right."

"Did you tell him about it?"

"I did."

"What did he say?"

"He said he felt the bump but saw nothing. He figured it was probably floating debris or the shadow of a passing cloud overhead."

"Were there clouds that evening?"

"There were."

"And was there debris in the water?"

He hesitated. "There was, actually. A long branch floated nearby."

I nodded, and decided not to point out the logic of his friend's theory. Instead, I did what any good investigator would do who could read minds: I dipped into his thoughts. I didn't have to go very far. Right there, front and center was the shadow moving under his boat. He was right. It was a damn big shadow, and it didn't look like any tree branch or reflecting cloud formation. It looked, if anything, like a giant worm. He was telling the truth. Then again, how trustworthy was his own memory? We would see.

Roy was saying, "Ms. Moon. This was no cloud shadow or tree branch. This was huge, and it was living, and—"

"And I believe you."

"I'm not crazy, Ms. Moon. I—I'm sorry, you what?"

"I believe you."

He took in some air, exhaled, then took in a lot more. "Wow. That's... that's refreshing to hear."

"I imagine so. Have there been any other sightings?"

"A handful of people have told me they'd seen something in the water."

"How many is a handful?"

"Three or four fishermen."

"Do you have names?"

"They asked me to keep them out of it."

"Why?"

"Because of the shit I've been taking. Well, from everyone but you. But they come to me, because they feel safe talking to me."

"And they've all seen something similar?"

"All of them."

"For how long?"

"Off and on for about ten years. The oldest sighting goes back over a hundred years, though."

As he spoke, I Googled Lake Elsinore lake monsters. And, sure enough, there had been a history of such sightings. The locals called the creature Elsie. Cute.

So I wouldn't appear rude, I showed him what I was reading, and then added, "It says here the lake has dried up a few times. The sixties was the last time."

He nodded. "Right. But that didn't stop the rumors."

"I would think an empty lake would put a stop to any lake monster rumors..."

"You would think. Keep reading."

I did, scanning the various articles quickly. And there it was. Sightings of a creature emerging out of the water... and heading for the local mountains, to hide within caves, only to return when the lake was full again.

I wanted to laugh it all off. Except I wasn't laughing, even when I excused myself to get a Mc-Refill. I'd certainly seen some strange things in my time. Hell, *I* was the strange thing. And there was the long shadow in his memory. When I returned, I said, "This was a week ago?"

"Right."

"Which is when the second boy disappeared."

"That night, in fact."

Two boys missing within a week of each other was big news, and the local police chief was under a lot of pressure to find them. The FBI was here, too, working right alongside them. I'd passed two news vans along the way to this McDonald's. So far, very few clues had turned up. And, certainly, no boys had turned up.

"Does Lake Elsinore have a history of violent crime?"

He shrugged. "We have our fair share. Elsinore is a rough and tumble town. A mixture of cultures. Our downtown isn't quaint or charming. Not for tourists. It's utilitarian. It's old. It features bars and bikers and gangs and the homeless. None in great amounts. But enough to cross paths. The lake attracts weekend warriors who drink too much, fight too quickly, and keep our police busy. Someone eventually ends up dead. Usually a fight. Usually over a girl. Occasionally, we have a murder. A body shows up dead and no one knows who did it. It happens. Our city is just big enough, hot enough, and isolated enough to attract enough people who may or may not do something stupid, or angry or vengeful. Or murderous."

"So what would you like for me to do, Roy?" I asked.

"I-I really don't know, Ms. Moon."

"Please call me Sam."

"I don't know, Ms. Sam. I mean Sam. I grew up

on this lake. I've lived here my whole life. This is my home. I love this place, and I'm just so pissed off that something seems to be trying to scare me away from my home. I don't know what I want from you."

"You want answers?"

"I guess so, yes."

Crackling, agitated purple flames now coursed through his aura. He sat forward and locked and unlocked his fingers. His right knee bounced. Try as I might, I couldn't keep the flood of his agitated thoughts out of my mind. He was feeling very strongly that this was all a mistake, that I couldn't help him, being a city girl and all. He was feeling that he should have just kept his mouth shut, that his business was going to suffer, that I looked kinda cute, that I sure looked pale for a Southern Californian. He also thought that his wife would be jealous if I came around, that he liked me, that he trusted me, that I seemed competent, that I was too small, that Sherbet had spoken highly of me, that Sherbet needed to lose some weight, that the disappearances had something to do with the shadow. He thought if he could just convince someone, anyone, to help, the disappearances might stop.

I pulled out of his thoughts, and shored up my mental barrier a little longer. Thoughts were living things, strung together to form new sequences, sometimes coherent, often incoherent, especially when someone was upset. And Roy was very, very upset.

I wanted to tell him that, more than likely, the disappearances had nothing to do with the shadow, except I couldn't. Not yet. Not until I checked out his story.

"What does your wife say?"

Roy shrugged. "Not much. But she believes me, I think."

His bouncing knee had picked up its pace, and his glancing eyes had turned furtive. He was beginning to look more and more like a cornered rat. Or, more accurately, feeling more and more foolish, and so I decided to reach out with my mind, which I did now.

Relax. Breathe. Good.

His knees stopped bouncing, and he blinked long and slow. As I reached out to him telepathically, I felt a stirring from deep within. The thing within me loved when I dipped into other people's thoughts. She especially loved when I manipulated them.

"I believe you," I said.

He nodded, expelled a long stream of air that reached me from all the way across the McTable.

"You do?" he asked. "You really do?"

"I really do."

"You have no idea how relieved I am to hear that."

"I have some idea. Now, show me where you saw this thing."

3.

While I drove behind Roy, I sent a text message to Detective Sherbet's super-secret cop hotline.

Queen of Strange, huh?

Yes, texting and driving is bad. Unless, of course, you are an immortal with reflexes that even a cat would admire.

At the next light, I got his reply. I imagined his fat, sausage-like fingers picking out the words on the keypad, and giggled. He wrote: *I thought you might like that, Laugh Out Loud.*

It's LOL, Detective. You don't spell it out. I wrote back, my fingers a blur over the keypad. *And I've been called worse.*

As the light turned green, I got his next message: *What do you think of his story?*

I think he saw something.

I do, too. Roy's a good guy. Salt-of-the-earth

type. Hardworking. Nothing to gain from this.

Except some added tourism? I suggested.

Mostly he's received ridicule from friends and family. Not worth the extra coinage. Plus, he does pretty well on his own. Doesn't need bullshit like this complicating his life.

Do I complicate your life, Detective?

Just help him. And it wouldn't hurt if you looked into the missing boys.

A two-fer, I wrote. *Or a three-fer.*

Something like that. His story really checks out?

It does, Detective.

You saw it? he wrote back. *Like in his mind?*

I did, I wrote. *Like in his mind.*

So there's really something in the lake?

I think so.

Holy sweet Jesus.

Laugh out loud, I spelled out, still giggling at the detective's faux pas. *Now get back to work and quit texting. Your fingers are probably tired.*

They are, he wrote. *They really are.*

We drove past rundown strip malls nestled between newer strip malls, past old homes nestled between newer housing tracts. A lot of the city of Lake Elsinore is hilly. In fact, one hill is a doozy, and seems to divide the city in half. Upon that hill sits some bigger homes with fantastic views of the lake. The homes don't exude wealth or abundance. It's as if they just happened to be big, and just happened to be parked on the hillside.

Many of the homes sat on multiple acres of

heated, scrubby, useless land. Only the heartiest of shrubs and twisted, sad trees eked out an existence here. And all within view of this shimmering, blue lake, truly an oasis in this desert outpost.

We followed a main road that curved around the lake. Cars along here drove much too fast, as if eager to get around the big, wet shimmering road-block. I got the feeling the lake felt unappreciated.

I followed Roy's old Ford truck with its missing tailgate. I wondered how useful a truck could be with a missing tailgate. As I followed, I stole glances at the glittering surface as often as possible, appreciating the hell out of it. It was just so unlikely in this dusty, forgotten, superheated city. But there the lake was, proud and magnificent and sprawling, and just owning this place. Hard not to love and admire Elsinore's unlikely hero.

We peeled off onto a side road, then another side road, winding down closer and closer to the lake. The vegetation went from scraggly desert brush, to dense lakeside foliage. Reeds and long grasses slapped at my van. Eucalyptus trees grew in abundance. I think the proximity of the lake had something to do with that.

The road ended in a parking lot of sorts. On one side was a grouping of lakeside cabins, and on the other was a beautiful Victorian home fit for a vampire. The home was nestled among the eucalyptus trees and a smattering of oaks that seemed to have forgotten they were in a desert. I felt as if I had pulled up into another world, far removed from the baking asphalts and tailgating cars and decrepit shopping centers. I could see why Roy loved this spot, and why he never wanted to leave, and why he was seeking help. There was, I suspected, no way in hell anyone was scaring him away from this idyllic, and hidden, piece of lakefront property.

There were eight cabins in total, each painted a different color. And when the primaries ran out, the colors didn't get much more creative after that. Each sported a chimney. Walkways led from the parking lot to the cabins. The walkways were beautifully manicured, with flowers and drought-resistant shrubs, all pruned neatly. Each cabin would have a beautiful view of the lake. I had a very strong desire to stay in one of the cabins, a desire that wasn't entirely work-related. And the image of Kingsley and I cuddled in bed, with the blinds open and the water lapping just outside was most certainly not work-related.

Before us was a private dock, upon which was tethered a wood-paneled longish boat that looked antique. It also looked very well-maintained.

"Built in 1947," said Roy, either picking up on my thoughts or following my line of sight. "My dad worked at the boatyard that built it, right here in Elsinore. You'll notice it's long and thin. The design was later used as the model for various ocean liners, back in the day."

I made appropriate noises that suggested I was suitably impressed. He next pointed out that he and his family lived in the big Victorian. Guests could come and go in the main house, as they pleased, where drinks and snacks were always made available. Breakfast was served up by his wife. Drinks in the evening were served up by him, he said, adding a wink and a smile.

I smiled, too, and inhaled the simmering, algae-scented air. Not a bad spot. Not a bad spot at all.

That is, until I saw the tall man moving between the cabins, pushing a wheelbarrow before him. He looked back over his shoulder, then continued between the cabins.

"That's Ivan, my groundskeeper," said Roy. "Doesn't say much, but does a helluva fine job."

I nodded, not saying much either. Mostly because I had noticed that Ivan wasn't giving off an aura.

"Now," said Roy, rubbing his hands, "would you like a tour of the lake?"

"Boy would I."

4.

The lake was quiet.

All those busy streets that surrounded the lake? Only a distant memory. And all those crazy drivers whipping through traffic? Part of another world entirely.

Here, in this gently rising and falling antiquated skiff, the world consisted only of a nicely tuned engine and waves slapping the wooden hull. In a blink, Roy went from client to tour guide. He pointed out a beautiful old plantation-style home overlooking the lake, once the home of Bela Lugosi. Clark Gable had come often to fish and duck hunt. William Hart, the top Western silent film star, lived there in that old house. And an old Moorish-looking castle was built by the founder of the International Church of Christian Gospel, Aimee McPherson, aptly called Aimee's Castle. I'd never heard of such a church or of her, but the massive structure looked beautiful. It had been privately purchased by an eccentric scientist nearly a decade ago. Lucky bastard.

More stories, and more celebrities. Steve McQueen had hung out just beyond there with his motorcycle pals, often frequenting a downtown bar called The Wreck. Frank Morgan, who had played the Wizard in the *Wizard of Oz*, vacationed here often. They referred to him as The Wiz.

Movies were filmed here: *King Solomon's Mines* with Richard Chamberlain; *Norwood* with Glen Campbell, Joe Namath, and Dom DeLuise; *And the Children Shall Lead* with Levar Burton.

These days, celebrities came for the speedboat races and to skydive. Once, a Kardashian had vacationed in one of his cabins. He hadn't known what a Kardashian was at the time. Still didn't.

We continued slowly, as the sun danced off the gently rolling wake. There were only a handful of boats out, being midday and midweek. Elsinore was, apparently, a weekend destination.

Earl Stanley Gardner, of *Perry Mason* fame, had sometimes set his novels on Lake Elsinore. Roy's now-deceased aunt used to work for Earl as his personal assistant. I thought that was kinda cool. I also made a mental note to check Amazon for some *Perry Mason* deals. With luck, there might even be a freebie.

There were certainly bigger and more interesting lakes in the world. Hell, I'd seen a number of them. But looking at Roy's content face, you wouldn't believe it. His look said it all: this lake, in this unlikely setting, was the most interesting thing around—and he clearly loved it.

Along the west side of the lake, Roy cut the engine. "It was here that I saw the shadow the second time."

Earlier, at the dock, he had pointed out where he'd had his first sighting, walking me through it. As he walked me through it, I relived it in his mind, confirming for myself that he wasn't full of shit and just looking for publicity. Yeah, he'd seen a long-ass shadow.

I'd half-expected the second sighting to be within a few hundred yards of his dock. Something to explain why Roy was the only one seeing this thing—or the only one reporting seeing this thing. But we were in the middle of the lake. His massive estate home was just a blip in the far distance. But we were quite a ways away.

"Just last week?" I confirmed.

"Yup."

I looked down into the glittering water, the sun hot on my neck, but not doing any real damage. Was I miserable? Yes. Mostly, the thing within me was miserable. Lord, how she hated the sun. Except her misery was my misery, too, the bitch. Her preferences were now my preferences. Except I did all I could to not give in to her needs. Her needs would lead me down a rabbit hole of murder and destruction, and would eventually unleash into the world one of the most powerful sorceresses of all time. True story.

And so I sat there, burning slightly, but not really. Any burns I received healed as quickly as they appeared. Had someone been watching my skin closely, they would no doubt see the burn appear, and then disappear, to be repeated over and over again, for as long as I stood out here.

So weird, I thought. *But kind of cool, too.*

It was just after noon. There was, precisely, not a cloud in the sky. Blue as far as the eye could see, all reflected in this big body of water.

"Clarity is one to three feet," said Roy.

"Which means the shadow had been close to the surface?"

"Probably. Then again, something that big could probably be seen maybe a dozen or so feet below, especially if it's moving, which it was."

"Could it have been a fish?"

"As long as my boat?"

I shrugged, playing devil's advocate. "It's a big lake."

"It's not that big. We're six miles long and not quite two miles wide. Forty-two feet at its deepest, but averages closer to thirty feet. Nearly three thousand acres of surface area. Big yes, but not that big."

"But yet," I added. "It's here."

He nodded at that, and kept nodding.

"Does being out here now make you nervous?" I asked.

He peered over the rail next to me and sighed. This close, I could smell his aftershave and some body odor. I could smell his hair gel and dirty cargo shorts. He smelled like a big kid. He said, "I don't know what to think or feel, Sam. Thinking there might be something down there makes me nervous; not just for me, but for anyone who uses this lake. I'm telling you right now, no swimmer would have a chance against it. Ten men wouldn't have a chance against it. It was that big and that fast."

"The two missing boys... were they swimming in the lake?"

"As far as I know, no. But I only know what made it to the papers." He was gripping the railing tight enough for his knuckles to show white. "I'm afraid for my friends, my family, for anyone who uses the lake, Sam. Except, I don't know what the hell to do about it. Everyone I've talked to laughs it off. Except now, two boys have gone missing, and I feel guilty as hell, somehow. I don't know who else to turn to. Sherbet barely gave me the time of day, but at least he recommended you. But unless you have some high-tech sonar equipment or you are an experienced diver, I'm not sure what evidence you can bring back. I'm not sure what I was thinking by bringing you out here. I'm sorry, but I think I wasted your time."

"Maybe, maybe not," I said. "I can't deny that I'm out of my element here. Then again, I have eyes to see, ears to hear, and I'm patient as hell. Also, I know how to follow clues all the way to answers."

He chuckled, then dropped his head down between his arms. His neck had the look and consistency of my leather satchel that also doubled as my laptop bag. "Maybe I'm losing my mind, Sam. No one else appears to have seen it. At least, not recently. Or they were smart enough to keep their mouths shut."

I said nothing. After all, I'd questioned my own sanity for at least a decade now.

He looked at me and added, "I need answers, Sam. I need to feel comfortable on this lake. And I need to warn people, if necessary. Okay, you're hired. Sherbet says you're the Queen of Strange, and this is the strangest thing I've ever seen in my life."

We discussed rates, right there on the open water, and he suggested a barter. Half my rates for a week's use of his best cabin. I grinned and thought about Kingsley, a fireplace, and more snuggling than any woman had any right to hope for. My own lake monster.

"You've got yourself a deal."

5.

Detective Hillary Oster returned with my driver's license and investigator's license. She had, I noted, made copies of them. She folded the copies and slipped them under her keyboard.

"You check out, Ms. Moon," she said. I couldn't tell if checking out was a good thing or a bad thing, based on her expression. Detective Oster was in her mid-forties and didn't smile much. In fact, she seemed to go out of her way to frown. Had I been sitting on my head, Detective Oster would be grinning like a fool. Right side up, not so much. I found all her frowning perplexing, since I'm adorable.

"I was holding my breath."

"I wasn't." She laced her thick fingers in front of her. No nail polish. No rings. Chewed her nails. She was the picture of calm, even while the department behind me was a beehive of activity. "Now, what's your interest in the missing boys?"

I slipped inside her thoughts and saw the wall. It wasn't directed at me, not entirely. She didn't like private dicks, but she mostly didn't like the FBI agents who'd come in here and taken over the place. She was the lead investigator for both missing boys, but now, she didn't know her place. She'd never before had a case that had interested the FBI, and she hoped she never did again. She was in a bad mood and not about to open up to me. It was time I exerted myself, to the delight of the demoness within me.

My reasons are perfectly reasonable, I thought, planting the words directly into her thoughts. *I have nothing but the boys' best interest and well-being in mind. Do you understand?*

There was a pause, necessary for her subconscious mind to realize it had just been taken over. A moment later, she nodded.

Good, I thought. *Now give me a smile.*

She nodded again, and her lips quivered in what appeared to be a rictus of pain.

Scratch that, I thought. *No smiling. As you were.*

Her lips dropped with relief, and all was right in her world again. I said, "Could you tell me more about the boys' disappearance?"

She nodded, blinked. "Their disappearances have been tough on everyone. We've been working overtime on this. I'm not sure I've slept in a week."

She gave me the rundown. The boys were the same age: twelve years old. Both were Caucasian. Both were troublemakers. Both had had run-ins with the police. Usually for smoking pot or ditching school. Once or twice for tagging. Once for a minor break-in.

"What's a minor break-in?" I asked.

"They broke into their history classroom and urinated and defecated on the teacher's desk."

"Hey, when you have to go..." I said. "They were friends?"

"The best of friends, apparently. Quite frankly, they were just rotten together, although everyone seemed to adore them."

"Who's everyone?"

"Teachers, fellow students, the girls in class. They were bad boys with a heart of gold."

"Even the teacher whose desk they turned into a toilet?"

"That's just the thing, Ms. Moon: the boys never did anything too outlandish, or too hurtful to get into any real trouble. Even when they were tagging they were simply tagging over other graffiti, and just using their initials. Anyway, they have been missed and, although they are a couple of bone-heads, there's great worry for them. Truly, they didn't deserve whatever has befallen them."

I nodded, and tried to think when the last time I'd heard the word "befallen" used in an actual sentence, and couldn't. I said, "Any chance they ran away?"

"Anything's possible. But why leave seven days apart? Why not head out together?"

"Maybe they went their separate ways."

"The possibilities for the disappearance are endless. We are following all leads, Ms. Moon. We've talked to everyone they've ever known. We actually talked to every single high school student at Elsinore High, every single teacher. Every relative we could find, every neighbor within one square mile. We've passed out flyers asking for tips. The local TV media have been a huge help, and so have the radio stations. And that's not taking into account the hundreds of follow-up calls, leads that don't pan out into anything, and just general agonizing over the case. The word is out there... but so far, nothing."

"It means a lot to you."

"It means a lot to all of us here. These kids were funny. They were clowns, yes, but they often had most of us in stitches. They were ruffians on their way to figuring out how life works, but meanwhile, having a little fun in the process. Sometimes, too much fun. Hell, it wasn't uncommon for those of us here at the station to share stories about those two. Story after story."

That last part got to her and she turned her head and collected herself. I waited. Some cases hit us harder than others.

When she had gotten control of herself, she said, "Anyway, we all have a soft spot for them. We all sort of looked out for them, too."

She continued. Johnny, twelve years old, had

been the first to go missing. From all appearances, he had been asleep in his bedroom, and simply decided to get dressed, put on his shoes and jacket and slip away into the night. No one had come to his door, no evidence of anyone coming to his window. His mother was asleep. They lived in an apartment complex. No one had seen him go. No surveillance cameras anywhere.

One man, a bum who lived on the streets, claimed to have seen Johnny heading down Lake Street, toward the lake itself. But that was it. No one else had heard anything or seen anything. No other leads. The bum had checked out, too. No indication of foul play. They dug deeper. No stolen cars reported that night. No evidence that Johnny had purchased a ticket at the local Greyhound depot. There were no trains into Elsinore. Neither Uber nor Lyft nor any of the taxi app services indicated they had picked him up. The last call on his cell had been to another friend in the early evening. According to the friend, they'd talked girls and a party coming up that weekend. His last text had been to a girl. It said "Sup?" Johnny had left his phone behind in his bedroom.

I blinked at that. A soon-to-be-teenager with no phone? A sure sign of foul play. I said, "Hitch-hike?"

"Possible. Might even be probable. Except he'd made no mention to anyone of wanting to run away."

"Teenagers are not known for planning ahead, at

least beyond their next Taco Bell run."

She shrugged. "He hadn't been fighting with his family, or with his friends."

"Girlfriend?"

"None yet, but he was trying. We read his text messages."

"Scary," I said.

"We had to bring in a translator. Literally."

"Who was the translator?"

"A local high school student."

"Any theories?" I asked.

"Someone picked him up. Someone had somehow made arrangements with him, outside of phone calls or text messages. Someone he perhaps knew on the streets. Someone offered him drugs or money or a good time, and Johnny got in the car with him." She thought about it, then added, "Or her."

I saw where she was going with this. "Perhaps an older man?"

"Seems probable."

"Well-to-do pervs with a penchant for young boys have been known to trawl high schools, and seem to have a knack for finding pre-teens up for anything. Usually there's lots of partying promised. The pre-teen quickly realizes he's in way over his head, that there's a lot more expected of him than he'd realized."

"Tell me about the bum who reported seeing him," I said.

"Known by the police. Harmless. Drunk most of the time. His statement has been agonized over.

Problem is, it's been changing with time."

"What's the gist of it?"

"Johnny was alone. Seemed to be walking in a sort of daze. Heading down toward the lake. The time ranges from midnight to four in the morning. His clothing went from shorts to jeans."

"What does that mean, a sort of daze?"

"Apparently, his arms were straight down, and so was his head."

"He was looking down as he walked?"

"Apparently straight down. But you ask me, it sounds like bullshit."

"Yeah," I said, thinking. "And Luke would disappear a week later?"

"Right."

"Tell me about Luke's disappearance."

She did. Detective Hillary was certain the clue to Johnny's disappearance lay with his friend. Surely, there was someone they'd met along the way, someone who had shown an interest in the boys, someone who had offered them the world... and all they had to do was leave with him for the weekend. Or just for the night. Hell, just for a few hours. But Luke was adamant: they'd met no one, at least no one he was aware of.

Detective Hillary had been knee-deep in Johnny's investigation when she'd gotten word that Luke was gone, too. Similar circumstances. The boy had left his apartment in the middle of the night, an apartment he shared with his mother. This time, there was footage: the apartment surveillance camera had caught the boy leaving at 3:18 a.m., walking alone, head down, arms to his sides.

I asked if I could see the video. She didn't seem so inclined. I gave her a mental nudge, and she inclined. She moved over and asked me to come around to her side of the desk. She spent a half-minute bringing down files and opening new ones, and soon, the video played out before me.

A blond kid, wearing jeans and a Beatles t-shirt and no shoes, emerged from an apartment complex. Arms straight down, head down, he also looked like he might be turning away from, say, a dust storm, or rain. But the night seemed clear, although the video was a little grainy. Most interesting was the boy's steady gait. He walked carefully, slowly, one big step after another, never looking up, never raising his arms, never appearing to see, in fact, where he was going.

He didn't have anything in his hands. No headphones. No shoes. No reason to be acting the way he was acting. In about twenty steps, he was out of frame.

"Play again?"

"Yeah."

She did... three more times, in fact; each time, it seemed stranger than the time before it.

"Looks a bit like a zombie," I said.

"You're not the first to say that."

"Sort of backs up what the bum saw."

"It does."

"Where's he headed?"

"The apartment's main gate."

"You seem pretty sure about that."

"Only feasible exit. Not to mention, he stepped on some glass. We followed a trail of blood for nearly a mile before it congealed or got clotted by dirt and grime."

"You're sure it was him?"

"We tested it."

"Okay," I said. "The suspense is killing me."

She waited, perhaps subconsciously getting me back for digging around in her brain. Finally, she said, "He was heading toward the lake."

I looked at her. "Just like Johnny?"

"Exactly like Johnny," she said.

6.

We were at Alicia's in Brea, our lunch head-quarters.

Alicia's is a cute place, which might be why maybe 98 percent of its clientele are women. Not that guys don't appreciate cute, it's just that, well, they don't. Not cuteness of this magnitude. There were flowers everywhere, on tables and counters and walls. There were paintings of flowers, and of grapevines. As in, grapevines crawling along the wall, with painted bunches of grapes. So. Damn. Cute. Yes, Alicia's might have been located in an industrial center—wedged between a computer repair shop and a photo studio—but she had done her best to help you forget that unfortunate fact.

"Since when were you so girly?" asked Allison.

"I've always been girly. Mostly."

Allison snorted. "Says the girl who's packing

heat in her purse."

"Old habit," I said. Concealed handgun permits were hard to come by in California. Luckily, I knew people in the right places. That, and I'm an ex-fed. Anyway, I didn't use the handgun much. Or at all. These days, I tended to be a hands-on kind of girl.

"Or fangs-on," said Allison.

"I don't have fangs."

"Metaphorical fangs," said my witchy-poo friend. "And why don't you have fangs? I thought all vampires did."

"All fictional vampires," I said.

"They don't even, you know, appear when you are, you know, feeding?"

"You should know better than me," I said. "Remember, I can't see myself. And I've fed on you God knows how many times."

She shook her head. "This conversation has gotten creepy fast."

"We are the Queens of Creepy," I said, continuing Sherbet's metaphor.

"Hard to deny that. And as far as fangs, you have none that I'm aware of. Besides, you usually opened my skin with your" she shuddered all over again—"crazy-sharp fingernails."

"Which, if you think about it, is more effective. Two puncture holes in the neck aren't going to yield much blood. And aren't the fangs, you know, plugging up the very holes they opened?"

"Are we really having this conversation?" asked Allison. "We sound like a couple of fanboys."

"Or fang boys," I added.

"Fang girls," said Allison. "And are we okay joking about this?"

"Why?"

"As you'll recall, not very long ago, we were both sort of addicted to the whole... process."

"It wasn't a very healthy process," I said. "And the more I don't drink human blood, the less I crave it. And the less I crave it, the more the bitch inside me disappears. The more she disappears, the better I feel. The better I feel, the more human I feel. The more human I feel, I *feel*."

"No, I get the idea. But isn't being human, you know, boring?"

"Being human keeps me from killing the UPS deliveryman. Being human keeps my kids safe at night. Being human keeps me sane. Being human is a godsend."

"Are you quite done?"

"I am."

Part of my attempt at normalcy was to keep any telepathic communication to a minimum. Allison didn't like it. She had gotten quite used to reading my thoughts. Or mind speak, as she called it. Apparently, this was how she communicated with her ghost friend, Millicent—a ghost who had once been my friend, too, although in a different lifetime. Many lifetimes, apparently. Rumor had it that we had all been witches. I had no memory of these past lives, and neither did Allison. For the most part, we were taking a ghost's word for it.

"Not exactly, Sam. I'm remembering more and more. And Millicent is giving me some of her memories."

"Ghosts have memories? And I thought we agreed no mind speak."

"I only half-heartedly agreed. And she's more than a ghost, Sam. She's a spirit, as in not bound to any one location, or even to this Earth, for that matter. She can come and go as she pleases. As such, she has access to many, many lifetimes of memories. And the three of us are most definitely in most of them."

"A trifecta of witches," I said, repeating her earlier words.

"Exactly."

"But I broke the circle, so to speak, by becoming a creature of the night."

"You did, Sam, and wouldn't this conversation be best discussed, you know, in our minds?"

"No," I said. "Not for me, not any more. And not if I can help it. I feel better and better these days. More alive. Happier. Lighter. I won't sacrifice that for convenience."

"Fine, except I'm pretty sure that redhead over there is listening to us again."

I recognized the slender, pretty redheaded woman from the last time we'd eaten here. Yes, we had her attention, but she was all human, with a rich and vibrant aura. How much she heard, I didn't know, but I wasn't worried. My inner alarm stayed quiet, which was always a good sign. I smiled, and she smiled. Hers wasn't an awkward smile either. Geez, did I know her from somewhere? I didn't think so. More than likely, she could read auras—and saw that I lacked one. But shouldn't that make her nervous? Perhaps even afraid? Not all immortals are as friendly and cute as me. Then again, not all people "get" their gifts. If this woman could read auras, she was probably curious as to why I didn't have one. Perhaps she had never seen a freak like me. I was her first. Lucky her. I dipped into her mind and confirmed my suspicions.

"She can see auras," I said.

"Or lack thereof."

I shrugged. "It's true. I am rather aurally challenged."

"That might be a double entendre. And a not very complimentary one, either. Sam, we should be having this conversation privately."

"Because of all your sex talk?"

"Because we can. Because it's safe."

I shook my head. "The less I use her..."

"I know, I know. The less you use her, the weaker she becomes, I get it. But there has to be a way to get rid of her once and for all."

Getting rid of her meant the demon bitch could possibly use my daughter as a host. Or my sister. Or any of my other blood relatives, quite frankly. I wasn't so sure it had to be a female. I opened my thoughts up enough for Allison to pick up all of that.

She did, nodding. "Let me ask around, Sam. I

might know someone who might know what to do about her."

"Would this someone happen to be a ghost?"

"Maybe, does it matter?"

"Nope, I'm all ears."

After the waitress delivered our food, we spent the next few minutes 'getting our eat on,' as Anthony would say. My sandwich was heavenly, and I could just kiss the Librarian all over again—not an entirely undesirable thought—for creating the medallion rings (one of which restored my ability to consume real food). But as I ate, Allison was harshing on my vibe, with bad vibes of her own. I could literally feel the pain leaking out of her.

"You still miss him," I said.

"I do, Sam."

"I'm sorry, sweetie," I said.

She nodded and looked away, a glob of mayo in the corner of her mouth. I didn't bother telling her about the mayo. It looked kind of cute on her. The tears in her eyes, not so much. It had only been a month since Allison's adventure in Oregon—an adventure that had seen her not only battle the Wicked Witch of the West, but also fall in love... and fall hard, too. To say that things didn't end well was an understatement.

"I dream of him, Sam. He comes to me in my sleep, and I wake up crying."

"It's still fresh, sweetie."

"He was a good guy."

"I know."

She wiped her eyes with her napkin. Allison was in top shape. She should be, considering the other half of her life was devoted to whipping the rich and famous in Beverly Hills into shape, too, being a personal trainer. She was dressed in a black t-shirt with a strange, triangle-shaped necklace resting on top of it, a necklace that I suspected had something to do with her other half... her witchy half.

"I bought it at Ross," she said. "Ten bucks. Nothing witchy about it. And your thoughts leaked out like they went through a sieve."

I sighed, took another bite. I might have made a moaning noise. Yes, the sandwich was that good.

She said, "Are you still having dreams about New Orleans?"

I nodded, my mouth too full to speak. I sipped from my Coke, washed it down. "Almost every night."

"Any answers yet?"

I shrugged. "None that I can put my finger on."

Over the past few months, I'd been having vivid dreams of life in nineteenth-century New Orleans. As in, the 1800s. As in pre-Civil War. True, I'd gone to New Orleans to work a missing person's case... but then came right home once the case was completed. Mere days. But since that time, I'd been plagued by dreams of antebellum mansions, too-tight corsets, slaves and voodoo. So much voodoo. I dreamed of a kindly colonel and ballroom dancing and slaves. Of a doctor in love. I dreamed of murder, too. Most interesting, perhaps, were the dreams themselves, as I rarely dream—and usually only when the dream is of the utmost importance.

"Maybe you should go to a hypnotist. Maybe they could help you figure out what the dreams mean?"

"Maybe," I said. "Except they would likely find out lots of other miserable things about me. Or accidentally release"—I paused, took in some useless air, and I might have said the next word through clenched teeth—"Elizabeth."

"Then give the hypnotist a suggestion of his own. Not to go there. Not to go anywhere but your dreams about New Orleans."

"Or maybe I should leave well enough alone," I said. "Maybe I don't want to know what happened in New Orleans."

After a moment of silent chewing, Allison said, "Millicent thinks you might be a bad influence on me."

I almost laughed. I almost had to block my latest bite from rocketing across the table... until I noted the somber quality in Allison's tone. "You're being serious?"

"I am."

"Bad, how?"

"First off, she loves you. Or she used to love you. We were closer than sisters. Really, we were. You have to believe me. But she no longer trusts you."

"Well, fuck her. She doesn't know me." I'd lost my appetite for the sandwich and pushed the rest of it aside.

"That's just the thing, Sam. She does. Better than you realize. She's been watching, for years now. And she thinks there is a chance of..."

"A chance of what?"

Allison looked away, tears suddenly in her eyes. "That we might have lost you."

"I'm not lost, Allie. I'm right here."

Now, the tears were streaming down her face. And I could hardly believe what I was seeing and hearing. "One of them is in you, Sam. And not just any one of them. One of the most powerful ever. Millicent says that maybe I can't trust you. Or even trust your thoughts. That maybe, just maybe, they have succeeded in taking you over."

"Are you hearing yourself?" I asked.

"Millicent thinks I should stay away from you."

"Screw Millicent—"

"I can't, Sam. She and I and Ivy Tanner... we are part of something big going on. Something powerful. I need them."

"What are you saying, Allison?" I felt sick to my stomach, which, for me, was saying something.

My friend took in some air and steeled herself. "I'm saying that, until I am a stronger witch, until I can protect myself, I need to stay away from you."

"Jesus, I only see you once a week for lunch."

"I'm sorry, Sam." She got up and dropped her wadded-up napkin on the table.

By the time she got to the front doors, she was crying pretty hard. She pushed through them, and was gone.

Just like that.

7.

I was sitting with Jacky in his office.

It is not much of an office. Stark walls. Simple desk. A printer that looked forgotten. Pictures on his wall. Famous boxers I should know the names of, but didn't. A series of photos of Jacky himself, fighting back in the day. In a number of the photos, Jacky was delivering a jaw-busting blow to his opponents. In others, his hands were raised in victory. All were in black and white.

"But he's a champion, Sam," Jacky was saying. I had just delivered the worst news, quite possibly, of his entire life. And Jacky had lived a long, long life.

"He'll always be a champion to me."

"Sam, you're not getting it... your boy... he's the best fighter I've ever trained. Ever. And that includes you. He can go far. Scratch that. He can go all the way. Your son, quite frankly, is unstoppable."

"I know that, Jacky."

"Maybe you're not hearing me, Sam. I've never seen a fighter so tough, so fast, so accurate, so strong, and at such a young age. Your son could fight now, at twelve, and beat ninety percent of the pros. Are you hearing me, Sam? At twelve, your son could go pro, and he would be a champion."

Jacky's face had gone red. So had his neck and nose. His hair was already red, so that didn't count. Wait for it... okay, now the tops of his ears were red, too. Yeah, he had gotten himself worked up, which concerned me. Jacky was not a young man, and his health seemed to be failing at an exponential rate. He still ran the club, and still worked with me at times, although he preferred to work with Anthony. Recently, he had made house calls to a disabled homicide investigator in Los Angeles. Blind, deaf, and mute—courtesy of an explosion I'd read about years ago—Jacky had taught the man to fight blind, so to speak. But after yet another attack that had nearly killed the man, Jacky swore the ex-investigator had developed a sixth sense or something. I thought maybe Jacky was losing it.

I reached out and took Jacky's hands in mine. His were about the same size, but gnarled. Some fingers had been broken, and his knuckles were thick and heavy. Street fighting, back in the day, without the benefit of gloves. Arthritis might have been a factor, too.

"Why are your hands so cold, Sam?" he asked.

He looked from my hands to me. I had made a point to close his office door when I came in to see him after our workout. I was still sweating, which I always found interesting. How could someone who was so cold, sweat so much? I wondered if it was an old bodily memory, maybe a conditioned response to working out? Or maybe that was one way I released any excess water weight since I rarely—ahem—used the bathroom.

Jacky had been pushing hard for the past few months to allow Anthony to work his way up through the amateur ranks in boxing. To the point he wouldn't let up, even when I kindly told him no. I liked Jacky. My son adored him. Jacky had taken over a fatherly role in Anthony's life, for which I would be eternally grateful; which, for me, actually meant something. The two usually spent a lot of time together after workouts. Jacky would drop him off later, often with ice cream or a Coke in hand. Anthony would tell me all about his time with Jacky, the workouts, the talks they had, Jacky's life as a young fighter. Anthony seemed less impressed about the boxing than the fact that a father figure had taken an interest in him. It wasn't so much about the boxing; it was about the bonding. And I didn't want to lose that for my son. But it was, perhaps, time for Jacky to know the truth about us.

I prayed—I hoped—Jacky would understand. I prayed I didn't have to resort to plan B.

"Jacky, you know how I feel about Anthony

fighting..."

He tried to move his hands, but I held them tight. Not too tight, but tight enough for him to know he wasn't going anywhere. He blinked when he realized he was staying put.

"Jesus, you're strong, Sam."

"That's not a surprise to you, though, is it?"

"Not really. I see how you hit. Your speed. Your son, he's even faster, I think. Maybe not. Hard to say, you're both freaks. *My* freaks."

I smiled at that. Sitting here, like we were, it would be easy to influence him, to dip into his mind and tell him what to think, to gently suggest that he back off about my son competing in boxing. Except... Except I had seen inside his mind... and it was tortured, deteriorating, damaged from years of taking punches. I didn't want to delve inside again, and I also didn't want to influence my friend either, not if I could help it, and certainly not someone who'd given my son so much attention, warmth, and love.

With Danny gone, Jacky had been there for Anthony. In fact, the two needed each other, and it was always special to see them together. Kingsley had been super kind to Anthony, too—to both my kids—going out of his way to bring them presents and spend time with them. But it wasn't quite the same. The connection wasn't quite there.

With Jacky, it was there, and it only seemed to be growing, and not because of Anthony's growing skills, either. I thought Jacky's diminishing faculties had something to do with it, too. Often, I would see Anthony helping the old man up into the sparring ring, and consequently, out of the ring. When they spoke, Anthony wrapped his arm around Jacky's shoulders, and I swear, he was holding the old man up. Already, Anthony was two or three inches taller than the little Irishman.

"Well, your freaks," I said, "are freakier than you might think, Jacky."

He squinted at me. More so than usual. His bushy eyebrows might have quivered. More so than usual. "That is a strange thing to say, Sam. Mighty strange."

"I'm a very, very strange person, Jacky."

"What are you getting at, Sam?"

Okay, this was harder than I thought it would be. I had known Jacky for so long... well over five years now. Maybe even six. Surely, he knew, on some level, that I was different than any of his other clients... or from anyone he'd ever seen before. Or maybe not. Maybe he was okay with a five-foot, three-inch tall woman kicking an undefeated Marine boxer's ass (I still don't feel good about that), or her son who routinely beat all the men in the gym. And when I say beat, I meant he beat the shit out of them.

"Jacky, a few years ago—ten to be exact—something happened to me. Something that makes me different from most people."

One of Jacky's eyebrows quivered like a caterpillar in the wind. Maybe Jacky was the strange one. "Different how, Sam?"

"I'm stronger than most people, for one. Surely you know that, Jacky."

"No one hits harder than you... except for maybe your son."

"No one, Jacky?" I asked. "No one you've ever worked with? Ever?"

"No one, Sam. Your speed and strength and timing and accuracy. I haven't stopped thinking about you since the day we first met... and your son is no different. And he's only going to get stronger."

"Why do you think that might be, Jacky?"

"Because you're freaks."

"Okay, but why us?"

"It's in your genes, I guess. Someone out there has to be faster and tougher and stronger than everyone else. I suppose it's you two. And for all I know, your daughter, too."

He seemed content with his theory: someone out there had to be the toughest among us, and I just happened to be it. Normally, I would have let him have his theory, his story, his explanation. Normally, I wouldn't have pushed. Except that Jacky was filling my son's head with dreams of boxing glory. Jacky, too, was already picturing Anthony in the ring with Floyd Mayweather, Jr. I could have let this play out. Maybe I could have let my son dominate the world of boxing. And maybe he might someday want to, for all I know. But, for now, my son was twelve years old and his strength was a fluke. His strength was supernatural. The fights would never, ever, be fair and, worst-case scenario, our family secret might just get out.

It wouldn't take much to give Jacky a subtle suggestion. But I respected him too much for that, and maybe, just maybe, he deserved some real answers, even if he never asked the questions.

I reached across Jacky's desk and picked up a letter opener. Now, you don't see those too often these days, but guys like Jacky still had them on their desks, and his was shaped like a miniature version of King Arthur's sword, Excalibur. In fact, it was even embedded in a mini-boulder. It came out easy enough. Maybe I was going to be the next king of England?

"What are you doing, Sam?"

For an answer, I placed my open left hand on his desk, palm up. There was the smallest of chances that the metal was made of silver, but I doubted it. Steel, I was certain. Well, I would just take that chance. I dragged the dullish tip of the mini-sword over my palm, deep enough to open the skin and for it to hurt. But I kept dragging, even as Jacky stood up abruptly, knocking over his chair and showing flashes of his old brilliance. He swiped my hand, knocking the mini-sword out of it, and flinging it across the room, along with some of my blood.

That I got some perverse pleasure out of seeing my own blood was enough to alarm me, and enough to awaken the bitch inside me. I literally felt her clawing her way up through the darkness, up, up...

Yesss...

Relax, you bitch, I thought. *This is just a demonstration.*

Still, demonstration or not, she liked the sight of blood, the feeling of pain—all of which seemed to give her subtle strength, encouragement, and a reason for hope. I never, ever wanted her to hope.

Suddenly, I had the very briefest of flashes of what it would be like to be trapped inside of me... forever. It would be hell. Well, not entirely. I was, after all, kinda fun. Not to mention, I didn't ask for this... she had brought this upon herself. And just as she receded back into the background, I heard the faintest wisps of what I was certain were her thoughts: *I am not evil...*

I nearly snorted, but I didn't have time for her. Not with Jacky standing over me, mouth hanging open, both hands holding his little chest, a look of anguish on his face.

"Why would you do that, Sam? Why?"

"It's okay, Jacky."

"Sam, my heart. I don't feel so good."

"Sit down, Jacky. Sit down and watch."

"Sam, we need to get you to the hospit—"

But he stopped talking—and for good reason. The wound in my hand was moving. Unlike special effects in Hollywood, where we watch, say, the Wolverine's many wounds seal up magically and seamlessly, my own fast-healing wounds are a bit more dramatic. Before our very eyes, the skin in my hand pulsed and moved like a living thing, as tendrils of skin reached out from each edge of the wound to meet in the middle and form a thin, crusty, strange, reddish layer of skin. The reddish skin soon formed a thick, pulsating scar before our very eyes. I knew from experience such scars would take a few days to completely disappear. But, for now, the wound was healed.

Meanwhile, Jacky held his chest—which worried me—and stared down at my hand. Sweat had appeared all along his high forehead, beading in some places and dripping in others. The skin along his cheeks and neck and the backs of his hands was splotchy and getting splotchier by the second.

"Sam, I don't feel too good."

"Deep breaths, Jacky. You're going to be fine." Indeed, his aura suggested he was going to be fine, although his heart center was pulsating at a faster rate. No, Jacky didn't have a heart problem; indeed, I'd noticed for quite some time now the dark spot in his aura where his liver was located.

That's what's going to kill him, I thought. *Someday.*

"I don't understand what I just saw, Sam."

"Sometimes, I don't either. Sit down, Jacky. Good. Deep breaths. Good."

"Your hand," he gasped as he righted his chair and sat down again. "The cut. What did I just see?"

It was her, I thought. *You saw her in action. Not necessarily me. Any powers, any strength, any rapid-healing, and anything and everything else...*

was all her.

No, I thought suddenly. That wasn't true. According to Allison and Millicent the ghost, I had been very, very powerful in my own right. Of course, I hadn't seen a whiff of such powers growing up. Or had I? Had I been more psychic than I was aware? Had I been more intuitive than I was aware? Had my witchy powers been growing, only to be cut off by my attack ten years ago?

I didn't know, and I might never know.

Although, I had a number of people I could ask. The librarian might have some answers, but there was someone else. Someone who had been with me for all eternity. Someone who had, apparently, fallen in love with me from afar. Or maybe from up close. I was thinking of my now-fallen guardian angel, Ishmael. He would know the life trajectory I was on. He would, in fact, know more about me than anyone.

Only problem was, I never knew where the bastard was. Was he watching me now? I knew he had taken up watching my son, who had subsequently lost his own guardian angel during those brief moments he'd been a vampire. Ishmael was a sort of surrogate angel... a job I had not asked of him.

Jacky was finally calming down, breathing easier, although the sweat and splotches continued forming and reforming, dripping and beading and splotching, like a live-action Pollack painting.

"Sam, please tell me that this was some sort

of..." he searched for words, licked his lips, blinked hard once, twice, three times, "some sort of magic trick or something."

"It's closer to the 'something' part, Jacky."

"What's happening, Sam?"

"To me, in general? I don't know. What's happening in here, in your office, to my hand, is a demonstration."

"A demonstration? I don't understand, Sam."

He was breathing hard again. Harder than I liked hearing. I decided to give him a small suggestion. *Relax, Jacky. Good. Deep breaths, calm down, down. Good.*

He took three hard, long, deep, steady breaths. Then looked at me and nodded.

I said, "You always knew I was different, Jacky."

"Yes, but—"

"A part of you, perhaps a very deep part of you, perhaps a part that you didn't listen to, always suspected I wasn't like anyone, ever. But you ignored that part."

"I did. I had to. You hit too hard. You move too fast. You punch through the goddamn body bags. Who does that?"

"I do," I said. "And I'm not even really trying, Jacky. I have yet to hit the body bag as hard as I can. I have yet to hit it with all my strength."

"What are you saying, Sam?"

What was I saying? How should I tell him? How much could I trust him with? I suspected I could trust him with as much as I wanted to.

"Look at my hands, Jacky," I said and turned them over and gave him a full view of my sharpened, thick nails.

"Oh, Sam. What's happening?"

I turned my hand over again for good measure, and the dark red, thick, pulsating scar was now pinker, and not so fresh-looking. It looked, if anything like a two- or three-day-old wound.

Easy, Jacky. Good, we are friends. I won't hurt you.

The bitch inside me liked his uncertainty, liked his growing alarm. The bitch inside me had issues.

I was having a different reaction, though. My little demonstration—and the growing horror on Jacky's face—was yet another reminder of the ghoul I had become. That I would forever be. No more sugarcoating. No more pussyfooting. Jacky had been around the block, had seen things, surely. Monsters were real. I was living proof of it. *And we are here, among you.*

"I'm a vampire, Jacky," I said.

He opened his mouth to speak, but no words came out. Just as well.

I continued: "Ten years ago, I was attacked by a very old and powerful vampire. The attack changed me forever, Jacky. In effect, it killed me, but I did not die. And now, something very dark and sinister lives within me, waiting to emerge. But I fight it every day. Every day, every hour, every minute is a fucking fight. I may not be a professional boxer,

Jacky, but I am in the fight of my life. And it never ends, and it will never end."

Jacky's lower jaw twitched, moving and jerking and spasming, but no words came out. His brightish blue aura had turned a tumultuous green, swirling and streaming and billowing. This was a lot to absorb, especially for a guy whose own mental faculties may or may not be one hundred percent. But Jacky was street-smart, worldly tough, a fighter in every sense of the word. Not a lot was going to shake him, which was what I was counting on. He had seen the evidence. He had seen my strength in action. He'd now seen the wound in my hand heal before his eyes. Now, it was just a matter of allowing the information to sink in, for understanding to dawn on him.

He wasn't there yet, and I didn't want to influence him or prod him. He needed to get there on his own terms.

Outside, through Jacky's closed office door, I could hear grunting and some *hee-yawing*. Jacky also ran a kickboxing studio. Jacky was a businessman, too, although I doubted he would go so far as to provide spin classes. I closed my eyes and saw light just behind my pupils, swirling and morphing and forming and reforming. Even with my eyes closed, I am never truly in darkness.

We are the darkness, Sam... came a distant, hissing voice in the deepest recesses of my mind.

"And your son?" asked Jacky.

I opened my eyes and the swirling stopped a

the old boxer came instantly, sharply into view. 20/20 vision for the rest of my life. Not a bad deal. Jacky had wiped his brow, and the turmoil in his energy field had steadied, although the occasional green spark blasted through it.

"My son is a lot like me," I said.

"You did say 'vampire,' right, Sam?"

"I did, Jacky."

"We know of vampires where I'm from."

I nodded, waiting, suddenly tired. It was still early afternoon. The sun was still out. In the gym behind me, my son was sparring with one of Jacky's top young recruits. My daughter, now a freshman in high school, opted to walk home with her friends these days. I had asked who her friends were, but she wouldn't tell me. Bad move. But I had my ways.

"We had stories from the town I grew up in. Rumors of a young man who may or may not have been a vampire. Some sheep had ended up dead. One person had gone missing. Months later, the young man went missing, too. Some claimed he was a vampire. I didn't know. I was only a kid. I didn't get out much. No TV, only newspapers, books and magazines."

I nodded, listening. I had no doubt that vampires have been among us for centuries. At least for as the great purging, or whatever the hell imus, aka The Librarian, called it. ject of highly advanced dark masters shed from the Earth.

How the hell did they get banished? And who had banished them?

The answer was an order of highly advanced alchemists, of which I was an extension. The Librarian was such an alchemist, too. Very powerful, very adept, and the son of Elizabeth. Yes, the same Elizabeth who currently paced like a hungry tiger within the cage of my mind.

There had been, I suspect, a great war of some sort five hundred years ago, a war of good and evil, a war that had set the stage for today's currently supernatural climate. A war that, I suspected, wasn't quite over. And somehow, I'd found myself in the middle of it, with a bloodline that went all the way back to the greatest Alchemist of all time, Hermes Trismegistus—and now, his greatest enemy was currently residing within me.

A tangled web we weave, I thought.

Except, of course, all I had done was gone for my nightly jog. I had been unaware of any of this. Unaware that vampires were among us. Unaware of werewolves and angels and alchemists. And witches.

I only wanted to go for a run, I thought. *That, and no more.*

"You say you were attacked ten years ago, Sam?"

"Yes."

"You want me to kick that sumbitch's ass?"

I laughed, but it came out kind of funny. I laughed again, and now it definitely came out funny. In fact, it came out as a sob, and now I quit trying to laugh and found myself crying into my hands, sitting there in front of Jacky, in his back office. Except, of course, he wasn't sitting there for long, was he?

No, he had come around the desk and pulled me in close and held me tighter than I deserved, and he kept holding me, even as I turned my face into his shoulder, and stained the crap out of his shirt with my flowing tears...

8.

"Are you done blubbering, lass?"

"No," I said, and held him tighter.

I heard him sigh, but he continued patting my head. I wondered briefly if my hair felt cold, then nearly laughed at the thought of it. These days, I kept a semi-permanent shield in place to block my thoughts. The shield was a bit of a pain, but better to keep it in place, then have errant thoughts slipping out.

"Did you just say something about your hair being cold?"

I sighed. Apparently, when I cried like a baby, my shield wobbled a little.

I pulled away. "No, Jacky. You heard my thoughts."

He opened his mouth to speak. Then closed it. Then opened it. Then closed it again.

I said, "Why don't you sit here?" And I eased him down into the chair I'd just been using.

"Sam," he said, finally finding his voice, "I heard your voice, but really. It was almost as if... you were thinking for me."

"A scary thought, to be sure," I said. "But yet, another example of who I am."

"So you're saying this is all real, Sam?"

"I am. Unless it's not."

"What do you mean?"

"I mean, a part of me thinks I might be imagining all of this. I might be, in fact, crazy."

He laughed and wiped his brow. He blinked a few times at his own pale hands, the backs of which were mostly covered in age spots. "Is there room in your padded cell, because I'm seriously thinking I'm losing it, too. I mean, did I just see what I thought I saw?"

"You did, Jacky."

"Your hand, let me see it again..."

I showed him my palm.

"You mind?" he asked.

I shook my head and he traced the rapidly-healing scar with a none-too-steady finger. He pressed the scar, pushed on it, and finally leaned down and examined it.

"Doesn't seem fake, Sam."

"Ya think?"

He next examined my nails, and I was certain no one, not even Anthony and Tammy, had examined them so closely. He ran an increasingly shaking finger over my right index nail. Tapping the tip. Looking under. Examining the cuticle. He saw, as I saw, a thickly grotesque nail that reached a little beyond the tip of my finger. A sharp triangle that I did all I could to hide from the world. Why the long, sharp nails, I didn't know. But it spoke of the evil within me. On that note, I thought of the man I'd met many months ago, a man I had not seen, a man who was not a man at all, but the king vampire, so to speak.

Dracula.

Wasn't he also called the Dragon? Wasn't Dracula, in fact, translated as "Son of the Dragon"? His father, if my shaky history was correct, was Dracul, which, I'm guessing, probably meant Dragon. And didn't dragons have claws, too? And didn't I sprout claws every time I summoned the giant bat within me, Talos? But maybe Talos wasn't a bat after all. Maybe Talos was a dragon, too. Or maybe something in-between.

I didn't know. But it felt right...

Jesus, was I, too, a dragon? Even if only sometimes? And what, exactly, was a dragon? A flying lizard? Did that mean, I dunno, that I could breathe fire, too? Or, rather Talos, could? And weren't Talos and I one and the same when I summoned him from his world into mine? Never mind what happened to my own body during those exchanges. I didn't really want to think about it. Such thoughts hurt my head.

A dragon, I thought.

Of course, I'd been turning into Talos now for years. That I turned into something epic and awesome wasn't the question. But going from a giant vampire bat... to a dragon, took some getting used to. I mean, dragons had cache.

I recalled again the flying creature I'd seen a few months ago, the creature that had been keeping pace with Talos and me in the skies high above. It had very much looked like a dragon. But it had been far away and there was a very real chance I had imagined it.

And didn't dragons guard, you know, treasures?

They also ate virgins, if I was correct.

"Sam," said Jacky, releasing my hand and sitting back in his client chair. I had slumped down on the corner of his desk. "That was a lot of dragon talk."

"Dragon *thinking*," I said.

"This is a lot for me to take in."

"I bet," I said, and zipped up my mind nice and tight. "Any chance you can forget that I can also turn into a dragon/bat thing?"

"I don't feel so good, Sam."

"I bet you don't."

I slipped into his mind quickly and gave his subconscious mind a suggestion to remove his memory from the last thirty seconds. The old guy didn't need to know about Talos.

He blinked and looked at me. "What were we talking about, Sam?"

"We were talking about my son, and how he has

an unfair—and supernatural—advantage over other fighters."

"Ah, yes. 'Tis a shame."

"It wouldn't be right, Jacky."

He nodded. "I know, and are we really having this conversation, Sam?"

"I'm afraid so," I said. "Can you keep this to yourself, Jacky? Not even your wife?"

He snorted. "I wasn't exactly in the church choir growing up, Sam. The wife doesn't know about half of what I've done."

"Well, she doesn't need to know this half, either. Deal?"

"Deal."

He looked at me. I looked at him. He said, "Your face, Sam, it was so cold. Even your tears were cold. Like ice, really."

I nodded. "Welcome to my life."

He nodded sadly. "Are you going to be okay, lass?"

"I hope so."

"If you ever need anything, Sam, come see me. I can still kick some arse."

"Thank you, Jacky."

"And your son..." his voice broke off, and he turned away.

"He's going to be okay, too," I said. "I think my son might, just might, be part superhero."

Jacky tried to smile, but all of this was just too much for him. Too much for anyone. He wiped his eyes and looked away.

"You care about him, Jacky."

"More than you know, Sam."

He nodded and now, I was the one swooping down, and holding the old Irishman tight, an old Irishman who had sort of adopted my son right here in his boxing gym...

God bless him.

9.

It was late and I was running.

The run had started as a jog, but I got bored with the jog. With my knapsack secured tightly to my back, I soon found myself sprinting down street after street.

It was just past 2 a.m. Probably not the vampire hour, but pretty damn close. I sped down Bastanchury. Had I continued for another five miles or so, I would reach Master Kingsley's stately manor. Except, of course, tonight was a full moon, and Master Kingsley—as Franklin, his butler, referred to him—would be highly indisposed. Kingsley, after all, dealt with a darkness of a different kind, a darkness that emerged once a month, every month. A darkness that took hold of him completely and totally. A darkness that would destroy anything living in its path, a darkness that preferred to feed upon the rotting dead.

And I kiss those lips, I thought, shuddering, as I turned left and headed up Imperial.

Kingsley had reached a sort of agreement with the darkness within. He fed it rotting meat (which Franklin hunted in the hills behind the estate home), and the thing within Kingsley left him alone throughout the month. How much inner torment Kingsley went through, I didn't know, and wouldn't ever know. But I suspected the darkness within him —a darkness I'd personally spoken to before—no doubt slipped into his thoughts here and there. Hard to say. On the outside, Kingsley seemed normal enough.

Of course, the very nature of Kingsley's super-natural existence—a werewolf—dictated that the thing within would make a full appearance each month. Kingsley, of course, didn't have to be so accommodating. He could have chained himself up all night, rather than let the creature roam within a secured cell. He could have denied it rotting meat, too. Kingsley didn't give it much, but the agreement seemed to work, and my werewolf boyfriend led a mostly normal life.

I, of course, had no guarantee that Elizabeth would ever relinquish her hold on me. I suspected her goal would be, and would forever be, to gain complete control of my body, mind and soul, forever and ever.

I shook my head at that, and picked up my speed. How I picked up speed, I don't know, since I was already blazing down the empty sidewalk. But I somehow willed myself to go faster, somehow willed my legs to run faster and faster, and they responded. Boy, did they respond.

Of course, my situation wasn't all bad. Elizabeth had given me much of her strength and supernatural abilities. From where she had gained such abilities, I didn't know. My guess: a pact with the devil. Or something damn close to the devil. Or not. Maybe they had tapped into humankind's limitless potential. Maybe she and others like her had figured out how to unlock the inner superhero in all of us.

Again, I didn't know, but I knew a handful of people who might know. And I was getting closer and closer to needing more answers. This was, after all, personal. Damn personal.

Anthony and Tammy were with Mary Lou tonight. I hadn't gotten to the point where I trusted the kids alone, all night. Okay, I didn't trust Tammy. Not these days. Not with all the skipping class and questionable friends. Not with the drinking last year and now the cigarette smoke I smelled on her. Not with her coming home way past her curfew.

I'm losing her, I thought, and somehow, some way, found yet another gear. I sped past parked cars and driveways and houses and lamp poles. I sped through green lights and red lights, through intersections and around bends and over hills. Imperial is scenic... and quiet at night. I soon found myself running through Brea and then, Placentia. Over the 57 freeway, which sped below me in a blur. At an intersection, I leaped over a car turning left in front of me. The driver never knew I was there. Hell, maybe I wasn't.

I'm here, I thought, and I was running faster than anyone had any right to run.

The speed. The wind. The pounding of my Asics. The streaking lights. Total control of my body, of my legs. Seeing everything. I could have been running backward through time, or forward. Everything a blur, a big blur. Yet, I saw everything, too. Everything.

Backward in time... something tugged at me, but I let it go, or tried to, and continued forward.

Faster, I prodded myself. *Go faster and faster.*

Time, I thought again. *Had I gone backward in time?* I didn't know, couldn't remember, but the thought felt right. What the hell had happened to me in New Orleans? I didn't know. Maybe I didn't want to know.

In one movement, I reached around and pulled off my backpack without breaking stride. And as I crested a hill and headed down toward Yorba Linda, I leaped as I high as I could, and saw the single flame in my mind. And the creature within.

A moment later, my clothing exploded from my body. I lost more workout clothes that way.

I gasped and arched my head back and felt myself become something much, much more—and caught my backpack with a curved, black talon. I thrust my wings and, just missing the concrete, flew low to the ground. I beat my wings again and again, and swept straight down the center of Imperial Boulevard, gaining speed and altitude.

And loving every second of it.

10.

Hello, Talos.
Hello, Samantha Moon.

I was flying high. The full moon appeared and reappeared through the stratocumulus clouds, blasting its reflected light over me. For someone who hated the sun, I sure didn't have a problem with reflected sunlight. I knew, deep down, it wasn't so much the physical light—after all, I lived easily within a lighted home at night. I knew, in fact, it was what sunlight represented: life, joy, community, love, companionship, support, working, playing, existing. All of which the creature within me shunned.

Samantha Moon, I repeated in my thoughts. *I didn't know giant vampire bats were so formal, Talos.*

I didn't know I was a giant vampire bat.

Wind didn't so much as blast me, as flow over me. The body I became—Talos's body—was perfectly, wonderfully, ingeniously aerodynamic. I glanced down at myself, over the thick skin, the thick, leathery wings, my massive claws far below —claws that had dismembered a demonic entity a few years ago.

I just always thought...

I know, Samantha.

But you never corrected me.

There was no need to correct you. Your interpretation was close enough. What I am, exactly, was far less important than you wrapping your head around our connection.

Well, I have wrapped my head around it. I love our connection. I love this body swap thing that we do. This merging that we do. I love that I can be you, and you can be me, if that's how it works.

Indeed it does. In a way.

I tried imagining my physical body on another world, in, possibly, another dimension, too. Then I nearly became dizzy. Not good when flying.

And what am I doing in this other world? I asked, as I flapped a little harder, gaining altitude and speed. *In your world?*

We are sitting together on a rocky crag.

Like before?

Like always, Samantha. You wouldn't fare very well in my world, I'm afraid.

What do you mean?

I live in a challenging world, to say the least, at

least, for land dwellers.

I knew that Talos and others like him were nearly immortal. I knew they were advanced spiritually, beyond our world. I knew they lived in peace, and I knew they lived in cities among the clouds.

Yes, all true, Sam.

And as I thought these thoughts, a mental picture appeared in my mind, and there I was, sitting naked on a rocky precipice, high above the clouds. Talos was sitting next to me, perched on a rocky overhang, wings tucked in at his side. My perspective was from his perspective, as he saw me. My arms were hugging my bare legs as I peered down, down over the ledge, down into the swirling misty depths.

Is that where your city is? I asked.

No, Sam. Look up.

And now, my perspective changed as Talos looked up and there... rising high above me, supported by structures that seemed oddly organic and rocky and fabricated all at the same time, were massive edifices mushrooming up into the clouds. They were of different levels, different shapes, different sizes. But all composed of the same organic material.

We work with the planet we live on, Sam. We work together. We construct together, and the planet yields to us what we want.

Winged shapes crisscrossed the sky. More creatures like Talos. Other creatures, too. Smaller animals. Oddly shaped, multi-winged animals.

Hundreds of different flying creatures, dotting the sky above.

You said man lived on your planet, I thought. *In one of our previous conversations.*

He lives below, Sam. Within the earth.

Why?

He so chooses.

Do they look like me?

Close enough.

I thought about all of this as I continued flapping Talos's massive wings, catching the air, holding it, and pushing it behind me. A wonderful sensation. Below me, the city lights of Earth faded into rolling hills as I left Orange County behind and headed over the Santa Ana Mountains.

Why are you sitting next to me? I asked. *You know, in your world?*

I'm keeping an eye on you, Samantha Moon, came his gentle words, and I sensed some mirth behind them.

Can I move around in your world?

Yes.

But I haven't yet mastered being in two places at once.

Not yet. It is a little like walking and chewing gum.

Because my focus is primarily in this world, on us flying, I thought.

Very good, Sam.

But if I were to land, and take my focus off flying, and put my focus on myself in your world...

You could move about.
But not safely?
Probably not without my help.
This is hurting my head, I thought.
My head, too, thought Talos, and I sensed a smile behind his words.
Will you show me your world?
Someday, Sam.
I took in a lot of air, using Talos's great lungs, filling his chest, my chest, our chest completely. As I did so, I held the air, held it and was aware of it, and then let it loose again. It came out hot. Very hot.
Are you a dragon, Talos?
Oh, yes.
A real, honest-to-God dragon?
Close enough to one, Sam. And so are you. We are, together.
I took in more air, held it, felt it brewing in my chest. In fact, I felt great power within my chest. I felt heat and gathering energy. I almost didn't dare ask the question, but yet here it was:
Talos, can I...?
Oh, yes, Sam. Oh, yes...
I felt the air churning inside my lungs, churn and heat and broil and metamorphose into something else, something not of this world, something alchemical and magical and exciting.
And when I opened my mouth, when I exhaled this roiling, burning air within, something orgasmic happened. Something explosive. Something terrible

and beautiful and deadly. Something I wasn't entirely prepared for.

Fire erupted from me, and it kept on erupting as I continued to breathe out, crackling and snapping and charging through the air before me.

11.

I breathed fire tonight, I wrote.

Is that a euphemism, Moon Dance? If so, you can keep your sordid sex life to yourself.

Sordid?

All that howling and panting and clawing.

Kingsley isn't a werewolf when, you know...

I wasn't talking about him, Moon Dance.

I shook my head and called him an asshole and he sent me back an "lol" which, in our newfangled world, meant that he had, apparently, laughed out loud. I secretly questioned most laughed out louds. Were people really going around and laughing that hard over texts and emails... and, in this case, IM messages? Call me a cynic, but I thought "LOLs" were making liars out of most everyone.

What's this breathing fire business, Moon Dance?

I told him about it. I told him about my gradual realization that I had been misidentifying Talos all along. What I had thought was a giant bat was, in fact, a dragon.

A fire-breathing dragon, I added.

There was a short pause, and then his name began flashing on my screen, signifying he was typing away over there. These days, I didn't worry so much about waking up Fang—or keeping him up after a long bartending shift. Now, as a fellow creature of the night, he was always up. Always wide awake; that is, until dawn, when sleep overcame both of us.

Fang had always wanted us to work. Fang, unfortunately, was a little creepy, although I adored him immensely. Then again, I'm a little creepy, too. Truth was, Fang was a cutie when he wasn't busy stalking me or killing girlfriends or prison guards...

Okay, that might be a little unfair. All of that had been in the distant past. These days, I knew Fang ran a blood bank. A very different kind of blood bank, where he paid mortals good money for their blood—and even paid some of them to be feasted upon directly by high-paying clients. As far as I was aware, no humans had been killed in the making of his business. Fang had quickly developed the ability to manipulate memory, and so most mortals went away thinking they'd really donated to a legitimate blood bank. All pretty much on the up and up. Anything less, and Fang knew he would have a problem with me. Not too long ago I'd shut down another type of blood bank... one where the donors weren't so willing, and they most certainly didn't walk away with a wad of cash. Most, of course, were hung from meat hooks where they had been drained dry.

Anyway, gone were the days where Fang lived in his tiny one-bedroom apartment, supporting himself with bartending tips. No, he was a real player in the blood trade... and had generated a lot of money. Blood money, as it were. In every sense of the word. Last I had heard, he was living in a familiar Gothic mansion in downtown Orange, the same mansion a client from Kingsley's past had lived in, a client I'd been certain was responsible for shooting Kingsley five times in the head. I had been wrong, of course. But that was another case for another time.

I always suspected you turned into a dragon, Moon Dance. There have been rumors and sightings of dragons for centuries, millenniums. There is always something to such legends. But you always seemed so sure that you were, and I quote, "a giant vampire bat."

How the hell would I know any different? I wrote. *I've only been recently communicating with Talos, and it never occurred to me to ask what, exactly, I was turning into. I mean, I knew I turned into something massive and winged. I just never thought of asking for a name.*

What was it like, breathing fire?

Honestly? I wrote, and found myself truly LOLing on my couch. *Kind of orgasmic. It felt so... fucking good coming out of me. It was a true release. Like it had been building up and needed an outlet.*

You make it sound kind of fun. And sexy.

I giggled on my end. Or GOL'd.

Oh, yes, I wrote.

Few of us can turn into such creatures, Sam. In fact, I am only aware of a handful.

I think, I wrote, *they choose us more than we choose them.*

They, being the dragons?

I wrote *yes* and added: *They do it for the experience, and they do it to help us, too. In fact, if I am correct, they are here to combat the darkness within us. Maybe combat is too strong of a word. To add balance, perhaps.*

Like your librarian friend.

Yes, like Maximus and the other alchemists.

Sam, do you and Talos switch bodies?

Not quite, I wrote. *We sort of combine bodies.*

But your human body gets transported instantly to another world, his world?

Something like that, I wrote. *But in Talos's world, we don't merge. Not yet, and perhaps not ever. Only in this world do we merge bodies.*

What happens when he's, say, in mid-flight and you summon him?

I asked him that. It's why I see the flame. He sees the flame, too, and knows I am calling on him. He will find a safe place for us to integrate, often high upon a rocky precipice.

So weird, Sam.

How often have we said that? I wrote.

Too often, but I wouldn't want it any other way.

You really do love being a vampire, I wrote. It wasn't a question.

More than you can possibly know, Moon Dance. He paused, then wrote: *How are you and the wolfman?*

We are happy. We are together. We might even be falling in love.

Oh, joy.

Don't be a sourpuss, I wrote. *Are you dating?*

Occasionally. Mostly, I work. There was a pause. *I miss you, Sam.*

We're talking right now.

I miss seeing you in the bar with your sister. I miss your smile and sometimes, the tragic look in your eyes. I miss lighting up those eyes with a joke or a drink or both. I miss watching you.

You're getting creepy again...

You know what I mean, Sam. I knew what you were. I knew why you were drinking the kind of wine you were drinking, and I knew why you never ordered appetizers. I knew why you looked tired before sunset, and why you suddenly looked so alive just after.

I exhaled on my couch, looking at his words. Of course, I hadn't known that our cute bartender was also the same Fang I'd often IM'd with. He had found me through various clues in our conversation, and eventually, had gotten a job at the very bar I frequented. Which got me thinking: had I dropped such clues on purpose?

I wrote: *I think our friendship was based a lot on you watching me, Fang. Watching me without me knowing it.*

Of course, he hadn't been a threat; at least, not to me. Never once had my inner alarm system warned me about him.

Not true, Sam. We spent many months and years getting to know each other. I loved everything about you. I still do.

Fang had, of course, nearly destroyed our friendship by going behind my back and teaming up with a woman who, eventually, not only had kidnapped my sister but had killed my ex. A woman who'd plotted to kill me, too. Of course, Fang had been under the control of a very, very old vampire who'd had the rare ability to control other immortals. A vampire Kingsley had disposed of.

Fang's end goal had always been to be a vampire. Growing up with two exceptionally long canines, being harassed and bullied along the way, and then developing the mother of all psychoses—a love for real blood—had ended badly for him and especially for his girlfriend, whom he'd drained of blood, effectively killing her. Fang's murder trial had been a sensation, and his ultimate escape from a high-security insane asylum had dominated the news for weeks. Finally, he'd managed to elude capture, and his story went away. Which is where I came in, years later.

I like our friendship, Fang, I wrote.

I do, too.

But you want more, I added.

Is that so wrong?

No, of course not. It's always nice to be wanted by a cute boy.

He gave me a capitalized "LOL" signifying that he'd really let loose with a guffaw. I wondered, just how hard did one have to guffaw to be deemed worthy of an LOL?

I am more than a boy, Sam.

In lots of ways, he wasn't, but I didn't tell him that. He seemed stunted at times. He seemed stuck in that ten-year-old's body, with his grotesquely deformed teeth, who dreamed of being a real vampire—only to discover that vampires really did exist. Who dreamed of acceptance and friendship and love.

Back in the day, I would have been worried about Fang picking up my thoughts... back when he was still mortal. But now, our thoughts were shielded from each other, which was a relief to me. No wonder why vampires hung out with other vampires and other creatures of the night.

It's late, Fang.

Although, of course, early to the rest of the world. By my inherent clock, the sun should be rising in less than thirty minutes. I might have a ring on my finger that helped me withstand the sun, but there was no denying the need for sleep at dawn.

Are you mad, Sam?

Mad that someone has feelings for me? Never. But sometimes, feelings need to be checked. I'm in a relationship now. A healthy one. A happy one. One that, I think, might be going somewhere.

Going where?

We'll see.

Marriage?

Now, I nearly lol'd him, but the thought had crossed my mind. The big oaf—that is, Kingsley— seemed to be dropping hints these days. I wasn't entirely against the idea. I was...intrigued, to say the least.

We'll see.

I wish nothing but the best for you, Sam.

I know.

But if you marry the bastard... I don't know if I can still be your friend.

You will, I wrote. *It's just hard imagining it now. Besides, it may not happen.*

Good night, Moon Dance. No snoring... you might just burn up your sheets.

I gave him a hearty LOL, which was well deserved because I'd just snorted embarrassingly. Good thing I was alone. Was there such a thing as SOL?

Anyway, when I was done snorting out loud, I shut my laptop and headed to the bathroom. I didn't wear much makeup these days—mostly because I couldn't see my face—although a little blush never hurt, especially when one had the complexion of a whiteboard. When I was done removing my makeup, I brushed my teeth and walked through the empty house. Truthfully, I got a little weirded out standing in front of an empty mirror.

Anthony and Tammy were with Mary Lou, as they often were. I tended to work the night shift. Someday soon, my kids would be old enough to take care of themselves. Anthony was already strong enough, certainly. And no one, but no one, was sneaking up on my daughter, not with her radar-like telepathic powers. Apparently, I was raising the X-Men. Complete with my own Wolverine.

Speaking of which, I wondered how Kingsley was doing. It was not yet dawn, so he would still be in his wolfie state. I wondered if he got tired of all that growling and pacing and feasting. Was he, even now, sitting up in his cell, just counting down the minutes until dawn?

I finished my home reconnaissance and spit the toothpaste in the sink, rinsed my mouth and spit that out, too. Long ago, I'd gotten used to making sure all the toothpaste was spat out. Even if a little bit found its way down my gullet, it hurt like hell. Now, thanks to the ring, I had gotten careless. I rinsed and swished and spit, and was soon lying in bed, on top of my blankets. Yes, I am often cold. No, blankets did nothing for me.

I didn't read myself to sleep or watch DVR'd episodes of *Modern Family* in bed until my eyelids got heavy and I finally dropped off to sleep.

No. Sleep started the instant the sun rose—as it was starting to do now—and it came over me rapidly, overwhelming my senses, my mind, my body, my entire being. A complete and total shutdown of all that I am. It was a form of micro-death. Yes, I could fight it if I wanted to, thanks to the day ring. I could even force myself to stay awake. But giving in was so much easier.

And so I gave in now, and felt myself die a little, all over again.

12.

I rarely dream when I sleep.

Mostly, I just lay there, comatose, not breathing, not thinking, not really sleeping. Perhaps I really do die a little. Perhaps I'm not anything. Perhaps there is no definition for what happens to me during the day. I don't remember any of it. Usually, I feel myself slip away, and then, my alarms are going off. Two of them, in fact.

Yes, it was hell getting up during the day. It was much better to awaken naturally at sundown. I could count on one hand the number of times I had slept through the day. I envied those creatures of the night who didn't have kids.

I set my alarm for 1:30. That gave me enough time to climb out of my sleep, to return to the land of the living—perhaps, literally—and then make some coffee, do some chores, and watch *Judge*

Judy, all before picking up my kids.

That was generally my routine.

Except on the rare occasions when I dreamed. And because I didn't really sleep, I didn't really dream either. I knew this because these weren't really dreams.

They were visions of the future. Prophetic visions.

And on this day, while others were working or in class or running errands or smoking weed, I was in my bedroom, dreaming of my daughter Tammy dying, over and over again.

The same dream, repeated over and over.

In it, I saw her being flung through a broken windshield, to lay broken and bleeding in the middle of the intersection... only to be run over by something, something big...

***

I shot up out of bed, fully awake, gasping and crying.

In my mind's eye, I saw Tammy, clear as day, lying in the center of the street, bleeding and cut and choking on her own blood, when a car—no a truck—ran her over. I heard the *thud, thud.* I saw the tires bounce, the shocks compress. I saw her jackknife involuntarily as her chest collapsed and blood burst from her mouth and eyes. Mostly, I saw the life escaping instantly.

Now, I paced, alternately running my hands

through my hair and shaking my hands before me, as if they were wet. My room was hotel-room dark. No light at all. I might as well be pacing in a cemetery in the dead of a moonless night. Even as I paced, I moved quickly, perhaps even supernaturally quickly. Pacing, turning, pacing. I didn't stub my toes along my smallish desk pushed up against the window. I didn't hit or touch anything. I was a spirit in my own bedroom. A wraith. A shade.

The dream or vision hadn't been very long. The car had been packed with kids. Teenagers. Older teenagers. Much older than my daughter, who was now a freshman in high school. The dream was seared into my memory. The details, too. And, unlike real dreams, I remembered everything.

As I paced, I relived the dream again and again.

I see the joints. I see someone raising something —a can of beer. A forty, they call them. It's a party in the car. I see all the faces. Hell, they are seared into my memory. And there is my daughter, riding shotgun, arms above her head and dancing in her seat, her seatbelt off. And then she screams, and I see why she screamed.

The bastard behind the wheel, the bastard drinking the 40, runs a red light.

Tammy screams, they all scream. Brakes squeal. The crunch of metal is terrible. No airbags. No seatbelts, and my daughter is launched out of her seat and through the windshield. I see this from seemingly many angles at once: her angle, the driver's angle, the passengers' angles. I am a wildly swinging point-of-view camera.

I shook my head and rubbed my eyes. I didn't want to see her get run over again. But I did. Over and over again.

13.

We were drinking coffee in her kitchen, something we didn't do nearly enough.

The first thing I'd done once I'd gotten control of myself was call my sister and confirm that Tammy was okay. Once confirmed, I threw on some clothes, ditched the makeup, pulled my hair back through an Angels ball cap, and was out the door faster than, officially, any woman ever.

I had precisely two more panic attacks before I finally pulled up to my sister's house. Once there, I rushed into the guest bedroom that Tammy shared with Mary Lou's own young daughter, Ellie Mae. My sister always loved her own two-word first name, and blessed (or cursed) her own daughter with one of her own. Anyway, both girls were sitting up in bed, texting. Perhaps texting each other. Kids these days. Tammy shot me a look that suggested she disapproved of my very existence on this planet. But she was alive.

I'd done my damnedest to shield my thoughts from my powerfully telepathic daughter, to bury my concern and panic, and I think I might have succeeded. "Love you," I had said, and she'd rolled her eyes.

In the kitchen, Mary Lou handed me an oversized mug that was, I was certain, exactly twice the size of my stomach. We sat at her cute little kitchen table that overlooked her cute little backyard, and three sips of perfect coffee later, I was bawling like a baby.

Mary Lou came over and took the cup from me. She set it aside and kneeled down and wrapped an arm around my shoulders. Our heads touched, our hair intermingled. Two sisters who had taken two very different paths.

She whispered some sympathetic words, instinctively aware that I wanted to keep this mini-meltdown from my daughter and my son, who was playing video games upstairs with his younger cousin, Billy Joe. Yes, Billy Joe. I think I might have cried a little harder with that last thought.

My face slid to her ample bosom, pulled down by the sheer gravitational force of her breasts. Had I been an air breather, I surely would have suffocated by now. I managed to pull away, just as a napkin materialized in my hand. Yes, Mary Lou was that good of a mother and sister and friend.

"She's fine, Sam."

I closed my eyes and looked away and made a small whimpering noise. The images of her dead in the street came flooding back and the whimper nearly turned into another bout of tears.

"Nothing's happened to her, Sam."

"Yet," I said.

"Don't talk that way—"

I raised a finger to my lips, especially since I knew my sister was about to launch into one of her Law of Attraction sermons.

"She can hear us?" asked Mary Lou.

My sister's home was big, maybe even twice as big as my own. Then again, that wasn't saying much. Danny had never really gotten his career going and the money had never really flowed in from his end. I'd made more than him as a federal agent which, I think, had gnawed at him. When I started working private, our money situation turned erratic at best. Maybe that was why the bastard had turned to his lurid side business. A side business that, as far as I knew, was still nothing more than smoking ruins.

To the world, Danny was still officially missing. And, since I doubted anyone would find his body buried deep within a cave, he would stay missing. I, of course, knew he was dead. So did my kids, and so did my sister. Most definitely my sister, as she had been a pawn in his plot to do away with me.

Anyway, few people asked about him, which spoke volumes of his futile life. My kids, it seemed, were the only ones who missed him. Little did they know he sometimes appeared in their bedrooms, or just outside their doors, or in the far corners of our house where he watched us silently, before disappearing into nothingness again. I never, ever mentioned his presence. His spirit haunting our place would do little to help them move on. I could see spirits, but I rarely interacted with them. It seemed that the interacting part was largely contingent on them. Few seemed to try. Most seemed content to appear, to watch, then disappear again.

Once again, I held the oversized mug in both hands, and looked at my sister through the steam that was still rising. Through her open sliding glass door, I could hear the birds singing and chirping and squawking. I knew she fed the birds each morning, and squirrels, too, I thought. She had not one but three birdbaths in her backyard, with small wooden bowls scattered around her garden for all the little critters. Her backyard was a veritable wildlife sanctuary. She had everything from raccoons to skunks to hawks showing up.

With all the chirping and chittering going on behind me, I said, "Truthfully? I'm not sure what Tammy's range is, but I suspect it's significant."

"How significant?" Mary Lou was dressed in mom jeans—she loved her mom jeans—and an old-school, sleeved softball shirt that was now wet with tears.

"I'm wondering if there is no limit," I said.

"What does that mean?"

I thought about that, as even this concept was new to me, too, but it felt right. "If she has established a prior connection with someone, I think—and this is just conjecture on my part—I think she has the potential to dip into their thoughts from anywhere on Earth."

"And you know this how?"

"Just a guess, but I've seen some evidence of it. She seems to know where I'm at most times, for instance."

"Every teen's dream."

"And every mom's worst nightmare," I added.

"We do tend to rely on stealth," said Mary Lou.

"Stealth is out the window with her."

"She can read other family members, but you can't?"

"Exactly. At least, not immediate family members. Never really tried third or fourth cousins."

"But she can?"

"Oh yes. And not just family members, but other immortals, too."

"Kingsley?"

I nodded.

Mary Lou said, "Does he know that?"

I nodded again.

"Good. Should keep the bastard honest."

Mary Lou hadn't been as forgiving as I had been of Kingsley's past transgressions. Mary Lou claimed it was her job to remind me of it as often as possible. Once a cheater and all of that.

"He's not a bastard," I said, then giggled. "And, yeah, he tends to stay away from her. I don't think he wants her to know all his secrets."

Kingsley, I knew, had lived an interesting life. Before he was a famous defense attorney, he had seen and done his fair share of questionable activities. And by questionable, I meant raiding local cemeteries and feasting on rotting corpses. You know, normal stuff.

"Is she listening to us now?"

"If she wanted to," I said.

I wondered if she could control thoughts, too. That gave me pause for thought. Hell, was she controlling me now? I doubted it, but that was just the thing with mind control, one never really knew.

"So it doesn't really matter where we have this conversation then?" asked Mary Lou.

"Not really."

"Or how low we keep our voices."

"Well, the others could always overhear us," I said. "You know, in the traditional way."

"We have the strangest conversations, Sam."

"We do."

"I'm not sure I enjoy them."

I waited, sipping, wondering again who those kids were in the car with my daughter. I hadn't recognized any of them. Then again, I hadn't gotten the clearest look at their faces. That was the thing with my prophetic dreams... they gained clarity over time. The closer to the event, the more details emerged.

"I mean, I enjoy talking to my kid sister—a kid sister who looks nearly a decade younger than me, mind you." My sister was six years older, and I'd been part of the undead club for a decade. "But I'm not sure how much I enjoy talking about all of this... craziness, you know?"

I nodded. "I know. You would prefer to talk about the kids and school and movies and *Game of Thrones*."

"Well, yes. Normal stuff."

"Mary Lou, normal flew out that window years ago. Like a bat. A vampire bat. I wouldn't know normal if it bit me on the ass."

"You see, it's these kinds of conversations. They are unsettling to me."

"Are you saying you want me to not talk about what I am, and what my family is going through?"

"Maybe just a teensy bit less? Is that too much to ask?"

I thought about getting mad. I thought about overreacting. But I thought my sister had a point. This past decade, our conversations had been dominated by what I am, what was happening to me, and the general weirdness of all things Samantha Moon.

"Let me get this straight," I said, my voice rising a little. I feigned righteous indignation. "Are you telling me that your life doesn't revolve around me?"

"That's what I'm telling you—"

I cut her off. "And that you have, in fact, a life outside of vampires and werewolves?"

She caught on. "A thriving life, in fact. A very fulfilling life."

I lowered my voice and sat back. My little faux tirade over. "I'm sorry, M-Lou," I said, using her high school rap name. Yes, she had a rap name, and, no, I never let her forget it. Ever.

"Thank you, Sam."

"So when's the band getting together again?"

"The band?" she asked, blinking, then put it together. "I was in a rap band for precisely two weeks, Sam. Two weeks."

"Two of the greatest weeks of my life," I said.

"You're terrible. Oh, no, you don't, Samantha Moon!"

And now I was off of my stool and in the center of her kitchen floor, going through her rap routine, a routine I'd watched her practice dozens and dozens of times with her friends; over and over they'd practiced their moves and flashed wannabe gangster signs.

"My name's M-Lou, and I'm coming for you," I rapped, and did their hop, skip, slouch dance perhaps a little too well.

"Sad that you still know that—"

I ignored her. "I drop sick rhymes for these scary times..."

"Oh, God. Kill me now..."

I did their routine, sliding right, then left, waving one arm, then the next. Now, elbows up, hands swinging. The robot zombie, as she used to call it.

"Mommy," I heard a small voice ask from the kitchen entrance, "what's Aunt Sammie doing?"

"Never letting me forget, baby. Never letting me forget."

"We like cute boys and we cannot lie..." I rapped, and accidentally slid into her stove. Ellie Mae giggled and ran over with me, picking up the dance moves quickly, or at least trying to.

Mary Lou shook her head. "My. Worst. Nightmare. Ever."

"Oh, stop, M-Lou," I said, sliding to the left, then to the right. Ellie Mae slid right along with me. "And join us."

"No."

"C'mon."

"Fine."

And she got up from her own stool a little too fast, I thought. In fact, it fell over. She ignored it and joined the two of us in the center of the kitchen. She fell into step smoothly and picked up where I'd left off, channeling her inner thug:

"We like cute boys and we cannot lie..."

14.

The dance party ended when Tammy appeared in the doorway, shook her head contemptuously, and pronounced that we were all lame.

I caught up to her in the living room. My niece followed us in, and I asked for some privacy. Mary Lou swept her up and hauled her deeper into the big house.

"Strong words for someone who used to call themselves Lady Tam Tam."

Tammy took to studying my sister's china hutch, which displayed anything but china... my sister, besides being a closet rapper, had been into all things medieval growing up. Dungeons & Dragons, fairies, sword and sorcery novels, Renaissance fairs. Yeah, go figure. I'd been told repeatedly that I'd been a witch in a handful of past lives. Maybe my sister had been Maid Marian or, maybe, a princess with an aversion to peas.

"You're funny," said Tammy, without looking around. She was eyeing a Knights of the Round Table display that, admittedly, looked pretty dang cool.

I said nothing, not because I didn't have plenty to say about my wannabe rapper, medieval-loving sister. But because the dream had come again, and I saw my daughter jackknifing in the center of the road as the truck's tires thumped-thumped over her exposed stomach. Crushing the life from her and bursting blood from every orifice.

"*Eeww*, Mom."

Yeah, I doubted that last vision—or memory—had stayed hidden. Too powerful, too painful, too fucking terrible.

"Such language, Mother." She had moved on to examining a fairy sitting on a crystal ball. The fairy had blue wings. I wondered if fairies were real, too.

"Of course they're real, Mom."

"Oh? And how would you know?"

She giggled and moved on to a red-winged dragon perched on a pewter rock. The dragon was eyeing the fairy. I came over and stood next to Tammy. We were both eyeballing twin swords sheathed in a wooden mantel of some sort.

"You kind of sounded like you knew what you were talking about," I said.

"I'm just joking, Mom. Of course they're not real."

But I wasn't so sure. I knew when my daughter

was lying. I sure as hell didn't need to be a mind reader for that. She had backtracked, but not very convincingly. "Fine," I said. "We'll talk about it later."

"You want to talk about the dream." She moved on to a display of tiny pewter figurines that could have been lifted from a *Lord of the Rings* board game.

"It's not a dream, young lady."

Tammy shrugged and touched the glass with her fingertips. She was going to be small like me. I barely scratched five foot, three inches. She had barely tipped the tape at five feet. She was thinner than I'd been at that age. She could thank Danny for that. I'd always had a little, um, padding. Even in my vampirism, some of the padding had stayed, although I was leaner and harder than I'd ever been.

"Okay, so a vision. Whatever."

"Not a vision. And not whatever. It was a premonition. A prophecy. A future happening."

She shook her head and I saw the smile reflected in the glass and I sort of lost it. Just sort of. I grabbed a shoulder and spun her around. When I spin someone, they spin. Big, small, in-between. And spin she did, nearly losing her balance.

"What are you doing, you freak?" she gasped, stumbling.

"This freak is trying to save your life."

When she righted herself, her face was flushed with embarrassment and anger. No reason to be embarrassed. We were alone in the living room.

"I'm not embarrassed. I just don't like being treated like a child."

"You're fourteen."

"Exactly. I know what I'm doing."

"No, you don't. You've seen my vision. You've seen yourself being thrown out of a car and being..." I just couldn't say it.

"Run over by a truck, Mom. Yeah, yeah, it's all you're thinking about this morning."

"Who are those kids in the car?"

"I don't know. I don't recognize them."

She was looking away from me. I still held her shoulder; she wasn't going anywhere. "Are you lying to me?"

Now, she turned and looked at me and gave me a half smile laced with lots of snotty. Lots and lots of snotty. "No, of course not. Then again, you wouldn't know if I were."

"I have my ways, young lady."

"Oh, you're gonna snoop on me?"

"I'll snoop if I have to."

She took in a lot of air. My daughter was very much mortal and growing and blossoming and looking too cute for her own good. Her mind read-ing gave her false confidence. And I wished like crazy it would just go the hell away.

"Not false confidence, Mom. Real confidence. I know what people are thinking around me. I've gotten real good at it."

"Mind reading won't save you from that truck."

She broke away from my grip, and crossed her

arms under her chest and stuck out a hip. There was a chance she looked just like me. "That's just the thing. I would never do that, Mom."

"You would never do it *sober*." And then it hit me. The look on her face just before the accident. The wild, jubilant, far-off look on her face. She wasn't drunk. The others weren't drunk. They were all on something.

"I don't do drugs, Mom. It's just a dream," she said, and gave me a small grin and was about to leave, when I caught hold of her hand.

"Wait," I said.

She sighed, already reading the question in my mind. "Yes, the fairies are real, Mom."

"How do you know?"

"Because I talk to them. I hear them singing at night, and sometimes in the morning, and then, they are gone."

"You have got to be kidding."

"Are they any less strange than vampires? Or werewolves? Or witches?"

"I... I don't know."

"They're not, Mom. They're real."

"Have you seen them?"

She smiled and cocked her head. "Oh, yes." And turned and left the living room.

15.

"We found him there, up against the reeds, face down in the water."

I was standing with Detective Hillary Oster on the southwest side of Lake Elsinore. A human-shaped form lay under a stain-resistant white blanket. The stain-resistant part was probably a good thing, from what I was hearing.

"Called you as soon as we got the call," said the detective. "Took you long enough."

"Sorry about that," I said. I had hit all kinds of frustrating traffic coming out here from Orange County. I'd nearly summoned Talos and sprouted wings through the driver's side and passenger windows, and flapped myself right out of the sea of brake lights. "Would have been more convenient if the body washed up earlier in the day."

"I'll make a note of it," she said, but I detected

emotion in her voice. She had grown to like the kids. And now, one of them was lying under a nearby blanket. That the shape only vaguely looked humanoid was troubling. At least, troubling to the sane, rational, loving person inside me. The bitch, on the other hand, was intrigued to no end. She said, "FBI is combing the area. So are my investigators. It's a real clusterfuck. No one knows who's in charge."

"He's missing his left leg," I said.

"And most of his right arm. Half of his right side is gone, too."

"Mind if I look," I asked.

"You really want to?"

I was intrigued. Too intrigued. I called it professional curiosity. But I suspected it was something. A dark compulsion. I nodded.

Detective Oster stared at me, sweating in the heat of the late afternoon sun, wiped her brow, then nodded for me to follow her.

***

The body was as described... and then some.

With the detective holding up the blanket, I leaned down and studied the wounds, fighting like hell the excitement welling up within me. Was the excitement her excitement? Or mine?

I shook my head. It was hers. Always hers. It had better be. I refused to believe that the mangled corpse of a boy could excite me.

I'm losing it, I thought, as I studied the wound to his upper right arm. The flesh was loose, pale, supple, and cut clean through with what appeared to be many serrated edges.

"Teeth marks?" I asked.

Oster leaned down next to me, still holding the flap of the blanket. "Would be my guess."

Damage to the boy's hip was similar. The detective had already provided me with a pair of latex gloves, and so I didn't hesitate to reach down and lift away some of the tattered and sopping jeans. Most blood had washed away. Most blood had drained away, too. The hip socket had been torn free, and the expulsion of tendons and muscle might have been enough for most people to lose their lunch. Except I had the opposite reaction. My stomach growled. Worse, I'm pretty sure the detective heard it.

"I might, ah, vomit," I said quickly.

"Not on the vic please."

I nodded, made a show of swallowing, and said, "I'm good."

The wound to his side—the very massive wound—was the most telling and the most perplexing. Although much of his side was missing, there was a very peculiar red ring around the perimeter of the wound. The serrated flesh was the same, indicative of teeth marks, but it was the red, dimpled flesh just outside the wound the held my fascination. I reached out and carefully ran my latexed finger over the indentations. Puncture marks, and just below these marks, the boy's side had been completely bitten through.

"Had we been in the Everglades, this would have been a no-brainer," said the detective.

"Alligator?" I said.

"Sure looks that way to me. Something took a bite of him. A few bites."

I nodded. The thing I'd seen in Roy's memory *could* have been an alligator. Long and cylindrical and missile-shaped. Yeah, maybe an alligator. Maybe.

I said, "What are the chances that, say, a rogue alligator is living in this lake?"

"A pet that got a little too big?"

"You hear about it all the time," I said. "Some yahoo comes back with something that looks like a gecko lizard, only to discover that it's eaten his cat. Rather than flushing it down the toilet, he drops it off here at the lake."

Oster shook her head. As she did so, sweat spilled onto her roundish cop sunglasses and streaked down over the lens. She ignored it. A true professional. "It would have been spotted. Alligators surface, and sun themselves. They're not exactly masters of camouflage."

"And we're sure it's an animal attack?"

"The medical examiner might have a different theory, but those sure as shit look like bite marks to me."

I nodded. They did to me, too. I continued examining the raw ring around the wound in his side. "Were his leg and arm found?"

She shook her head, and more of the sweat that had been building up at the bottom of her lens flung free. "Not yet."

"Which boy is this?"

"Johnny."

"He was the first to disappear?"

She nodded. "And no, we haven't seen or heard from Luke."

I stared down at the face that seemed peaceful and passive. Surely, he had been anything but peaceful and passive when whatever it was had come up on him. Had the boy been swimming in the lake, when something came up from underneath, *Jaws*-like? Or had he been fishing and caught something too big to haul in—something that had, in fact, pulled him into the lake? Except the boy had been missing for over a week now. I doubted he would be out swimming or fishing, not with the whole town looking for him and his friend.

"How long had he been in the water?"

"Hard to say, but my guess, not very long. Maybe since this morning. None of the critters had gotten to him."

"Who found him?"

"A fisherman."

"Statement?"

"He's giving it to the feds now. From what I gathered, he'd found the body floating face down in the reeds."

"Did he see anything else?"

"No."

We were both silent, but I was picking up her thoughts. I was picking up the horror she felt. The fear she felt for her own kids. For the public at large. How she was going to break the news to Johnny's mother that her son had been eaten alive. How she was going to convince her police chief to shut down the lake. How she was going to get through this without crying in front of me. But most predominant in her thoughts was finding Luke.

"How does a boy who's been missing for a week, wind up in the lake, half-eaten?" I asked.

"Million-dollar question," she said. "We've scoured the area. I have personally searched the entire perimeter of the lake a half-dozen times."

"Maybe he was *under* the lake."

"Trapped on something?"

"Maybe."

She shook her head. "We hired divers. We used sonar. We covered likely spots, and checked out abnormalities in the lake. We didn't find anything."

"No lake monster, either?"

"Nothing. And certainly no twelve-year-old boys."

We both thought about that as a distant speedboat slapped the water and the sun beat down on a partially devoured boy.

16.

I was waiting in my minivan for the sun to go down.

Lake Elsinore wouldn't be my first choice of a place to live, or second or third. Not because of the heat or isolation, or even the high-crime rate. But because of the damn mountains.

Although having the sun dip behind the mountains hours before the actual sunset gave me some relief, it was a false relief. It was, quite frankly, confusing. My eyes told me it was dusk. But my internal clock told me not yet. And, of course, it wasn't my internal clock, was it? It was my internal demon who knew all too well where the sun was in the sky.

In my book, when the sun disappeared behind anything, it was called sunset. Not in her book, though. Nope. Her rules dictated only when the sun disappeared beyond the horizon. Granted, it was a moving horizon. After all, when I was recently in New Orleans, I noted that my internal demon adjusted instantly to the geography. Apparently, there was no jet lag for the evil.

Now, with the shadows deepening around me, and the lake darkening in my rearview mirror, I waited in an apartment parking lot, on a slight hill. I waited to feel good, to feel strong, to feel more alive than I ever had before. At least, that's how it always felt. With each sunset, I couldn't imagine ever feeling this good, this strong, this free. That is, until the next sunset.

I waited for it now. Yearned for it. Hungered for it. I sat forward in my seat, gripped the steering wheel, closed my eyes and breathed and waited. It was as if I'd had all the sun I could handle, all the light I could manage, and another fucking second of it would drive me ape-shit.

C'mon, I thought. *C'mon!*

I released the steering wheel and shook my hands and breathed faster and faster, and hated the bitch inside me, hated her fear of the sun and light and anything happy and loving and real. I hated her control over me, her hold on me. Who the fuck was she to do this to me? *Just who the fuck was she?*

My head dropped, my chin pressed into my sternum, breathing, breathing, now wringing my hands, knowing that, to all the world, I might have looked like I was having a seizure. Which was why I stayed in the minivan. The windows were tinted, of course. After all, I often used the van for surveillance, too.

Her name had been Elizabeth—and maybe it still was. Then again, maybe she went by something new now. Like Zoran the Invincible. She had been the Librarian's mother. And that's about where her humanity had ended, as far as I knew. I hadn't gotten the full scoop on her life on earth as a dark master. I also hadn't gotten the full scoop on what went down and how it went down and how many good people had died in what must have been one hellacious battle of good versus evil.

She had fought her son, I knew that. And others like him. Alchemists, mostly. I myself was from a long line of alchemists. From the original alchemist, Hermes Trismegistus.

I wondered if my bloodline flowed through all my incarnations, or if it was isolated to just this current one. That is, my current and *last* incarnation on Earth.

My bloodline was highly valuable, I'd discovered. Which was why I had the pleasure of being targeted by Elizabeth, one of the strongest of the dark masters. My bloodline and her dark mastery were enough to turn the tide of power. That is, if I let her out, which I never did.

I say one of the strongest, because there was another, of course. The entity that currently resided in none other than Dracula himself, a prince of a man I'd encountered a few months ago—and a unique warrior who had saved my ass. Dracula, the original vampire. Dracula, who had given himself up as a vessel to the strongest of the dark masters. A dark master who just so happened to be the love of Elizabeth's immortal life.

What tangled webs we weave...

The entity within Dracula had made it known that it wanted time with the entity within me. By time, I figured they meant some hot and sweaty dark master sex. After all, it had been centuries since they had been, ah, united. Centuries that Elizabeth had waited for me to be born. Why me, I didn't know. Why not, say, my mother? I didn't know that either. My mother's bloodline would have been even closer to Hermes, and less diluted. Then again, imagining my mother as a vampire nearly caused me to have a fit of semi-hysterical laughter in my minivan.

No, I thought. She waited for me for a reason. Perhaps it had something to do with my witchy heritage.

I nodded, knowing that was the key.

I continued breathing, sucking in lungfuls of worthless air, but not knowing what else to do. The sun was just minutes from disappearing from a distant horizon that I could not see—not with the damn mountain in the way.

Why did she hate the sun so much anyway? What was the deal with that? Kingsley operated in the sun, and he had a similar highly evolved dark master residing within him, too.

The answer came to me as an impulse, and it

came to me from her, I knew. The thing within Kingsley was a different kind of dark master. A lower form, in fact. Okay, that made sense, although I would never tell Kingsley that. Then again, maybe he knew. The thing within him was hungrier, angrier, wilder. Hence, the beast he turned into each full moon.

I wrung my hands, breathed, rocked.

The sun, the sun, the sun...

I gripped my steering wheel. Too tightly. It creaked in my hands. Bent inward, threatening to snap. I didn't care. I hated my skin, the sun, the light. I felt myself losing it, going crazy, completely fucking losing it...

And then it happened.

It was gone and the crawling sensation between my shoulders stopped and the air hissed out of my lips and I hung my head and found myself weeping... for joy.

Then, I sat back and found myself smiling, knowing I was surely losing my mind, but I didn't care. Not in this moment of pure relief.

The sun was gone, and I had never felt so alive.

17.

There was a chance I might have been in the bad part of town.

The complex was tucked away at the end of a cul-de-sac. Anyone on this street meant to be on this street. No one came through here. And those who did were high or wasted or up to no good. Okay, that sounded sort of judge-y.

The apartment complex itself was sprawling, with many wings and buildings and covered parking lots and entrances. The apartment was gated, sort of. Heavy iron gates blocked the entrances, opened by, I presumed, a scanner card. But the rest of the complex was fenceless. Foot traffic could get in, but cars couldn't. Seemed sort of half-assed. If you're going to gate a place, then gate it.

And here, there was foot traffic aplenty. Teen-agers lounged in groups of three or four. They did most of their lounging around an old Mustang fastback, which, when you looked at it sideways, seemed to be lounging as well. Grown men lounged in front of their apartments, or on their narrow, feeble-looking decks. Two kids on trikes lounged near the main entrance into the complex. An old woman watched me from a chair, a wooden cane in her hands. Come to think of it, she was lounging, too. Exactly half of all males within eyeshot, from the very youngest to the very oldest, were shirtless.

The apartment complex boasted a network of catwalks, wobbly-looking railings, and stone pebble stairs with chunks missing. This was, I was certain, an insurance company's worst nightmare.

There was a general shift in attention and body language as I moved through the parking lot. The closest group of teens seemed too young to be trouble, but not too young to be crude. I heard "MILF" and "booty" and "dat ass" as I moved past them, and, for some reason, I was grinning all the way up the ramshackle stairway of doom.

Somehow, I made it up without plunging through a step, or careening off a broken rail. Up here it was a bit livelier. The smell of barbeque and beans and curry filled the air. Cigarette smoke, too. And weed. And meth. Kids riding on plastic toys, moms talking out front, laughter and TV. Someone shouted from the far side of the complex. Someone shouted back. Human beings are weird.

I counted down the apartment numbers, moving past a little Hispanic girl standing out in front of an open door, chocolate on her face, eyes round and distant. I smiled, she didn't. At the door in question, I rapped loudly enough to be heard by just about all in the complex. There seemed, if I was correct, to be a general hum in the air, and it wasn't because a vampire was among them. Something seemed to be going on. People were on edge, lively, talkative, connecting. Perhaps more so than usual here in the complex? I didn't know.

The door opened and a cute woman in her thirties appeared in the shadow. Correction. Not very cute, once I saw past the shadows and into the haunted eyes, the scars, the acne, the paleness.

"Police?" she said.

"No."

"Come in."

18.

She didn't offer me a seat, which was fine. The place was filthy, the broken couch was stained, and the single chair pushed under the dining table looked questionable. Yeah, I was good.

"You're here about Luke."

"I am."

"The cops were just here."

Ah, I thought. That explained the nervous buzz in the complex. There were a lot of drug dealers, drug addicts, hookers and petty criminals breathing a sigh of relief.

She picked up a broken, stained, half-finished cigarette, lit it with a match that seemingly came out of nowhere, and inhaled on it. Waste not, want not. She said, "You look like a cop."

"I'm a private investigator."

"Whatever. Why are you here?"

"My case might overlap your son's case."

"Stupid fucking kid."

"Missing kid. Alone kid. Scared kid."

"Whatever. He got himself into this shit, and I'll be damned if I'm going to worry about him another second."

"That'll show him," I said.

But she wasn't really listening to me. She was sucking on the filthy cigarette that may or not have been found in a street gutter, and looking blankly into the far corner of her apartment. I wonder if she knew the sheer amount of spirit energy collecting in that very same corner. My guess, three or four spirits were vying for space. One was a new spirit, a young man wearing, big surprise, a wife beater. There was a bullet hole in one of his eyes, and a bigger hole in the back of his head where the bullet had exited. The other three were amorphous and not fully formed. There was other activity in the room, too. Spirits appeared through walls, swept across the room, and then exited again through the TV. Some of the faces turned to us as they slipped by. The apartment was a variable superhighway of the dead. Noticeably absent was the spirit of a young boy, who may or may not have returned to be with his mom. That absence gave me hope. Maybe, just maybe, he was alive.

"What did the police say?" I asked.

"That Johnny was found dead by the lake, an accident of some sort, and that they will be doing all they can to help me find my son. Same old shit."

"Yeah," I said. "Same old shit."

"Fucking cops. Full of promise. But they never deliver. Except to harass hardworking people just trying to make a living on this shitty rock."

"Rock?"

"Planet Earth."

"Silly me. Did they tell you any more about Johnny?"

"Only that they would know more later."

Probably for the best, although Carol Jensen probably could have handled the news that her son's best friend had been eaten alive by a lake monster.

"What else did the police talk to you about?"

"Why do you fucking care?"

She had finished what was left of the cigarette, which seemed to irritate her further. These days, I smoked because I could. I smoked because any cancers would get obliterated the moment a mutation reared its ugly head. I smoked because, back in the day, it was one of the few things that helped me stay grounded, connected. It was also one of the few things I could put in my mouth that didn't cause me to get violently sick.

Now, I did it because it helped focus my thoughts. Like alcohol, nicotine had no effect on me. Just as well. I didn't want to be hooked on cigarettes for all eternity. For now, they were a pleasant distraction, and my "thinking cap," so to speak.

I wasn't sure what had prompted me to grab two cigarettes from my not-so-secret stash in the minivan's center console, but I fished one out now from my back hip and handed it over to her.

She lit up in more ways than one. First, her eyes, and then, her lighter, which appeared in her hand like a magic trick. Before I could take a step back, she had already taken, precisely, two hits.

I sent her a small prompting that I was a friend and that I had nothing but her son's best interests at heart. Unfortunately, while I was in her thoughts, I caught wind that she was hoping I would leave fast because her next john was due any minute.

Yeah, eeew.

She nodded after the small prompting and said, "They wanted to know if I could remember anything else, anything at all that might help them locate my son."

"Detective Oster?"

"Yeah. Her, and another cop. I've talked to her. A dozen or so times. Her and the fucking feds. Feds! They all keep fucking coming here and shaking up this place. My neighbors are beginning to resent me."

"Are your neighbors aware that your underage boy has been missing for two weeks?"

She shrugged, sucked, exhaled, looked at the front door, adjusted her tank top. No bra. Nearly see-through. *Eeww, again.* She shrugged at my question. Sucked long and hard on the filter, closed her eyes. Seemed to enjoy the moment. The calm before the storm, perhaps. The storm being whoever was going to show up next at her door.

"Did you provide any new information to the police?" I asked.

She shook her head. "Nothing I haven't already told them."

"And what did you tell them?"

She looked at me. "You got another cig?"

I did. And handed it to her. She placed it on the edge of the dining room table, ready for a quick draw, so to speak. "I remembered that he started a new lawn-mowing business a few months ago."

"A business?"

"Yes. The little fuck wanted to make his own money. Legal money. Clean money, he called it. Judgmental shithead."

I took in some air, and it was all I could do to not slap the woman. If I had, I might have slapped her too hard. I might have just knocked her eyeballs out of her head. Instead, I exhaled and said, "Does he own a computer?"

"No."

"Do you know who his clients were?"

"Oh, fuck no. I'm too busy to care about his stupid fucking job."

"Of course you are," I said. "Would anyone else know about his business?"

She shrugged.

"Try again," I said, and gave her a prompt.

"Fuck you. And get the fuck out of here. I've got paying work..." She took in some air and her eyelids fluttered a tad. "Maybe the guy he rented the lawnmowers from."

"Rented?"

"You think we have a lawnmower parked on our fucking balcony? Anyway, some old guy down on the corner, Raul or something. My son gave him a sort of kickback or something. Whatever. Now, are we done here?"

We were, and I couldn't leave fast enough, passing a heavyset man coming up the stairs, a man with a hat pulled low over his face and sweat on his upper lip.

Again, eeww...

19.

I spent the next twenty minutes knocking on doors and getting cold shoulders—and promptly warming cold shoulders with my fancy mind tricks, until I found Raul's house, who most certainly didn't live on a corner.

Raul did have a collection of lawnmowers and, according to his wife, Raul had been helping the missing boy. By helping, he'd loaned one of his older lawnmowers to Luke. Raul, unfortunately, was in Mexico for the week, helping a sick brother, and I suspected Raul wasn't that bad of a guy. His wife didn't know anything more about Luke and his clients. I asked if Raul had a cell phone. She said Raul was seventy-eight years old. I guessed that meant no.

I thanked her for her time and headed back to the vampmobile—my 2002 Toyota Sienna with a dent on the passenger side panel. A dent had been placed there by Anthony's soccer ball a few months back. A dent that would set me back $500, according to my insurance agent.

A dent that would just have to stay there.

***

I parked high up on a winding road that led to the nicer and newer homes, all of which seemed to sport a magnificent view of the lake below. At least, it was magnificent to my eyes.

To mortals, the water would be nothing more than a black swatch in the center of town. But to my eyes, oh, to my eyes, the lake was teeming with life and energy and vibrations, with flowing particles of light that pulsated along the surface of the water— and just under, too. Light that wasn't really light. It was energy, I knew. The energy that powered this Earth, this universe, energy that flowed over everything and anything, constantly, unendingly, flowing, flowing. From where it came, I did not know, but I had my ideas and a single word appeared to me now as I sat there in my front seat.

God. Or something close to God. The Creator, the Source, the All That Ever Was. And each light particle was, I suspected, a part of God, to be used and gathered and collected as we see fit, to be harnessed as we see fit. It is the driving force of creation. It is the thing that holds our world toge- ther, keeps its place in its orbit around the Sun, and the Sun in its place in our Galaxy, and our Galaxy in its place in the known Universe. It is creation and love, and it flows and is there for all of us to be used, or not used, to experience or to not experience. It is inspiration. It is love. It is life. It is health. It is great ideas. And it is always there, flowing, moving, adapting, growing.

And I can see it.

Lucky me.

Within this energy, I see other fragments of light. Brighter fragments, and sometimes, duller fragments, too. Spirit energy. Such energy weaves through the constant bombardment of universal love, which is what I think of it as. Spirit energy sort of rides the waves of these eternal, flowing particles. Surfing the cosmos.

It all made for a spectacular light show, especially when combined with the chaotic, zigzagging lights that skimmed the surface of the lake—insects would be my guess. Even from up here, I could see them swarming over the lake. Brighter objects darted just below the surface, especially along the billowing reeds. Fish. Slower, pulsating light seemed to indicate frogs, especially on the north side of the lake. All of it pulsating, emitting light, flowing with the light of the Universe, merging and blending and giving depth and profundity to the night.

I stepped out of my minivan.

Up the street behind me were rows of backyard fences and elaborate decks, all designed to give the owners magnificent views of the lake below.

Magnificent *daytime* views. Now, not so much. Some of the decks sported outdoor grills big enough to feed an army, or Anthony, and long stone counters that put my own kitchen to shame. Hell, my family could live comfortably on most of those outdoor decks.

A Porsche whizzed past, clearly going faster than the posted 35 MPH speed limit, and headed to the really big homes higher up. Yes, there were Porsches, even in the desert. I briefly considered following him home and feasting on him. Maybe that would teach him not to speed.

As they say, speed kills.

The day's events had permitted my inner bitch witch to slip out more than I was comfortable with. Her influences always permeated into my life in negative and hateful and angry ways.

Maybe if you weren't such a bitch, I thought as I began to disrobe right there on the side of the road, my minivan shielding me from the majority of the homes above me, *I would let you out more. Something to think about, lady.*

Another car came by, this one slower and a little closer to the posted speed limit. The mom in me approved of the safe driving. The vampire in me could give a shit. Still, I suspected Elizabeth had heard me. I suspected she was mulling over my offer. Or not. Maybe she was seething deep inside me, wherever it is that she resided. Seething and planning a very hostile takeover.

You catch more flies with honey, I thought, and

tossed the last of my clothes onto the back seat. I double checked the hide-a-key. It was still there, just inside the front left wheel well, magnetically secured and ready for action.

Once the minivan was locked, I headed over to the guardrail. The drop-off down into the gulch wasn't too steep. Maybe twenty feet, maybe less, at a slight angle. Not straight down, but it should be sufficient. Especially these days. I was getting faster at transforming, at summoning Talos.

I stood up on the slightly dented guardrail, proof that it had served its purpose at one point in time. Although twenty feet wasn't much free-fall space, it would have been a helluva long drop for a mom in a minivan. Or a speeding Porsche.

The wind was mild and warm and brought with it the fragrance of the ancients: dusty hills, dusty plants, dust of the forgotten. All sweeping past me, for my senses only.

Yes, it was time to get to the bottom of this lake monster story, once and for all. And to the bottom of the lake, too.

I balanced easily on the thin lip of the guardrail. Perched might have been more accurate. But I am a lady. I don't perch. But I do stand naked on the side of the road, my black hair billowing around me, my arms now spread, my head tilted back... a single flame now appearing in my thoughts.

And there, in the flame, is the beast.

I leapt out into the night as far as I could, away from the sloping earth that came at me quickly...

20.

The transformation was faster than usual.

A good thing, because the stony, scrubby ground was coming up on me fast. But in one instant, in one mind-boggling, supernatural, super-incredible, super-cool moment, I went from falling... to gliding.

From gliding to now racing over the curve of the sweeping drop of the hill, the very contour of the Earth itself. I altered in mid-flight, defying physics and natural laws, to bank right, to drop down into a gully, then flapped hard to climb over a rocky protrusion, skimming scrub brushes and elderberries and twisted junipers, scattering jackrabbits and kangaroo rats and skunks. I shot down a narrow ravine, my wingtips just missing the rocky protrusions on either side. A hawk screeched from a dark crevasse, probably scared shitless.

I grinned and flapped and picked up speed and, like a cannon blast, shot out into the night sky.

***

Greetings, Talos, I thought.

Greetings, Sam, came the voice in my head, so strong and sure and calm. *A lovely night for flight.*

Oh, we will be doing more than flying. Care for a swim?

Your wish is my command, m'lady.

Is that another idiom you picked up from my thoughts?

Indeed.

I circled the perimeter of the lake far, far below. In this form, my eyesight is many times better. Maybe up to fifty times better. From up here, I was certain I could see the lights of Los Angeles, over a hundred miles away.

Below, the glowing fish in the lake took on actual form and shape. The bigger bugs, the dragonflies and mosquito catchers, grew legs and wings. I was hundreds, if not thousands of feet up. I appreciated Talos and all he could do, all over again.

And I appreciate you, Sam.

For what?

Your company. Your wit. Your eagerness.

I don't bring you down?

With these wings? Would take a lot to bring me down.

I laughed, although the sound came out more of

a roar, with a chaser of smoke. *Who knew dragons had a sense of humor?* I thought.

Perhaps you are rubbing off on me.

A scary thought, I said. I continued banking around the great lake, looking for signs of something bigger on or under the surface. I saw a group of brightly lit people on a short dock. Some of their laughter reached my ears. Or Talos's ears, which were much better than my own ears. Lots of laughter. Good friends and liberal libations... and not necessarily in that order.

I continued my slow sweep around the lake, flapping occasionally to maintain altitude, but mostly allowing the warm updrafts to keep me aloft and to keep my wings full.

The stars were bright up here. Who would have thought that Southern California, with its smog and bright lights, could have access to so many stars? Of course, it took coming out into the desert, and gliding many thousands of feet up, to actually see the stars... but still. They were here.

There wasn't much on the surface of the lake, or along the perimeter, to suggest that a young boy might soon be a late-night snack to a creature from the deep. On this night, at this time, the lake was quiet. At least, on the surface.

You ready, Talos?

I am all yours, Samantha.

And with that, I tucked in my massive wings, and shot down toward the phosphorescent lake... with its millions and millions of bright little lights...

21.

The splashdown was smooth.

In fact, I suspected we barely made a splash at all, so aerodynamic was Talos and his giant, torpedo-shaped, fire-breathing, winged body. And my own night vision, combined with the dragon's super-deluxe sight, well, it made it possible to see into the murky lake.

A good team, came Talos's thought.

Yes, I thought, and oriented myself. After all, Talos gave me complete and total control over his body. In fact, I suspect he just sat back and watched. I imagined a bemused expression on his giant dinosaur face; if, in fact, that's what he looked like.

Close, came Talos's thoughts, as I flapped my wings smoothly, pushing through the water with ease. *Your original image of a giant bat isn't too far off either.*

A giant dragon-shaped bat?

A small chuckle inside my head. *Something like that, Sam.*

Okay, now that's a scary thought.

Welcome to my world, he said.

And to mine, I added, grinning inwardly.

I flapped my wings and felt less like a giant dragon bat and more like a giant manta ray. My eyes felt clear and protected, and I suspected Talos sported a sort of natural shield over his eyes. A clear lid perhaps.

Indeed, Sam. Protection from water and heat.

Your own heat?

And the heat of others.

Now, I had a picture of two giant dragons battling in the skies high above, blasting each other with great gusts of streaking fire. Talos chuckled in my head.

Perhaps long ago, Sam. We are a little more evolved now.

So you are telling me that in your history, you have had dragon wars?

Many wars, Sam. But all long, long ago. Every world has an evolutionary process. You are just emerging from the beginning of yours.

The beginning?

Humans have a ways to go.

I couldn't argue with that, so instead, I focused on the task at hand, flapping his wings and gliding through what surely would have been impenetrable black water to anyone other than, well, us.

Yes, I thought, *a good team.*

The lake was big by Southern California standards. To the rest of the world, not so much. Still, at over three thousand acres, and just over six miles long and nearly two miles wide, I had plenty to explore. Thankfully, the lake wasn't particularly deep. Rather quickly, I was skimming over the lakebed with its seemingly moving floor of flowing and waving plant life. I wasn't expert enough in lake plants to know what the hell I was looking at, but my general impression of them was that they looked... well, icky. Slimy and alien, too.

More chuckling from Talos.

There was also enough debris down here to shame all lake-goers. Beer cans and bottles, and plastic wrappers of all sorts. I saw more than one Starbucks cup. I also saw two or three shipwrecks. Or boat wrecks. Whatever. Mostly small dinghies and rowboats. One was a damaged Jet Ski lying upside down. There was more: a toilet seat, a baby stroller, a mountain bike, car tires, a paperback novel fluttering in the current, a desk fan, men's shoes, a lifejacket (which made no sense), and countless other tidbits that I ignored, but all of which made me sad. The lake needed a good dredging. A damn good one.

What I didn't see was a giant, snake-like lake monster. At least, not yet. There was still more lake to cover...

I flapped and glided and banked and searched,

ignoring the debris and focusing on the beauty around me. Lake Elsinore had a surprisingly large fish population. Maybe that was common knowledge to fishermen. I didn't know, but small schools of fish scattered continuously before me. Bigger, lumbering fish patrolled the lake's bottom, fat catfish that freaked even me out. Some were quite large, well over three or four feet, mostly hidden in the deeper regions of the lake, and looking about as alien as a creature could look. I considered one large creature in particular, bigger than any fish I'd ever seen. It moved slowly in the darkness, almost majestically, easily the biggest fish in the lake. The sensors or whiskers around its snout quivered in its search for its next big meal. I circled it, dipping a wing and flying around it, and watched as it pounced on a rotting bass hovering along the lake floor. It attacked it heartily, voraciously, and not very prettily. Fish bits floated in the water around it, and soon, it was moving again, scanning and searching, not aware that a much larger predator was presently watching it. Or maybe it did and didn't care. Surely nothing messed with this big boy.

But was it big enough to consume a twelve-year-old boy? It might just be. And it also just might be big enough to pull free a limb or two. There was, of course, one way to find out. I could catch the fish, gut it, and see what was inside it.

Or... yes, I had another way. A way that wouldn't kill it, although killing it and gutting it would have excited the thing within me. Except, except... I couldn't feel her excitement. In fact, I couldn't feel her at all. I thought about that as I continued to circle the lumbering and yet somehow graceful beast.

It is because she is not with us, Sam, came Talos's words. *In this form, you are free of her. But you gain me.*

A welcomed relief, I thought.

I'll take that as a compliment.

You should, I thought, grinning inwardly. *I assume she is with my physical body?*

Not quite. She was temporarily ejected to another place, a place where others like her dwell.

Where is this place?

It is safe to say you will find out some day.

Fine. Do I still have some of my vampiric powers, Talos?

You have your night vision, do you not?

Yes.

Then that should answer your question.

I nodded his great head and closed my eyes and projected my thoughts out around us, using a trick I had used to see through cave walls and homes, and now *into* a giant catfish.

My range is limited to maybe twenty feet, and it acts as a sort of sonar that returns clear images to me. How it works, I don't know, but I could see why it would have been of great use to Elizabeth and her posse of highly evolved dark masters. To know where the enemy was at all times, to spy and watch and creep and control.

Well, it was serving a purpose now, even if it was a weird and gross purpose, for the images that came back to me now, as I circled with my eyes closed—but yet, seeing everything around me at the same time—made me want to lose my lunch. Or Talos to lose whatever lunch he'd eaten.

Now, as I projected out, I focused my attention on the meandering, powerful catfish, the obvious king of the lake. If ever there was a lake monster, he was it.

Correction... *she.*

Almost immediately, as I plunged through the powerful, rippling pink muscle, I saw that the creature was heavily laden with a thick cluster of blood-red eggs—within which I could see hundreds of smaller movements.

I shifted my focus to her other organs, each pulsating and quivering with the flow of life and power, all in perfect harmony and rhythm, flowing, churning, pumping. Each organ pulsed with its own inner light: bright blue for intestines, red for the heart, bluish for the liver, bright white for the brain, and a pulsating, throbbing yellow for its massive stomach, which ran along the bottom length of the fish.

I plunged into the yellow light.

***

It was later, and I was perched high above Lake

Elsinore, on a rocky ledge along Highway 74. Below me, the lake was iridescent and alive, and if I looked hard enough, I could probably see the great, lumbering beast swimming in its deepest depths.

The catfish.

Color me a city girl—or a suburban girl—but I didn't know much about catfish. Or, more accurately, *anything* about catfish. I knew they were bottom feeders, but that was about it. I had seen the pictures of the giants caught in lakes and rivers, and this giant was nearly as big. Certainly big enough to drag a boy below the surface and keep him below the surface... until said boy drowned.

But its stomach was the giveaway, and then, later, its teeth, which were nearly nonexistent. Its stomach had been full of reeds and smaller fish (and even a duck or two). No arms, no legs, no shoes. Just a fish that appeared opportunistic. I suppose there was the off-chance it could have gripped an arm or a leg, and sort of done a death roll, but there had been no evidence of the limbs being twisted off and, more important, there hadn't been any evidence of limbs in the creature's stomach.

Are we okay sitting here a while longer, Talos, I asked.

He knew my meaning, and answered from deep within me, his voice booming and comforting at the same time. *You are safe in my home world, Sam. You are with me.*

What are we doing there?

We are sitting on a ledge much like this one, but

much, much higher up, enjoying the view, sometimes watching the flying shadows below us, and sometimes looking up at our cities.

That is so weird.

Maybe.

I never remember any of it.

But you can.

I thought about that, and looked down at another city, a human city, and wondered again what could be in the lake, what had killed the boy, and what the hell was going on.

It was then that I sensed something high above —or perhaps Talos had sensed it. I looked up and saw something pass beneath the stars. Something massive. Something winged. It wasn't quite as iridescent as the lights below, as the living creatures in the lake. It emitted a softer light, and I was reminded of some of the spirits I sometimes saw and their sporadic energy.

The winged shape blotted out the stars and now the moon, and banked gracefully and I could see its long neck and diamond-shaped head.

I tensed until I felt Talos's soothing touch on my mind, reminding me I was safe with him, and that, perhaps, I was safe with this other.

The winged creature angled down, flapping glowing wings. Dust and hot wind swirled around me, rising up like a living thing to form around me, as the creature turned tighter and tighter circles, and finally alighted on the ledge next to me.

A moment later, a very naked man was squatting next to me. A man I recognized all too well. Dracula.

22.

"Excuse me for my, ah, indecency," said the pointy-faced man, who didn't seem to really care that he was, in fact, squatting before me naked as the day he was born. A day which just so happened to be half a millennium ago.

Talos's eyes were better than mine in every way; indeed, through his eyes, I could even see the vampire's dull aura, which pulsated weakly from his body in a bluish light. With my own eyes, I could never see another immortals' aura.

"I'm pretty sure you can understand me in this form, but I won't be able to understand you. Try as I might, I don't speak screeching dragon."

I considered transforming, but I doubted Kingsley would be okay with me and the King Bad Boy Dragon himself hanging out on a rocky ledge in the buck. Dracula had come here to talk. So he could talk, and I would listen.

Truthfully, the Count made me a little nervous. He did, after all, host the most powerful of the Dark Masters—and Elizabeth's lover. Of course, Dracula had been nothing but a gentleman; indeed, he'd saved my hide just last year when I'd found myself in an arena full of ravenous werewolves. Dracula had proven to be scary deadly. Within minutes, the arena had been full of *dead* werewolves.

To his credit, Dracula wasn't giving me the full show now. He mostly kept his hands laced over his groin, and mostly presented me his side, rather than the full monty.

Dracula was not a big man. Well under six feet, I suspected he was closer to maybe five-nine. He didn't need to be tall, or hulking. He had an undeniable presence, even when buck naked. *Magisterial*, came to mind. He had been, after all, a warrior king for Romania. He had commanded thousands—and many thousands more had worshiped him. And he had, by all accounts, watched many thousands perish in gruesome deaths... and had enjoyed every minute of it.

Yes, he had been a fitting host for the worst of the worst, the most powerful of the Dark Masters.

But something seemed to happen on the way to the twenty-first century. This Dracula seemed surprisingly banal, shockingly well-mannered, and, pray tell, polite. Dracula wore his hair long, most of which was presently billowing in the hot wind. He was muscular enough, but a little scrawny for my tastes. Then again, Kingsley had something to do with that, meaning, the big oaf had somehow altered my tastes in men. More and more, I find myself attracted to bigger guys, hairier guys, hulking guys. The Liam Neeson types. The Jason Mamoas of the world. Lord help me, the son on *Pawn Stars*. Then again, few stacked up against Kingsley. Correction, no man did.

Dracula didn't need to be big or hulking to command my presence. He also didn't need much clothing, and, polite as he was, I still saw his junk more than one time.

Which led to this surreal thought: *I just saw Dracula's junk.*

My life, I thought, and shook Talos's massive, diamond-shaped head.

"I hadn't realized just how, ah, intimidating our winged friends are, Samantha Moon. My God, you are massive. And frightening. And beautiful."

He kept his hands clasped before him, but had taken to pacing along a very small area on the ledge next to me. I turned my head to watch him, my claws digging deep into the earth. At some point in time, someone was going to stumble across these very claw marks—and wonder what the hell had been watching them.

If they only knew, I thought.

I suspected that Prince Dracula, or whatever he referred to himself as these days, had seen plenty of dragons in his day. I suspected he had, in fact, seen it all. Tasted it all. He had five hundred years under his belt at this undead business. I had ten.

I suspect Dracula had journeyed to his dragon's home planet, had shifted from this world into the next. I suspected he was only now trying to seem accommodating, normal, real, approachable. I also suspected he had done things and seen things that no one would ever know—or would want to know. The killer was still in him, I had to remind myself of that. I also had to remind myself of the ease with which he had dispatched the pack of werewolves that night. He had killed easily, wantonly. Yes, he had saved me, but he also hadn't hesitated or tried to negotiate. Dracula, in short, had been a killing machine.

He moved over to the lip of the cliff and stared out over the sparkling light of Lake Elsinore. That Dracula was here, on this forgotten cliff face, facing a mostly forgotten city, at this time and place, was beyond surreal. It was unreal.

Now, he folded his arms over his chest and just let it all hang out, exposing himself to the world but, luckily, not too much to me. "It is a strange world we live in, Samantha Moon."

He let his words hang out there. There was a lot of hanging going on at the edge of the cliff. I waited, unmoving, my leathery wings rippling in the wind. Overhead, a single-engine airplane droned on, its safety light pulsing. There had been no airplanes in Dracula's time. Hell, there wouldn't have been significant transportation improvements for nearly 250 years, with the advent of the steam engine. The man next to me had truly seen it all.

Now, he was just a naked guy with nice hair and a decent-enough body, although he was no Kingsley.

"I assume you have seen the other worlds? Or, at least, caught a glimpse? They are beautiful, and very evolved. They are perfect in their own ways, but they are boring. There is no room for improvement. Yes, perfection can be boring. There is little room for expansion, which is why some of them come here and connect with us. My dragon is such a creature. And so is yours. Whether they admit it or not, Samantha, they seek excitement. They seek to live. Why do you think they are always ready at our beck and call? It is because there is so little for them to do in their home world. Why? Because everything has been done. All obstacles have been removed. Nirvana is everywhere.

"It is only in the lower worlds, the lesser-evolved worlds, that monumental leaps of evolution can occur. And therein lies the excitement of living, Samantha Moon, the juice of life. It is in the *taking* of the step. Not *where* the step is taken."

He squatted down and ran his surprisingly long fingers through the loose dirt at the cliff edge, his skin pale, smooth and blemish-free. Muscles rippled as he trailed his fingertips in the dirt.

"I did not ask for Cornelius to join me." Cornelius, I knew, was the name of Elizabeth's love interest, the entity who had possessed Dracula so many years ago. "But I was not surprised when he did so. I had been asking to be given the secrets of eternal life. I had been asking the sorcerers and charlatans alike. I had been praying to God, the devil, you name it. I sought to live. I sought to continue to expand, to improve, to spread, to..." He caught himself, but I knew what he was going to say next.

To kill.

"I was a wild man back in those days, Sam, reckless and full of anger and hatred. The anger and hatred is long gone. But the desire to expand, to grow, to challenge, to change, and, believe it or not, to help, never leaves. And I suspect if it did, I would die. One way or another, I would die."

He rested both elbows on his bare knees, his legs spread away from me, sitting casually, relaxed, never mind that he was naked or sitting next to an honest-to-God dragon.

"So where does that leave us, Sam?" he asked, not bothering to look at me, his voice barely above a whisper. Turned out, Talos's hearing was rather exceptional, and I suspected Dracula knew that, hence, the near-whisper. "Of course, there would be no we, if I hadn't appeared suddenly in your life. Or if I hadn't helped you. But that sounds manipulative. I have manipulated my way over this planet, and I refuse to do so now. You might have handled those werewolves fine, especially in your change-ling dragon form. I cannot take full credit for your getting out alive. But perhaps I can take a little.

Again, that sounds manipulative and, well, a little needy. I would like to think that I am beyond such base needs. Then again, I know what you are. I know who is in you. And I know the deeper importance of our meeting, our connection, our past and what might lie in our future. I know all of this and more, and it is bringing out, within me, a juvenile need to be accepted by you, to be held in some esteem, to be valued and appreciated. I hate that I think such things. I was a king, for Christ's sake. A warrior. I killed with reckless abandon. I took what I wanted, when I wanted, and then I took more for no good reason at all. I killed for no good reason at all. I was terrible and I hope to never be that man again. Power is a terrible thing, especially for those with little patience and bloodlust."

Dracula spoke crisply, enunciating perfectly. A hint of a European accent of the likes I had never heard before. Then again, I didn't get out much. But still...

"I have been a bastard. I have been a devil. I have been a saint, too, but few know that. I have stopped advancing armies with blood in their hearts and, yes, I saved all of Europe, but few remember what it was like in those years, with an enemy breathing down one's neck. I did what I had to, and I destroyed many lives in the process. I believe many more would have been destroyed, and much of the landscape of Eastern Europe would have been changed, too, if not for me. But how many blood-lines have I ended? How many good people met their end, often on my silly whims? Too many. I was a true psychopath, I believe. But over time, I started to feel. I started to care, and I am haunted every hour of every day for my past transgressions."

The wind whipped up some of the dust along the ledge. The dust swirled and danced and formed mini whirling devils, then dissipated again.

"So where does that leave us, Sam? It doesn't have to leave us anywhere, quite frankly. I could leap from this cliff and fly off and you would never hear from me again. Perhaps this is something you wish. If so, I do not blame you, or anyone. I am hardly anyone's type. You surely did not ask me to be here, or to help you, or anything. Yet, here I am, shoehorning myself into your life. Or, at least, entertaining the idea, and asking you to entertain the idea, too. Maybe. Quite frankly, I am not sure what I am asking of you, or even of myself. I am truly thinking out loud; so perhaps, it is a good thing that you are in your changeling form. It helps me do all the thinking and talking. Trust me, I have spent decades alone. I do not mind your company, even if it's silent and regarding me with big, monstrous, black eyes."

Beauty is in the eye of the beholder, came a voice in my head. *Beware of this one, Sam.*

You know of him?

I do, of course. There are only so many of us who connect with you. And those that do have been specially selected. I am told that the entity within the one you call Dracula is particularly dark, and particularly cunning.

I had no doubt about that, being, from my understanding, the strongest of the dark masters. I thought: *Can you tell me more?*

Like you, Dracula is free of the entity within while in his changeling form. Unlike you, the entity within has control over much of what he says in his human form, although the man called Dracula does occasionally break free. It is only when he has transformed into one of us that he is truly free, and even then, it takes many minutes, often hours, for Dracula to find himself again. It is only in the brief minutes following his return to human form that you are most likely to trust the man, as is the case now. It is only then that he is, as you would say, his old self again.

Until the entity within regains its grip on him, I thought.

Correct, Sam.

I thought about this. Indeed, the man before me seemed clear of mind, clear of speech. I didn't sense an internal struggle. Then again, he had also just transformed into his human form.

I waited for Dracula to continue, and as he continued squatting on the cliff edge, free as a bird and as naked as the devil, I couldn't help but note that the hands that had been idly running through the loose dirt, had turned into something closer to claws. Now, they dug harder, leaving deeper furrows.

He's fighting it, I thought.

I believe so, Sam.

"So why am I here, Sam? When I have not much interest in you, although, from all appearances, you seem a delightful creature."

I continued waiting, noting the blood that now trailed in the dirt, blood that poured from his bloodied fingertips.

"Why am I here when I have much better things to do? No, that's a lie. I have done everything I wanted to do. I have seen everything I wanted to see. I have killed and raped and pillaged the entire fucking world, Samantha Moon."

Dracula shook his head and his long hair billowed forward. Now, I could see red splotches appearing over his bare skin, along his arms and cheeks. This was a first for me. I had not seen such splotches before, even on myself. What it meant, exactly, I didn't know.

It's indicative of his internal struggle, Samantha Moon. There is a war going on for his mind and body, even now.

Dracula continued, unaware of my internal dialogue with Talos. "But I am here because *he* wants me here, Sam. *He* wants me to appeal to your sensitivities. *He* wants me to persuade you to allow us into your life, into your world. To allow us to be a part of what you are building."

I wasn't aware that I was building anything. But I was aware that Dracula's voice was changing. He was going from mild-mannered and, dare I say, polite, to something closer to agitated. The smoothness of his voice was giving way to something gravelly and angry.

"I want in, Sssamantha Moon. Whether you allow it or not. I want in, and I want my Elizabeth."

Okay, there it was. Dracula shook his head and grabbed at his hair, pulling. Large, bloody chunks tore free. He threw both handfuls of long, black hair fluttering over the cliff face and I watched, in amazement, as the skin healed over... and fresh shoots of hair sprouted free.

"Forgive me, Sam. Forgive me. As the good book says, I know not what I say. Usually..." He twisted his head, stretched his jaw, showed his perfectly white teeth. His eyes rolled back into his head. "Usually my host and I get along swimmingly. But not always. Sometimes, I want the limelight, as they say. Sometimes, I want to be free. Sometimes, I want more time. But he gives... so little. His roots run deep. His hold... tenacious. My fault, all my fault..."

I watched him turn his head this way and that... and I watched as his body seemed to swell, as if he were taking in more air, his lungs and chest expanding. Or...

Just maybe...

He was growing a little before my very eyes.

Indeed, that seemed to be the case. The once and past king, who had been, by my estimates, standing at around five foot, nine inches, now stood well over six feet tall. Maybe even by an inch or two.

"Never mind him, Sssamantha Moon," came a soft and hissing voice, spoken from lips that, as far as I could tell, hadn't moved. At least, not by much. "He is a good enough vessel. We have shared many adventures. We have feasted on many, and, I suspect, we will feast upon many more. But he needs to remember his place. He needs to remember he summoned *me*, he called to me, and I fulfilled his heart's desire. I gave him the very thing he wished for, and he, in turn, has given me a perfectly suitable vessel. He is, of course, listening to us, wishing to make his presence known, but even I was getting tired of his doggerel, as I'm sure you were, too, Samantha Moon. You see, I think he might fancy you, which could fare well for me. Because, you see, I fancy she who is within you. And not just fancy, Samantha Moon. I need her. I need my Elizabeth. We need each other. We have great things planned for this world."

Careful, Samantha Moon, intoned Talos's words.

"Let me speak to her, Samantha Moon. If for only a few minutes. If for only a few seconds. I want to see her. Hear her. Touch her. Taste her."

Talos's words came to me again: *I can teach you how to safely release her, Samantha, if you should so desire. But now is not the time and place. You will need careful training.*

I nodded at his words, although the naked man before me would not know why I nodded, and if he did, I didn't care.

"It is not so much to ask, is it? You have already heard her. Felt her. You know her deeply, Sam, for she is the reason you are alive now. She is the reason you are not dead and buried. The reason you can see your kids. The reason for, well, everything. Do you not think you owe her this small favor? Is it not so much to ask?"

I continued staring down at the man who had gone from medium-sized to extra-sized within minutes. His chest was full. There was more body hair on him, but not much more. And his jaw, if possible, seemed slightly straighter, his nose a tad smaller. He still looked like Dracula, but he had taken on the semblance of another. Cornelius, I presumed. I could expect, I figured, Elizabeth to take on a similar look, too. Taking over not just my mind, but my body, too. My very shape.

"Please, Sam. I am humbly requesting an audience with my beloved. Surely, you have been in love? Surely you know the private hell I am going through."

I continued doing nothing, as a hot wind rose up from below, and pummeled us cliff-dwellers.

"Do it now, you fucking bitch!"

With one clean swipe, I unfurled my massive wing, and sent Dracula/Cornelius tumbling over the cliff face, to ricochet off the many boulders below, and to land in a heap in the deepest of shadows.

No, I thought. *Fuck you.*

I took in some air that I doubted Talos needed, and leaped off the cliff edge, flapped once, twice and was soon rocketing high above the desert landscape...

23.

We were in bed together.

I'd made a big dinner for everyone. Spaghetti, and lots of it. Between my son and Kingsley, we had gone through three bags of organic noodles and a massive, bubbling cauldron of homemade meat sauce. Maybe I *had* been a witch in a past life. Even after all the spaghetti, and garlic bread, salad, and homemade chocolate pudding—I caught my son in the kitchen, scraping the cast iron pot clean with the wooden spoon.

"Your son can eat," said Kingsley, one arm under my head and curled around my shoulder, exactly where it should be. "Maybe even more than me."

"Now, that's scary."

"He's a growing boy, Sam."

"Growing into what, though?" I asked.

"I think," he said, turning onto his side and resting his massive, lion-like head on one paw, er, hand, "that remains to be seen."

I nodded, suddenly concerned about the sheer amount of food my son was eating—where did it go? And how was I going to afford it all? Mostly, I worried about my daughter and her friends and how I was going to hack into her phone with or without her knowledge. Okay *with*, since nothing got past her. I worried about Luke still out there and, presumably, alone. Whether he was alive or dead, I didn't know.

"You got quiet," said Kingsley. And for the umpteenth time, I was relieved there was at least one man (two, if you counted Fang), who didn't have access to my thoughts.

I had spent the evening mostly avoiding any talk of work, of the mutilated boy, or of my latest prophetic dream about Tammy. Especially the latest prophetic dream of Tammy. If anything, it had been even more detailed: the blue eyes of the big rig driver, his mouth opening in a scream, the *whump whump* of the tires going over my daughter's torso, the blood bursting from her eyes and mouth, her body broken beyond repair, dead instantly.

"I'm not sure I want to talk about it yet," I said.

He reached out a hand—it could have been a low-flying eagle coming at me—and swiped away some of the stray hair hanging over my face. "I'm here when, or if, you're ready."

Okay, that was damn sweet of him. Truth was, I

wasn't ready to discuss the dream. Short of kidnapping my daughter for the next week—which was what I very well might end up doing—there wasn't a damn thing anyone could do to stop the accident. In fact, I knew from past experience, only I could stop the probable outcome. No, that wasn't necessarily true. In the past, I had acted alone. But couldn't I recruit a team to watch her around the clock, whether she knew they were there or not?

I mulled that over. Another immortal, someone proficient at keeping their mind sealed off from her, could keep an eye on her. I knew only two immortals well enough to even ask for help: Kingsley and Fang. And Fang was still a newbie, as I liked to remind him as often as I could. Kingsley, on the other hand, was quite adept at shielding his mind. One problem, he was as big as the Matterhorn. She may not read his mind, but she would spot him a mile away. Two miles away.

That left Fang—except Fang, so far, could not go out into the light of day. And if he did, not for very long, and not very effectively. Of course, the accident would happen at night. I knew that much. The exact time, not so much.

That was the thing with these prophetic dreams: the more I dreamed them, the more the details came to me. For instance, I was just beginning to see the shape of what appeared to be mountains behind the vehicles. Mountains to where, I didn't know. So far, no street signs had appeared, or any recognizable landmarks.

I don't know where the accident is going to happen, at least, not yet.

Or I could just lock Tammy up in Kingsley's dungeon of horror for the next week. She could hate me for the rest of her life, but at least she would be alive.

Kingsley had rolled onto his back, which meant he was, officially, taking up more than half of the king-sized bed; hell, two-thirds. Honestly, he was bigger now than even when I'd met him four years ago, when he'd first appeared in my office, looking for help. I knew that with each full moon—and each subsequent turning—he gradually grew closer and closer to the beast within. It made sense. The closer he was to the size and shape of the creature within, the easier the turning, the faster the turning, the quicker he could hunt—or, in Kingsley's case, unearth dead bodies to feast upon. Thank God for Franklin, Kingsley's faithful butler and assistant, who locked him up each full moon, and provided Kingsley with the rotting corpses of local Chino Hills State Park deer. I was certain that hunting wasn't permitted. Say that to the werewolf, and his faithful assistant who might or might not be the real Frankenstein's monster. There, I'd said it.

Anyway, I thought of the missing boy, the giant catfish, and my daughter, as Kingsley now snored quietly next to me, his great, hairy chest filling and rising and expanding. Yes, Kingsley needed to breathe; I didn't. All told, we were both damn weird. We were both products of the powerful entities within us, as were all those whose lives we touched. A sort of spilling over of power, a leakage of dark energy.

I tapped Kingsley's slowly rising bare chest. Of course, bare was relative. It was covered in thick hair that you either loved or hated. Trust me, on him, you loved it. It fit him, his persona, and his wolfish yellow eyes, perfectly. He continued snoring lightly, his wide nostrils flared, sucking in most of the oxygen in the room. Indeed, I watched the finite particles of swirling luminescence rocketing up his nose with each inhalation, and blasting out with each exhalation. Yes, I can watch people breathe. No, I am not happy about it, although it can be fascinating... for about a half minute.

I patted his chest again, this time a little harder. He snorted and was about to swing his wide shoulders around to move away from me, except I held him down and shook him. Maybe a little harder than I should have.

"You awake?" I asked.

"I've never been more awake."

I sidled up next to him, pressing my mostly naked flesh against his. Mostly. My kids were home after all. His body was, as usual, gloriously warm. I was addicted to the warmth. If I could wrap myself around him all day and night, I would. And the big oaf would probably not even miss a step.

I said, "I'm ready to talk about it."

He sat up a little, his arm flexing powerfully, and his belly shifting. Yes, he had a belly, and yes, I loved it unendingly.

"Okay," he said, rubbing his eyes, "let's talk."

24.

I spent ten minutes telling him about the dream.

Kingsley, true to form, remained quiet, listening —or maybe asleep. One thing the man had going for him: he always, always listened to me carefully, processing everything I said, before responding. Perhaps it was the attorney in him, and the need to know his client's story intimately, perfectly, exactly. Of course, in the past, he had represented the scum of the Earth, and I let him know that, and let him know that I was not happy about it. To date, the quality of his clientele had improved, but Kingsley, in no uncertain terms, reminded me that people were innocent until proven guilty, and that one shouldn't jump to conclusions, and to let him do his job and let justice take its course. Oh, and to not control him; that he was, ultimately, going to do what he wanted, and I had to respect him and his choices.

It's hard to rail against such logic and, ultimately, he was right. He was his own man. I didn't have to be with him, and I shouldn't want to change him...

Too much.

Maybe a few tweaks here and there.

So, yeah, I've come around. I've turned a blind eye to some of his more objectionable clients. Hard as it was, I let him do his thing... and he let me do mine. Life, admittedly, was easier that way. I learned to trust him and his choices. Truth was, I had enough to worry about. And Kingsley was a big boy. A very, very big boy. Maybe the biggest boy ever.

"How long until the accident?" he finally asked.

Hearing the certainty in his deep voice was jarring; it gave my dream a legitimacy that I wasn't entirely prepared for. Prior to this, the dream had existed only as a fantasy, a flight of imagination, a memory. Perhaps I had been wrong. Perhaps I had read too much into it. Perhaps it was only a dream. Except I knew the danger of entertaining such thoughts. When I dream, I dream hard, and I dream of the future. Ignoring the dream would be foolish, and would almost certainly not end well for my daughter. It would end, in fact, tragically.

Before answering, I scanned my home and saw that my daughter was fast asleep. She was. Or appeared to be.

"Hard to say for sure," I said, and found myself

clinging to Kingsley's arm like a lifeline. That is, if lifelines had the size and girth of low-hanging tree branches. "The dreams are getting sharper, clearer, more real. My guess is about three or four days. Maybe as little as two, or as long as a week."

To know that if I did nothing, my baby girl would be dead within a week was too much to bear. A really, really high-pitched squeak escaped out of me, involuntarily, an inhalation of air through restricted throat and chest muscles.

Kingsley squeezed my shoulder, and somehow, managed to pull me in even closer. Had I been a mortal woman, he might have broken my collar-bone. "We could always lock her in my cellar," said Kingsley. "She won't like it, but at least she will be alive."

I shuddered again at the thought of my poor daughter a prisoner in Kingsley's werewolf-proof "cellar." Prison was more accurate. How many dead and putrid carcasses had he consumed down there? Was the interior furrowed in deep claw marks? And just how clean was it? I shook my head, and shuddered. The thought of it repulsed me all over again, but yet...

Yet...

It could keep my daughter alive.

As I contemplated this terrible answer, I heard the footsteps a fraction of a second before my bedroom door was thrown open, and there stood Tammy in her sweats and t-shirt, her hair pulled back and her makeup off. Her chest rose and fell, and I could see the heat around her cheeks and the wetness in her eyes.

"If you lock me in that place, that filthy, terrible place, I will never forgive you. Ever. I will hate you for the rest of my life."

"Sweetie... no one's locking you up—"

"You lie, Mother. You lie, and he's a monster. I will run away and you will never, ever find me again."

And with that, she turned and left, leaving the door open, which was just as well. There were no secrets in my room. Perhaps ever.

25.

"You sure this is a good idea?" asked Allison.

"Us spying on my daughter or you hanging out with me?" I asked. I might have had a 'tone' in my voice.

We were in my Batmobile, which was what I'd come to call my minivan. Granted, now that I'd recently learned that I didn't, in fact, turn into a giant bat, but something closer to a dragon, the novelty of the name had worn off. But old habits die hard. So the Batmobile it would remain; that was, until I could finally afford something newer. Then again, something newer wasn't necessarily better in my business. The business of investigations, that is. A worn-out looking minivan, sitting nondescriptly on a street was less likely to draw attention than something flashy. Then again, I'd never owned any-thing flashy. Ever.

"I'm sorry about all that, Sam."

Allison and I hadn't spoken since she walked out on me at lunch a few days ago. Granted, I had been too busy looking for lake monsters and trying to get a handle on what to do about my daughter, to worry much about Allison. But she'd always been there, at the back of my mind. And not in the back-of-the-mind way that I'm used to, when I could catch hints of her thoughts, even from a distance. No, she had been silent, uncommunicative, closed. Gone, for all I knew.

That was, until she'd called me this afternoon and wanted to talk. It was Saturday and Tammy had said she was going to the movies. Gone were the days when she, you know, *asked* to go to the movies. I offered to drive her, and she let me know, in no uncertain terms, what she thought of my offer. Then, being the child of a freak that she was, she immediately caught a not-so-fleeting thought of mine.

"And don't follow me, Mom," she had said. "I'm not a criminal. And it's only a *dream*. Gawd!"

I reminded her that my dreams were much more than dreams. They were prophecy. She rolled her eyes at that. "I don't even know those kids, Mom. So your dream is wrong." Yes, she could see their faces in my memory. I had the same ability. Someone needed to only recall an event, and I could recall it right along with them.

"That doesn't mean you won't meet them at some point—"

"Please, Mom." Another eye-roll. I had a bone to pick with whoever invented the eye-roll.

Shortly, a friend's mom had picked her up. I was okay with a friend's mom picking her up. And I was okay with her riding in a car during the day. The accident happened at night, after all. Within view of a distant mountain chain with a distinctive peak in the middle. I wasn't familiar with the peak, and I wasn't familiar with the people she was driving with. Maybe it was just a dream, after all.

But why did I keep dreaming it over and over? And why did it come into even starker clarity upon each awakening?

Because it wasn't just a dream. It was a future happening. Eye-roll or not.

"Sam, can we talk?" asked Allison now, as we sat in the front seat of the minivan. We had been quiet for many minutes. In fact, we had been quiet the whole drive here from my house. Allison called shortly after my daughter had left, asking if she could talk with me. I told my *friend* to get her ass over here if she wanted to talk, because I was heading out on a stakeout. Perhaps the most important stakeout ever. Anthony was boxing with Jacky, who had picked up my son himself, and I had no intention of not following my daughter, whether she liked it or not. Anyway, Allison and her too-fit ass had gotten to my house in record time. So far, we hadn't said much.

I looked at her now, and scanned her thoughts again. Or tried to. "Seems that talking is all we have, since your mind is closed off. Let me guess: Millicent's idea?"

We were parked outside the AMC Theaters in Fullerton, about halfway down a row, with a mostly clear shot of the theater entrance. That was, if my daughter decided to use the front entrance. The theater also had side entrances. The side entrance part concerned me.

"Sam, her reasons are valid. And so were yours. You wanted to shut down that aspect, as well, to keep the demon bitch within you weak. So don't blame this all on Millicent."

"My reasons are very different than her reasons."

"Sam, we are essentially at war with the entity within you."

"You do know that you are a psychic phone operator in L.A., and a part-time fitness instructor."

"And a full-time witch, who's part of a powerful triad of witches. Sam, more and more we are facing —and battling—demons and monsters. And the thing within you is one of the most powerful of all. I am only just beginning to understand the depth of the darkness within you."

"Gee, thanks."

"Not you, Sam. *Her*, the thing within." She paused, gathered herself. "Sam, Millicent is certain that Elizabeth is in communication with others like her."

"Other dark masters?"

"Yes."

This was news to me. "How?"

"When you sleep, Sam. It gives her the escape she seeks. It is why sleep is so powerful, so necessary. It's not necessary for you. It's necessary for *her*. It is only then that she is given reprieve from the prison of your mind."

Okay, that made some sense. I said, "And where does she go?"

"I do not know, Sam. Perhaps from where she came."

The Librarian, Archibald Maximus, had suggested that it was another dimension, or perhaps a parallel world overlapping our own. Talos had suggested something similar, too, regarding his own world.

"So you're suggesting she always knows my secrets, and is, you know, spilling the beans to her cohorts?"

"Millicent thinks so."

I thought about this as I watched moviegoers pouring in and out of the theater. One thing Allison could provide was a big shield around both of us, which she had done using her witchy powers. A much stronger shield than I could conjure. True, my shield was strong enough for most people, but apparently my daughter saw through it with ease.

"So you can see why Millicent wants me to be careful around you, Sam."

I nearly snorted. "Geez, you make it seem like all we do is talk about demons and dark masters."

"Often enough, Sam."

J.R. RAIN

"So this shield of yours is permanent now?"

"I think so."

Sneaky bitch, I thought to Elizabeth. *Who knew you were sneaking out at night and boogying with your demon friends.*

"Fine," I said. "That still doesn't explain why you are here. Or why you're talking with me now. I thought I was a bad influence and all that."

"Millicent agrees that you are an invaluable ally —and understands that you are my best friend."

Hearing that caused a ripple of satisfaction—a ripple that I desperately needed. "What about your triad of girlfriends?"

"One is a ghost, and the other's a pampered Hollywood star. Neither are exactly best friend material."

"And I am?"

"Yes, Sam. And I'm so sorry if I made you feel bad about yourself."

I shrugged. "I've felt worse."

"I'm still sorting through all of this, Sam. So much of it is new to me, too."

I added I got that and soon we found ourselves hugging and there might even have been some tears.

Allison finally pulled away and said, "I've never been part of such a tightknit group of women before. We are doing big things, Sam. And soon, we will be going after the worst of the worst."

"But without me."

"For now, Sam."

"Fine," I said. "Just be careful."

172

"Say that to the bad guys."

I raised an eyebrow. "You ladies are that powerful?"

"And growing more powerful all the time."

I nodded, impressed. "I'd like to meet Millicent someday. And Ivy Tanner, too."

"You will, Sam. Someday. Now, tell me about this dream."

I did, and it was so damn nice opening up to my friend again—a friend who sometimes frustrated me to no end, but my best friend none the less. When I was done explaining, Allison said, "This is terrible, Sam."

I nodded. I could only agree.

"And I only added to your problems," said Allison.

"You did," I said. "And you should feel bad." I winked.

She reached over and gave me another big hug, pressing her closed-off head against mine. She smelled of incense and other witchy kitchen ingredients that I couldn't quite place. "Nothing's going to happen to her, Sam. Not with us on the watch."

"Thank you."

"We good?" she asked.

"Yes," I said. "Unless you ditch me with the bill again."

She pulled away, nodded. "I owe you lunch."

"You do."

She reached out and took my hand, then looked

forward through the windshield at the theater before us. "Does this place have side exits?"

"It does."

"Can you reach them with your mind?" she asked.

"No."

"Okay, I'll head out on foot and keep an eye on them. We'll text as soon as one of us sees her."

Now, *that* was an idea I could get behind.

She slipped away into the night, and I turned my attention to the brightly lit front doors.

26.

Thirty minutes later, she appeared.

I watched her laughing and hanging on to the arm of a boy who looked like nothing but trouble. He also looked like no one in the car, either, and so I breathed a sigh of relief. I sent a text to Allison: *The eagle has landed.*

Of course, my daughter would know I was here watching her. She might not know *now*, but she would know later as she picked it up somewhere in my thoughts. I was thinking about that, as Allison appeared at the driver's side door, ducking and trying to look inconspicuous, but she really was too cute to be inconspicuous, ever. Still, it gave me a small chuckle.

"Who is she with?" asked Allison, a little out of breath.

"I don't recognize him."

"So he's not from the dream?"

"No."

"That's good, right?"

"Maybe. He's too old for her. And I don't like his skinny jeans. Or skinny jeans, period."

"I wear skinny jeans."

"Okay, his skinny jeans. Or him."

Allison laughed a little, and patted my hand.

"And I also don't like hiding from my own daughter. She should know that I care. She should know that I am watching her. She should know that I am doing what I can to keep her safe."

"What are you saying?"

"Allison, lower your shields," I said. "And, yes, I heard Captain Kirk's voice, too."

"Are you sure, Sam?"

"About Captain Kirk?"

"The shield, silly."

"I am."

Allison closed her eyes and dropped her head a little. A second later, she raised it again. "Done."

The Skinny Jean Punk Ass leaned down and gave my daughter a small kiss. She veritably melted. His friend hugged my daughter's friend. Skinny Jeans gave Tammy's hand a squeeze, which was kind of cute actually, and then left with his friend. When they were out of sight, the two girls turned to each other and giggled, holding hands, and I remembered the feeling of a first kiss. Although I suspected this *wasn't* my daughter's very first kiss. Still, the first kiss from anyone was, well, pretty damn special.

And here I was watching her like a peeping Tom.

No, I thought, *watching her like a concerned mother.*

Shortly, while the girls continued holding hands and talking into each other's ears, followed by what I assumed were high-pitched squeals, another minivan appeared, pulling up in front of the theater. Her friend's mother's van. The girls each checked their texts. Tammy showed her friend her texts, covered her mouth in what might have been a hypersonic squeal, and they both started running toward the van.

At that moment, as Tammy was coming around to the driver's side cargo door, she looked up from her phone, much like a dog catching a trace of something on the wind. She paused, frowned, scanned the parking lot, and then settled on us, parked a hundred feet away, tucked under a scraggly tree. By all rights, she shouldn't be able to see us, or make us out. But she did.

She paused and stared, and no doubt scanned the entirety of my mind. I had nothing to hide.

Tammy shook her head, then slipped into the cargo van and slammed the door shut.

27.

With my daughter safe under the watchful—and witchy—eye of Allison, I soared over Orange County, high enough to not be seen but just below the low-hanging cumulus clouds.

As I flew steadily along the 91 Freeway, looking down into the many vehicles cruising even at this late hour, I was horrified to see that, precisely, half of the drivers were texting or looking down at their phones. Yes, Talos's vision is that good. Hell, if I squinted, I could maybe, maybe just make out a text or two. How we weren't getting into even more accidents, I don't know.

Actually, I kind of did.

After all, I knew firsthand that guardian angels were real, and, I'm sure, cell phones and driving were keeping them busy as hell. Which made me wonder, as I sped swiftly over the freeway, sometimes flapping, sometimes gliding, just what the hell Ishmael, my own guardian angel—ex-guardian angel—was doing these days. He claimed to be watching over my son, who himself had lost his own guardian angel, thanks to his brief trip down vampire lane. Whether or not Ishmael was keeping his word, I didn't know, but if he was keeping an eye out for my son, well, that was kind of sweet of him.

I considered: did angels live on yet another plane? Another dimension? A higher dimension perhaps? Did the banished dark masters live in a lower dimension?

I wondered if Elizabeth could just up and leave me. I doubted it. I suspected very, very dark mag- icks were at work here, and such magicks didn't let go of their hold very easily. But if she did, if she was ever to relinquish her hold on me, what would happen to me? Would I die? Was she, in fact, the one thing keeping my immortal body alive? I suspected I would very much go back to being normal. Or perhaps I would age rapidly, sort of catch up to where I should be. Of course, that would be a problem a few hundred years from now, wouldn't it? Or not. Maybe I would just revert to the age I was when she first possessed me. Twenty- eight.

Of course, there was always the diamond medallion, created by the Librarian, a relic that promised to remove the entity from me, and to revert vampirism altogether. Except, of course, I knew it wasn't as easy as that. I knew there was a likelihood that some of her dark powers would remain. None of this was an exact science. A lot of this, I suspected, was new even to those who were immortal.

Everyone's learning as we go, I thought.

I also knew that, should Elizabeth be released from me, there was a very strong likelihood she would next go after my sister or my daughter. Which was why the diamond medallion presently resided safely with the Librarian, Archibald Maximus, unused.

Keep your enemies close, as the saying goes.

Well, Elizabeth couldn't get any closer. Actually, I was wrong. She *could* get closer. She could take me over completely, and I would be the one looking out from the shadows of my own mind.

I banked away from the freeway and aimed for the hulking dark mass to the south, the Santa Ana Mountains.

Elizabeth, I knew, wasn't going anywhere. I knew that, and she knew that. We were in this together, forever. And like the saying goes: *forever is a very long time for a vampire.*

28.

I have a question, Talos, I thought as we circled high over Lake Elsinore. The moon was in its waxing state, about a quarter full. The stars, much brighter and numerous up here, twinkled and flashed and generally gave one a sense of infinite space.

Let's hope I have the answer you seek.

Do you not know my questions before I ask them? I suddenly asked, switching gears.

Is that your question?

No, that was an addendum.

Then to answer your addendum... I prefer to not pry too deeply.

But you could if you wanted to?

I choose not to. I have, as you might guess, perfectly good thoughts of my own.

Very well, I thought. We were banking steadily,

circling widely. The wind was cool, with the occasional updraft of thermal blasts. All of which were absorbed easily by Talos's massive wings. Nothing threw him off course. *How do you protect yourself from me taking over your body completely? After all, what if I never choose to go back to my own body again? What if I never summon the single flame again and remain, well, you?*

I am always in control, Sam, whether you know it or not. You might think you are in control and that's because, for the most part, I give you that impression. How do you think you learned to fly so quickly?

Um, at the time, I didn't know... but now I'm thinking you had a lot to do with it.

Everything to do with it, Sam. No one can take permanent control of your body, no matter how much they may want to do so, or how much they think they can do so, or how much they were trained to do so. Your body is yours and yours alone.

Say that to the bitch inside me.

She's not inside us, Sam. Not in this changeling form. This is your safe place. Remember that. Just as it is for the human called Dracula. It is a place where you can be free of her, and free to explore decisions of your own, without her input or knowledge.

Good to know, I thought.

Yes, came Talos's words. *I imagine it is.*

But won't she know any of my plans once I

182

transform back?

The mind is a mysterious thing, Samantha Moon, capable of shielding and boxing and fragmenting.

Fragmenting? Are you suggesting multiple personalities?

It is an idea, Sam. You can safely keep her in one area of your mind, and you can live your life in another area, free of her input, free of her snooping. Free of her completely. She could be, in effect, locked up for all eternity.

This is quite a concept.

Indeed.

And scary as hell.

It doesn't have to be.

I am afraid of her, Talos.

Only your own fear can keep you from reclaiming your body, and your mind, Sam. Dracula is evidence of it. He is afraid of the entity known as Cornelius. And thus, Cornelius has control over him.

I nodded. I had seen it. Heard it.

And you will help me, Talos?

I am here to help and to serve.

Let's talk about this later, I thought. *It's hurting my head.*

My head, too, came the deep reply, followed by an internal wink.

We flew in a slow counterclockwise circle, and I searched the landscape for a boy-shaped bright light—or for a monster-shaped bright light swimming in the deeper waters. So far, nothing. Not even the big female catfish. Maybe she'd been caught. Or maybe she was hidden, or had burrowed into the silt. Then again, this was a big lake. I couldn't see everything at all times, try as I might. And I did try. For the next half hour or so. Circling, circling...

Later, along the north side of the lake, moving through what I knew to be tall grass and low scrubby trees, were four figures. Human figures. Adult human figures. Who they were, I didn't know. What they were up to at this time of night, I didn't know that either. I figured it was time to get some more answers.

I touched down not too far from them. I shifted, and donned my crime-fighting outfit: jeans, sneakers and a t-shirt.

Ready for business...

29.

They were drunk. As skunks.

They had with them a bevy of weapons: two rifles, a shotgun, a high-powered BB gun, and a hunter's bow. Four guys, four weapons, and lots of bullets and booze. And all piling into a shaky rowboat at best.

This isn't going to end well, I thought. I didn't need a prophetic dream to know that.

As I stepped out of the reeds and into a small clearing, one of them saw me. "Whoa. You here to find the monster, too?" he asked.

As soon as he did so, the other three turned and saw me, then raised their weapons high and gave a sort of drunken, hillbilly cheer. It combined whistles and catcalls and something that could have been a yodel. One guy, I was certain, was making a bovine mooing sound. All of it involved inebriated, uninhibited exuberance. And wild optimism, too. To the man, they believed they were going to find the lake monster, and put an end to it and its reign of terror.

Yes, just today the word had gotten out about the attack in the lake, an attack that had left one boy dead with missing limbs. The city was on high alert, and, I suspected, the rest of the country was perking up, too. I had even seen one or two news vans parked around the lake during my flyover.

"Yes," I said, as I approached them. "I am."

That got another rousing round of high-pitched war cries. Weapons were pumped into the air. One of them accidentally went off. The high-powered BB gun, with a muffled poof, and the others laughed and chided the guy for bringing his BB gun. The boat rocked and wobbled.

"Well, make room for the missus," said the loudest of them all, the guy waving the shotgun. The guy who clearly meant business. The biggest gun and all that...

I brushed off the suggestion, and asked, "What do you boys know of the lake monster?"

"Tore up some kid!"

"Been hearing about it all my life!"

"Dunno, but its ass is grass!"

"Reminds me, who brought the weed?"

"We will drink from its skull!"

I sighed, not sure this was going to go any-where. "Has anyone here actually seen it?"

That quieted them down, and I noted they all

turned to a big guy wearing suspenders, the guy who was sporting an actual bow over one meaty shoulder. Actual arrows spouted from a quiver strapped to his back. He looked like Robin Hood and the Merry Men all rolled into one.

Now that the spotlight had caught him, he shrugged shyly. I took a step closer and under his weight, the rowboat of fools almost capsized.

"I saw something," he said, shrugging. "The other night."

"What did you see?"

"Who wants to know?"

And then the others chimed in, in full herd mentality, which might have been the reason for the mooing:

"—yeah, who the hell are you?"

"—and what the hell are you doing out here alone?"

"—you a reporter?"

"—say, did I used to date you?"

"—in your dreams, Jimbo."

Enough, I shouted. Or, rather, projected loudly, in my mind.

And that seemed to do it. All four men reeled, blinked, and stared at me, not sure what had happened, or why they had a sudden need to be silent. I'd never done a group suggestion before, so this was fascinating.

They continued blinking and breathing loudly, and smelling of beer and cheap booze, and way too much sweat. There was something else in the air, too, and not the stinky lake.

Testosterone, I thought. I hadn't known I could actually smell it, but I think that's what it was. A mix of nerves and hot air and wasted energy.

I focused my intent on the big guy in overalls. *Talk,* I commanded.

Back in the day, I'd had a problem with taking over someone's will. Now, not so much. I saw it as useful, and even kind of fun, which worried me. But in doing so, I gave the bitch within me hope and strength, which was why I didn't do it too often. At least, that was what I told myself. Truth was, I feared I might start enjoying it too much. Or she might. And that's when things started getting murky. When did I drop off and she begin, and vice versa?

"I was out last night," said Hillbilly Hood. "Fishing the spillage pipe, when I saw it."

"Walk me through it."

He did. He was fishing here on the bank when he heard a splashing sound coming from a spillage channel that was nearby. The Redneck of Sherwood hadn't heard about the attack yet—no one had; in fact, it had gone a full day without word being leaked out—and so he hadn't thought much of the sound. He investigated anyway, and what he did see was the world's biggest catfish (his words) in a sort of death roll with something big and slithery. He hadn't, admittedly, seen what it was struggling with. But he'd caught something gleaming in the light of his flashlight, and then it was gone, dragging the catfish down with it.

"Then this morning, I hear about a kid getting all ate up. And I figure I must have seen the thing. Or part of it."

I gave him a sort of mental release, a mental snap of my fingers, and he blinked and looked at the others, all of whom were staring forward at me. Oops. I'd released them as well, and now they all were shaking their heads and running their fingers through their hair, far less subdued than they had been just minutes earlier.

I should have felt badly for zapping their enthusiasm, but I didn't. At the rate they had been going, one of them was bound to blow a hole in the bottom of the boat—or lodge an arrow in a friend's neck. At least now, they wouldn't be lake monster food.

Let's hope, I thought, and turned in the direction of the spillage tributary.

30.

Fifty-odd years ago, Lake Elsinore had run dry.

That hadn't been good for business, and the city had taken measures for that to never happen again. One such measure was for water to feed continuously into the lake from a regional water reclamation plant. Indeed, something drastic had to be done to replenish a lake that loses 14,000 acre-feet of water a year due to evaporation. That's the equivalent of 4.56 billion gallons a year. The lake is, after all, right smack-dab in an honest-to-God desert. And, yes, any good private eye uses the crap out of Wikipedia.

Now, as I stood behind a protective chain-link fence, I could see the highly purified reclaimed water pouring into the lake along a cement channel, itself heavily overgrown with grasses and reeds, which acted as a final filtration process for the water.

I had dipped inside Friar Huck's mind as he relayed his story. Yes, he had indeed seen what he'd claimed to have seen. He had even shone his high-powered spotlight on the crazy battle. He had just caught the massive catfish in a sort of death-roll... with something. Something big. Something black and shining and rubbery-looking. Serpentine.

Here be monsters, I thought, as I looked down into the overgrown ditch, and listened to the rushing flow of highly-filtered water into the lake.

In the night, I saw many bright spots of light. Smaller creatures. Jumping creatures. Frogs, and lots of them. All shining with their own inner light, and all visible to me. But that was it. Nothing bigger than a frog.

I waited another hour, searching, scanning, listening—and worrying about my daughter. Then I felt a strong need to move on. There was, after all, one man I had my eye on. One man who might shed some answers to Luke's disappearance.

I pulled out my cell phone and brought up the Google map app, and saw that a jogging trail followed the overgrown ditch to the water reclamation plant, and beyond. In fact, the path and ditch led directly to Luke's apartment complex, which sat, coincidentally, at the far end of the path. I also noted something else along the path. A certain popular landmark. It was situated about a mile or two from Luke's apartments, on a hillside overlooking all of Lake Elsinore.

Aimee's Castle.

31.

We were in his living room, drinking black coffee, and not having a very easy time of communicating.

Raul Cruz was in his late seventies, according to his wife. And although spry and spunky, his accent was so thick that I was having a devil of a time understanding the man. When he'd answered the door—holding an aluminum baseball bat over one shoulder—I had explained who I was and said I was looking into the disappearance of Luke Jensen. I next showed him my private investigator's license —the one where I'm covered in a half pound of make-up. He read it carefully, nodded, and invited me in. He eased the bat down into an umbrella holder. Side note: there were no umbrellas in it.

That's when our communication started to break down. He said something, and I nodded and smiled politely, and he shuffled off into the kitchen. I might have heard the word *café*, which seemed safe enough. While he clanged about, I studied the many portraits of Christ that adorned the living room walls above the many low bookcases. I even stood in front of a beautifully ornate crucifix and noted, once again, that I felt nothing. No repulsion. No angst or anxiety. Jesus, I think, was all right with me.

Soon, the scent of coffee wafted from the kitchen, and with it another question from Raul. At least, I think it was a question. I gave a noncommittal—and perhaps even nonhuman—grunt, and shortly he returned with two steaming mugs of black coffee. Damn, I could have used some cream and sugar. Stupid language barrier.

Now, as we sat in his living room, I noted the distinct absence of a TV. I also noted a lack of any computers, laptops, tablets, iPhones, Xboxes and Kindles. Just books, and lots of them. Most of which had Spanish titles. A comfy-looking chair sat under a reading lamp. A book was propped open over one the chair's plush arms. His reading nook looked so inviting that I wanted to curl up with one of his books, even if it was in Spanish.

He tried English again, and I tried listening again, but I was quickly beginning to realize my Spanish was better than his English. And I didn't speak Spanish. I considered my options, and decided to go within.

I took Raul with me.

***

Can you hear me? I asked, projecting my thoughts.

Raul's eyes widened.

I mean you no harm, I thought.

Who are you?

I nodded, pleased. I knew that with a meeting of the minds, language was clarified, intent was emphasized. I still heard his accent, and I still felt him struggling with English, searching for the words. With intent, the meaning was clear. There were no hardened, strained vocal cords to get in the way.

I considered a white lie, but then shrugged. After all, there was a very good chance I was going to wipe his memory clean of my visit anyway. Besides, I was sensing that the old man could handle the truth. Why I sensed that, I didn't know. Maybe he had strong faith. Maybe something else.

I'm a vampire.

Everyone reacted differently to me slipping into their minds. Some let me in easily, and didn't skip a beat. Others were on guard, their bodies tense, their internal selves ready to fight me off as best as they could. Most couldn't fight me off. At best, they could clutter their minds so full of nonsense that I couldn't read their thoughts, as had been the case with the old man in Fullerton, a few years back. Others slipped into a semi-hypnotized state. Raul was vacillating a little between the last two: on guard one moment, eyes drowsy the next.

I thought you looked different, Senora Moon.

Señorita, I thought, and wished I knew the Spanish equivalent for *Ms.*, if there was one. *Different, how?*

I could not see your body light.

My aura.

Si. Yes, your aura.

You can see those?

He nodded, then surprised me with: *I am a brujo, Señorita. Among other things.*

I knew the term well. Mexican witchcraft. I had a friend out of the City of Orange. A sister private eye who, after a few drinks, had admitted to me one night that she came from a long line of *brujas*. My friends are weird.

He nodded, picking up on my own thoughts. *Si. Señora Cruz. Mi sobrina. My niece. She is, ah, how do you say? Muy powerful. Very, very powerful. Perhaps the most powerful of us all.*

I looked around his house, at the crucifix and portraits of Christ. *You are Catholic, too?*

He grinned and sat back in his comfy chair and his perfectly positioned lamplight caught his surprisingly smooth face. Late seventies, but he had the skin of a forty-year-old man. Or of a vampire.

No, senora. No vampires. And I am not afraid of you. Indeed, you would do well to tread lightly here. He tapped his skull. *You might very well find something here that you wish you hadn't.*

Message received, I thought. *I am here only for information.*

Very well. And to answer your question: the paintings you see are my personal visions.

You painted these?

Si. I have, what you say, a personal connection to He who is called Christos. I've had it from an early age. I have it today. I paint and carve the images I see. I sell them. I speak to Him, too. Often. Every day.

And he, ah, Christos, doesn't have a problem with, um...

Witchcraft? he asked.

Si, I thought, then added: *I mean yes.*

He shrugged. *It's never come up. Truthfully, I do not practice it much. The power is strong with the females in my family. I have only gotten a whiff of it. But enough to repel you, if need be.*

Fair enough, I thought.

You wish to know about the boy?

Raul told me what he knew of Luke Jensen. The boy was a good enough boy. He'd always been trouble, but Raul had seen some changes in him. Positive changes. Raul spent most of his time on his front porch, with his friends and family. (His wife was presently asleep in the back room.)

He kept an eye on the neighborhood, and had seen it go through many changes. Most people kept a wide berth of his home. Most knew of his family's history in Mexican witchcraft. Most wanted no part of it. People, Raul said, were smarter than they looked. But one kid kept coming around. Luke Jensen. He would sit with Raul and tell him about his day, about school, about his mom and her many boyfriends. Raul knew what was going on with his mother, too, knew she was turning tricks, and gave the boy a safe haven. He'd watched Luke get into much trouble. He'd also seen Luke do a lot of good, too. A number of times, Raul had scared off the local bullies.

Once or twice, those same bullies didn't learn their lessons. Those same bullies didn't come around here again. Those same bullies were long gone. To where, I didn't know, and didn't ask. But in Raul's mind, I sensed the bullies had brought out a darkness in Raul that he was not proud of. I slipped away from those darker, hidden thoughts, and eased back front and center. Raul nodded, and we continued our internal dialogue. I noted that his wide-eyed look was softening. He was getting used to me being in his head, trusting me. Good.

Of late, Luke had started his own lawn mowing business. Which was a good thing, according to Raul. Luke had also been hanging out with a troublemaker. A real honest-to-God troublemaker that Raul didn't like. Johnny. Yes, Raul had heard of the incident on the lake, an incident that had left Johnny partially consumed. Raul, if you asked me, didn't seem too torn up about it. I let that thought go, too.

A few months of honest work had done wonders for Luke, Raul thought. It had started shaping the boy into an independent young man and Raul couldn't have been more pleased.

I saw in him something special.

Special how?

The boy, Luke, has a special gift. I can see it within his aura, as you call it.

What do you see?

Better I show you, Samantha Moon.

And he did, giving me a peek inside his memory. Seeing memories is tricky business. Many memories were amorphous and subject to change over time. Memories were often infused with other relevant memories... and sometimes not-so-relevant memories. The greater the impact, the sharper, more accurate the memory. Major, life-altering, or powerful things were emblazoned quite accurately.

His memory unspooled before me. There was Luke Jensen sitting right where I was sitting, listening to Raul and nodding, and smiling and holding a can of Coke. This was Luke's safe place, away from his whoring mother, abusive johns, local gangbangers, drug dealers and addicts, and trouble-makers in general. Here, Luke was coached by Raul, taught by a kindly old man, to think for himself, to work hard, to believe in himself, to find the good in all things, especially in himself. Hell, I wouldn't have minded a lecture from Raul myself. The man was inspiring, and I could see the brightness on Luke's young face as he took it all in.

Most important, I could also see Luke as Raul saw the boy; in particular, the bright aura that surrounded the boy's body. The aura itself consisted mostly of primary colors, with only a few strands of brown and black. The darkness represented natural fears and doubts and perhaps evidence of something or someone clinging to him. Something was attached to the boy, but I had seen it dozens of times with others. Many people had many such unhealthy attachments.

If they only knew, I thought, as I looked deeper into his aura, through the murky reds and blues and patches of yellow. I could have been looking at a living, pulsating painting. But this was no portrait. This was a living, breathing, and highly active aura, itself described to me as energy leakage. Spillover, so to speak. Of the soul.

I didn't know, but I could see it, and so could Raul, and what I next saw weaving through it was a first for me. As the shape wove in and out of the boy's light body, it occasionally turned to look at me. Well, at Raul, at the time.

Yes, turned and *looked.*

Attached to the boy, was, I was certain, a serpent. And not just any serpent. It was a silver dragon.

***

What does it mean? I asked Raul, as the memory ended, and I blinked my way back to my senses and equilibrium. It was always jolting to exit another's mind.

I wish I knew, Samantha Moon.

Did he ever talk about running away?

Not to me. But did he had a reason to run away? Yes. Many reasons, in fact.

Luke recently started a lawn mowing business?
He did.

When was the last time you saw Luke? I asked.

The day before he disappeared. He had just returned from a day of mowing lawns.

Would you mind replaying that last conversation for me?

He didn't mind and opened up, and I watched a very sweaty Luke Jensen pushing a grass-covered lawnmower into Raul's garage. Raul chastised him for not cleaning the machine, and Luke got right to it, using a rag to wipe it down, and then a broom to sweep up the refuse. The boy was bright-eyed and talking quickly. I wondered how much Raul understood of the excited boy. But through the muddled memory and all the jabbering, I heard one name clearly: Aimee.

Raul's memory trailed off, and I waited. I let him work through his emotions, and when he was done, I had a bright idea. I brought up a Google map of the local area, chose the satellite view, expanded it, and had Raul touch all the houses that he was certain were clients of Luke's lawn mowing business. As he touched the homes on the aerial map—none very far from this location—Google was nice enough to drop down pins on each, marking the homes for me. Technology at its best.

After seven such pins were dropped, I held my tongue, and my mind, when I saw the eighth pin drop down on Lake Elsinore's famous landmark.

I shouldn't have been surprised, but I was.

Before I left, I asked Raul a question. I asked if he could see my aura, as well.

The old guy looked at me from under thick, wiry, gray brows. He held my gaze for a moment, then shook his head. *No, Samantha. You have no aura.*

I nodded. I knew that, of course. Allison couldn't see it either. But I just chalked that up as her being closer to something like men, than to her human self. She was, after all, a reincarnated witch of considerable power. I had been one, too.

Still, I had held onto hope that others might be able to see my soul. That there was evidence of it somewhere. But first Allison, and now Raul. No, aura. No soul. What the hell did that mean?

Do you believe in monsters, Raul? I asked at his door.

Oh, yes.

Lake monsters?

All monsters.

I thought about that as I stepped away from his dimly lit front porch and headed out into the night.

32.

The Castle.

Everywhere I turned, it seemed to come up in this investigation. That could mean something, or it could simply mean that Lake Elsinore wasn't a very big city, and the structure itself dominated the landscape. One couldn't help but see it, or cross paths with it.

Still, I knew that when something comes up more than once in any investigation, that something needed to be investigated. And I needed to investigate the crap out of this place. Besides, it's a castle, for God's sake. It was just begging to be checked out by an ace vampire detective like myself.

The waning moon was out. So were about seven stars. The sky was clear, which was no surprise. Wind tugged at me, and brought with it the small stink of the lake, which stretched out far below. I wondered how the four yahoos were faring in their search for the lake monster. And just as I thought that thought, I suddenly had a very bad feeling. A premonition? I didn't know.

Before I knew it, I found myself approaching the biggest house in Lake Elsinore. And that's because it wasn't a house, was it?

No, I thought, as the white structure came into view from around a corner. The massive white structure.

It was Aimee's Castle.

***

The castle itself rested upon a hard-packed dirt hill, high above Lake Elsinore, and looked more like a medieval fortress than a home in Southern California.

Then again, if I let my imagination really run wild, I could almost imagine camel caravans trucking through here with their bundles of spices and cloths and mohair rugs. Where that image came from, I didn't know. But it was real and exciting, and called to my heart. Called to what, I didn't know. No, I did know, as I stood there, looking up at the massive structure on the hill. It called to me of adventure and distant lands. It was, I was certain, the first time I had ever felt such a calling, and I suspected it might have something to do with a past life.

I listened to the water lapping along the rocky shore far below. From my aerial reconnaissance, I knew the hill sloped steeply down into the lake. Had this been a seashore, the castle might have been a lighthouse. A high stone wall surrounded the property, with a main gate opening up onto the sidewalk. Another gate opened for cars to enter through a side entrance.

I wasn't tall enough to see over the wall, but the structure itself continued up a hill, and was easy enough for anyone to see from the street. There were no other homes on the hill. Just the castle, and it was hulking and brooding and oddly ominous, despite the white façade.

The high stone wall wasn't quite high enough. I landed on top smoothly, easily. From here, I had a view of the surrounding gardens and footpaths. All of which looked inviting.

Invitation accepted, I thought, and dropped down inside the fence.

33.

I had that tingly, slightly disorienting feeling I sometimes get when I'm somewhere I shouldn't be; i.e., when I'm trespassing.

Perhaps more disconcerting was my inner alarm. That sucker had been buzzing just inside my ears, the closer and closer I'd gotten to the castle. And now that I was inside the fence, well, it continued at a steady, nearly painful hum.

I scanned the empty gardens around me. Nothing and no one. And yet, the humming continued. More so now than ever.

"Okay then," I said to myself, opening and closing my jaw, trying to ease the uncomfortable vibration in my inner ear. But the hum was not to be denied.

I reminded myself that it was meant to be uncomfortable, and it was meant to keep me on high alert. Oh, I was on alert, all right.

I headed up toward the castle.

***

The slapping waves grew louder as I mounted the hill. The wind grew stronger, too, whipping my shirt and hair around me. I fished a hair tie from a front pocket and pulled my hair back tight.

It was coming around midnight, and the night air felt just about perfect. In fact, I felt as strong as I'd ever felt, and a little hungry, too. The two or three bright spots moving through the plants—field mice and kangaroo rats—were looking mighty tempting, which was a terrible thing to say. Who looked at a mouse and licked their lips?

Monsters did.

I sighed and continued hoofing it up to the castle on the hill.

***

The castle. Up close, up here, I could feel the weight of it, heavy on the earth, built to last even the coming zombie wars. It was massive and foreboding and, well, kind of badass. And it had been here for nearly half a century. And it had been built by a preacher's daughter, of all things.

I took it in: the massive bricks, the soaring minarets, the mosque-like dome that capped the whole structure. I was briefly reminded of a well-known structure in Riverside, The Mission Inn, another vaguely medieval building that had no place in our modern times.

But this, well, there was nothing vaguely medieval about it. This was full medieval, and it took my breath away.

I followed a path that led away from the well-watered gardens and brought me closer to the cliff's edge. The wind was stronger up here, whipping through the scraggly grass that somehow clung to life upon the hard-baked, dry soil; soil that sometimes saw temperatures climb over 110 degrees. The deserts just outside of Los Angeles and Orange counties were no joke. They meant business. And they would kill you dead. Especially vampires.

That so many people lived here was a testament to, well, housing prices in Orange County. The high prices pushed people further and further away from metropolitan areas, all the way out to a desert outpost, into the kind of remote wilderness that could wipe a man off the face of the Earth, bones and all.

Of the many such desert outposts, where developers had thrown up all sorts of strip malls and grocery stores and Home Depots, where people tried to forget the heat and the two-hour commutes to work, Lake Elsinore boasted a beautiful lake. From here, with the castle rising behind me and the lake spread before me, I could almost forget I was in the middle of fucking nowhere.

As my hair whipped in the hot wind and low

clouds scuttled across the sky, my inner alarm reached an all-time high, a crescendo of ringing and humming. I spun, searching. Something was coming for me. And it was coming now.

I saw nothing, just the long sweep of grounds that led back to the castle. I looked to either side, nothing. I looked into the sky, nothing as well.

The ringing, the ringing...

When I turned again, I caught a brief glimpse of something appearing over the cliff's edge, something bounding, loping, and moving faster than anything I'd ever seen run before, even the werewolves, and it was upon me.

34.

I sidestepped to the right, and it sidestepped with me, altering course in a blink, and before I knew it, the damn thing hit me full on, harder than anything had ever hit me before. And it didn't just hit me. It lifted me up in the air, and drove me down into the hard-packed dirt.

The sheer speed, the ferocity, the power. The thing kept me pinned to the dirt with one hand, an iron grip to my throat that crushed tendons and windpipe and my spine itself, while it delivered lightning strikes to my face, faster and harder than anything I'd ever felt before. Blow after blow after blow, shattering cheekbones and my orbital ridge. A particularly strong blow shattered the right side of my skull. He drove his knees into my chest, drove them and drove them, until I felt my sternum collapse and my lungs burst.

Air and blood burst from my mouth...

And still, he punched me, over and over again... all while screaming something I couldn't quite make out, a guttural, primal, animalistic scream, asking me something over and over. Demanding something I couldn't quite hear, but that was because my eardrums had burst and a loud, *whooshing* sound of escaping air filled my head, and I knew that if I didn't do something now, I would die here on this hill, on this night, at the hands of this thing. He would, I knew, tear me to pieces.

I did the only thing I could think of.

I focused the bright light that now filled my head into a single flame, and with each punch, the flame wavered and snapped, but still, I focused on it. Just when I saw the bastard above me raise both fists together, in a blow that I knew would concave my face and drive me into the hill itself, I saw the great flying beast within the flame.

***

The transformation was instant.

Talos, unlike my broken body, was powerful and whole. And now, so was I, so to speak, although I was still disoriented and reeling from the ferocity of the attack.

One moment, I had been lying on my back, watching a pair of massive—and oddly misshapen hands—hurtling toward my face, the next, I was on my feet and screeching loudly into the night.

The thing that had been on top of me, backed away, and as he did so, I saw him clearly for the first time. A big man, but his proportions were off. One arm was longer the other. Hell, the skin itself was darker than the other arm. Scars crisscrossed his neck and face. He was naked, and the scar tissue on him could have been a roadmap to hell. He continued backing away, limping due to his legs being of different lengths. He was, I was certain, composed of many different body parts.

He continued backing away from Talos, as well as he could. He stumbled over a low wall, and soon found himself in the perfectly manicured gardens of the castle estate.

I bore down on him, step for step, still trying to wrap my brain around what just happened, still grappling with who and what he was. Rather than attack, I studied and fought for clarity.

Perhaps I should have attacked.

But I didn't, and soon, the creature pulled open a concealed basement door in the ground, and dropped down into the darkness.

35.

The flight back was spent in silence.

I had abandoned my minivan on the side of the road. I had to. There was no way I could transform into my broken body. Not out there, and not alone.

Later, as I flew in slow circles high over my house, dreading the return to my abused —and quite possibly dying—body, I waited for a late-night dog walker to continue past my home and move up the street. The dog looked up, once, and growled. While I circled, I prayed that my broken body was doing some healing in Talos's world.

When the coast was clear, I dropped down into my backyard—not the first time an actual dragon had appeared in my backyard.

I paused, waited, summoned my courage, along with the single flame, within which I saw my broken body. I saw my concaved head and crushed cheeks, and soon I found myself in the grass, gasping and writhing and weeping.

***

It didn't take long for my daughter and Allison to hear my cries for help. A light turned on in the backyard, and there was Tammy, then Allison, and now, Anthony... all rushing toward me...

Allison pulled a sheet from the clothesline and threw it over me. I felt strong hands carefully lift me off the wet grass, and realized it was only wet because of my own bleeding, and as Tammy shrieked hysterically, I heard Allison take control of the situation and order Anthony to bring me into my bedroom.

I rested my shattered skull on his shoulder, and soon, I was resting on a soft pillow of daggers, and that was all I remembered of that night.

36.

I spent that night and all the next day gone to the world. Or dead to the world. To Allison, I was nothing more than a corpse, and a mangled one at that. No breathing, no real pulse (although if you wait long enough, you'll find one). That is, until she finally saw me healing in my sleep. Right before her very eyes.

When I finally opened my eyes, I saw again the monster pummeling me into mush, and shot up screaming. Allison screamed, too, from her chair next to me, dropping her Kindle reader. She rushed over to my side.

I babbled incoherently about the monster and the beating, and Allison took my hands and told me I was okay.

I touched my face, my cheekbones, my eye ridge, the side of my skull. All intact. I took in some air... my lungs were working again, my sternum strong and sure.

I pulled Allison into me and held her tightly and wept into her shoulder. She patted my head and made soft, reassuring noises. "The kids?" I said, mumbling the words into her now-wet neck.

"Are with Mary Lou."

I nodded, then said, "Is it..."

"Yes, Sam?"

"Is it too early to drink?"

***

"My poor kids," I said, drinking wine that did nothing for me. "I can't imagine what I looked like."

"You looked like pulp," said Allison. "Bloody pulp with arms and legs. If you would have told me that a train hit you, I would have believed you."

"Worse," I said.

"Worse than a train?"

"I think it would be easier to show you," I said, and tapped my head.

I opened my memory to her, reliving the most violent night of my life, violence that should have left me dead, many times over. I heard her gasp once or twice. She was probably covering her mouth, but I wouldn't know it. I kept my eyes closed, concentrating on the details of the attack and, in particular, the details of my attacker.

When I was done, Allison and I did another

round of hugging. And after just reliving every horrid detail again, I really needed that hug.

"He looked like a science experiment gone wrong," said Allison.

"Or right, depending on how you looked at it. Do you have any idea what he was saying?"

"His speech wasn't normal. Or human. But I think he was asking something over and over. Let me listen again. Try to isolate his speech."

"How the devil do I do that?"

"Just think about his voice, his words, nothing else."

"Do I have to?"

"If you want my help."

"Okay, fine."

I closed my eyes, and replayed the sound coming from his lips, as best as I could recall.

"Okay, got it," said Allison. "He's saying 'I know what you are. I know what you are.'"

"Okay, okay." She mimicked the voice a little too well. I got chills just hearing it. Truth was, I couldn't for the life of me discern what he was saying. If that's what Allison thought, so be it.

I asked, "Did English seem his first language?"

"I'm not sure he had a first language. The noise coming from him was very primal, almost ancient."

"Speech impairment?"

"Something like that. Or..."

"He was never taught to speak," I said.

She nodded. "I was thinking the same thing."

"What do you make of his scars?" I asked.

"I'm not sure what to make of them. Do you?"

I gave her a glimpse of another memory: this time, of Kingsley's butler, Franklin, and his strange scar that circumnavigated his neck. I also gave her a snapshot of his mismatched ears, and strange, loping walk. I also replayed his speech for her, to compare. I usually kept the very strange Franklin out of mind, rarely asking Kingsley about his man-servant, mostly because I didn't want to know the answer... whatever it might be. And these days, I had a very sneaky suspicion of what the answer might be.

Allison, who had been following my trail of thoughts, said, "Are we really suggesting that he might be..."

"I don't know what you're suggesting," I said. "Your mind's closed off to me."

"Well, I can see what you're suggesting."

"And are you suggesting the same thing?" I asked, not bothering to hide the mild irritation in my voice.

We both stared at each other. Finally, Allison asked the inevitable: "Is Franklin... Frankenstein?"

***

"I've been thinking the same thing," I said. "And Frankenstein was the doctor, not the monster. Get it straight."

Allison ran her fingers through her hair, then grabbed a thick handful of it and pulled. "What

217

have our lives come to, Sam?"

"To the place where butlers are Frankenstein monsters, defense attorneys are werewolves, psychic phone operators are witches, and private eyes are sexy vampires."

"You did not just say that."

"I did. And I meant most of it."

Allison finally giggled. "But Franklin... he seemed so well-spoken."

We had refilled our glasses and retired to the east wing. Or, as some people called it, the living room. I nodded, and said, "Better than I. Or me. Whatever."

"Better than most," agreed Allison. "But this thing that attacked you the night before last... it could barely speak. And was a veritable roadmap of scars."

"Evocative," I said. "Maybe Franklin is similarly road-mapped."

"You could always check."

"Strip him with my mind?"

"Well, you can see through things."

"I don't really see through things. I see beyond things. There are no barriers."

"Seems the same to me."

"Yeah, you're right. Forget it." I drummed my pointed nails on the glass, careful not to shatter yet another one. "The thing last night was closer to Frankenstein's monster than Frankenstein's butler."

Allison shrugged. "There's one person who would know."

I didn't have to be a mind reader to know who she was talking about. "Kingsley," I said.

37.

Kingsley, my hotshot attorney boyfriend, wasn't such a hotshot these days.

These days, fewer and fewer scumbags passed through his office, and that was all right by me. Early on, I had been having a real hard time respecting him. Kingsley, to his credit, got the picture and cleaned up his business. By doing so, he took fewer high-profile cases, and, as such, found himself less and less in the spotlight. Again, that was all right by me, especially since I had an aversion to spotlights, and tended to not show up in pictures.

I waited outside his office while he consulted with a client. Kingsley charged $1,000 an hour consulting fees. I did the math. That would be $8,000 a day. I did some more fuzzy math. Over a $175,000 a month. Or $2.2 million a year. Not a bad living.

I'm in the wrong racket, I thought.

So while I digested the fact that my boyfriend earned more in one hour than I would all week, I found myself in his lobby, flipping through a *People* magazine, occasionally tearing pictures of one Kardashian after another. Funny how the tears were only on the Kardashians. Silly, sharp nails.

I tossed the magazine aside and smiled at Kingsley's latest secretary. A man this time. A gay man. He glanced at me occasionally from behind his desk, working the phones and tapping into his computer and letting people know, in no uncertain terms, that Kingsley Fulcrum was a very busy man and they would be extremely lucky if he eventually called them back.

Kingsley's office was, in fact, fully staffed with interns and assistants and clerks. Most were youngish. Some seemed like career assistants. Many seemed bright, and most seemed stressed out. I wondered if Kingsley was a good boss. Did he give them a hard time when they needed days off? Did he pressure them into working late nights, weekends, forsaking kids and family and friends? Was he jovial? Was he in good spirits? Did he joke with them, or laugh at their jokes? Did he take the time to get to know them? Or was he an asshole boss?

Kingsley could be very serious. He had to be. He fought to keep his clients out of jail. He fought to make their stories known. As such, he was an investigator himself, and so were some of his staff, digging deep into police reports, interviewing witnesses, anything they needed to do to punch holes in a prosecutor's case. Yes, serious stuff. Lives were on the line. Truth had to be discerned. Laws followed, laws bent. Loopholes discovered. Meetings after meetings.

Kingsley, I knew, loved the courtroom. He had a flair for it. I had sat in on a number of his cases. No one, but no one, could take their eyes off him. His own amber irises were hypnotic, and he knew it, and he used them to his advantage. Was he controlling the jury? I didn't know. Could he read their minds and know what they were thinking? Maybe, although he never admitted to it.

One thing I had learned was that immortal powers were not constant or consistent, even from one vampire to another vampire. And that was probably because we reflected the entity within us. The more powerful the entity, the more powerful we were. I'd also since learned that my attacking vampire—that is, the person who had transformed me—had transferred some of his own power to me. Who he was, exactly, I never did find out. At least, not yet. Additionally, one's own bloodline could affect one's supernatural powers. Apparently, I came from a long line of alchemists. Those who fought on the side of good, those who resisted—and subsequently banished—the dark masters. That I had been reborn throughout time as a witch, along with Allison and Millicent, was a whole other story. My current bloodline reached all the way back to a very powerful and famous alchemist, the first alchemist, Hermes Trismegistus. As such, my own family shared the bloodline, which potentially put them in danger. Why danger? Because only some-one from Hermes bloodline could open the gates of hell, so to speak, and allow the dark masters back into this world.

I thought of all of this as I flipped through the next magazine, which featured, surprise, a whole new brood of Kardashians. Apparently, they were attacking us in waves.

At the far end of the hall, Kingsley's office door opened and out stepped a lovely woman in her late fifties, dressed immaculately. She seemed upset. I could poke around her mind to see what was bothering her, but I had enough on my plate. Then again, it might be because she had just forked over a grand to sit across from Kingsley for an hour.

When the big lug saw me, he smiled wolfishly, flashing white teeth and amber eyes all the way down the hall. He waved me in. He shut the door behind me and caught my hand and pulled me into him. All in one perfectly rehearsed motion. This might not have been the first time he'd done this, with or without me. I nearly resisted, nearly pushed him away, until I felt his warmth through his custom-made long-sleeved shirt, and the raw power in his arms and chest, the love in his big, dopey eyes. Oh, and some pretzels in his shaggy beard.

I picked out the crumbs for him. "I can't take you anywhere."

"Food and beards go hand in hand."

My laugh was muffled by about three or four feet of muscle and bone and hair, as I did my best to wrap my arms around him. No such luck. If there was ever a place in this world that I felt safe, it was right here, inside these arms, and covered in all that hair.

When we were done, he pulled away and offered me a drink and I considered, then shrugged. Why not? Kingsley always enjoyed his high end booze, especially here in his office. I secretly suspected the booze kept his clients talking, and kept them on the clock.

"To what do I owe this surprise?" he asked, his hands sliding suggestively down to my waist after handing me a glass of something caramel-colored. Whiskey, if I had to guess. I gripped him by his oversized gorilla thumb and pulled his hand away. I spun out of his grasp and hopped up on the corner of his leather-tooled executive desk.

"I need to know about Franklin."

"Franklin. My Franklin?"

Interesting way of putting it, I thought. "Yes, *your* Franklin. Who is he? What is he? How long has he been employed by you?"

He looked at me, then rocked back on his heels, his wing tips gleaming brightly under the fluorescent lighting. His glass hung loosely in one hand, ice clinking. "Any reason for the sudden interest?"

"I've always been interested. It was just never

the right time and place."

"And now is the right time and place?"

"What can I say?" I said. "I'm unpredictable."

He raised his eyebrows that, I thought, were even bushier since the last time I'd noticed them. The man was a walking, talking hair-producing factory.

"Can I ask what led to you wanting to know?"

Which was fair enough, and so I told him about my attack the night before last, and since Kingsley couldn't read my mind, I left out much of the gruesome details. I didn't need to relive that again, thank God. Or get him too worked up. Yet.

As more of the details of my story emerged, Kingsley paced faster and faster in the spacious area before his desk, even shoving some of the client chairs out of his way. One toppled over. He didn't seem to care. Okay, so much for him not getting worked up. He paced the length of his conference table. I knew he sported an even bigger conference table in another room. I was pretty certain it was attorneys who kept conference table makers in business.

When I finally got around to describing my attacker, Kingsley stopped pacing and stood before me, his shaggy hair hanging forward. A row of untouched law books lined a couple of shelves behind him. Ditch the fancy suit, strap on a broadsword and loincloth, and he could have been Conan the Librarian.

"And you're okay now?" he asked.

"All healed," I said. "It's a miracle!"

"And this thing that attacked you looked like Franklin?"

"Kinda sorta. Built like him, if you know what I mean. Walked like him, too."

He nodded, although one hairy eyebrow now seemed permanently arched at this point. That was his pissed-off face. It was also his sex face. Trust me, I've gotten them confused.

Kingsley nodded and drained his glass, ice cubes and all. Kingsley, I knew, didn't take kindly to anyone—or anything—beating his girl to smithereens—and I hadn't even given him the half of it. Little did he know how truly beaten I'd been. Anyway, judging by his arched eyebrow, and the way his hands opened and closed, there was going to be blood. Or sex. But probably blood.

He went over to his desk phone, pressed the red intercom button and told whoever was listening on the other end to hold all calls and to cancel his 2:30. He didn't wait for an answer. At the bar, he poured himself another whiskey, this time, neat. He knocked it back, poured another, then sat across from me in one of his client chairs, which he filled to capacity and then some. He crossed one leg, absently adjusted the drape of the seam, wiggled his oversized foot once or twice, and finally began his tale:

"I've known Franklin for a long, long time..."

38.

Kingsley's tale:

As you know, Sam, I'm no spring chicken. And neither is Franklin. And neither is, I suspect, the thing that attacked you out at Lake Elsinore. Of course, Franklin would take exception to one of his brothers being called a *thing*, and, by extension, him as well.

What they are, Sam, has all the makings of a great horror novel, which Mary Shelley captured so eloquently and at such a young age, too. Did you know she wrote *Frankenstein* at age nineteen?

Right, sorry, a tangent. Truth is, I'm organizing my thoughts here. I haven't told this story... ever, actually. This will be my first telling of my meeting with Franklin—and others of his ilk.

Yes, Sam, *ilk* is a word. And yes, old fogeys like me still use it today.

Anyway, Dr. Frankenstein was a real person. He was an instructor at a boarding school in Ramsgate, where Mary Shelley spent about six months of her time. This was as close to a formal education as Mary would ever receive. She benefited from being raised by a writer of high standing, surrounded with books and interesting people who took an active interest in her. Of course, at the age of eighteen, she would marry Percy Shelley, the great Romantic poet; indeed, he encouraged her writing and often edited it. It was while vacationing with friends on Lake Geneva one summer, Lord Byron—yes, another great Romantic poet and good friend of Percy's—proposed that they all amuse themselves by creating ghost stories.

While the others concocted elaborate and, quite frankly, terrifying stories, Mary found herself unable to play along. In fact, she seemed distressed and disappointed in herself. What kind of young writer was she, if she couldn't think up a simple ghost story? Percy and Byron came up with tale after tale, regaling their friends around fires, often telling their fictions late into the night. And after each night, Percy would ask his young bride if she finally had a story of her own, and, each night, with some shame, she would admit to not having one.

That is, until the fourth night.

It was then that Mary decided to not tell a ghost story; after all, no such stories were coming immediately to mind, and certainly not clever enough to compete with those of Percy and Byron, wordsmiths revered even to this day. No, she had a different tale in mind.

And it wasn't so much a tale, as a secret. A secret she was finally ready to share.

You see, young Mary had been given a glimpse into a world of horrors—real experiments by a mad scientist she renamed Victor Frankenstein. The man was real, the name wasn't. Indeed, she'd had the good decency to protect his privacy, even as she exposed his work.

After all, she was desperate; that is, desperate to tell a good tale. Perhaps, in hindsight, she shouldn't have let the cat out of the bag. Or the Frankenstein monster off the operating table.

But in her need to save face, her very strong desire to be accepted by these great, great poets, she'd created for these masters a horrific tale. Except it wasn't so much of a tale, as it was real life. It was, in fact, a nearly exact retelling of the real-world scientist she had come to know at a young age, and to love.

He was thirty, and she only sixteen. Even back then, the age difference was just too great. Mary considered eloping, until the good doctor revealed his true self... and revealed his experiments.

***

Kingsley paused and stood and refilled his glass, this time, adding a couple of perfectly cubed, perfectly clear ice cubes from a brass ice bucket. He eased next to me on edge of the desk, leaning a meaty hip against it. His aftershave smelled perfect. He stared down into his glass and continued his tale:

***

His name was, in fact, Edward Lichtenstein.

Edward was many years Mary's senior. He was from a prestigious Swiss family; indeed, he used his family's vast resources to build his secret laboratory... and to bribe the local constables and gravediggers and anyone else who might stand in his way.

Yes, I said gravediggers. As you can imagine, reviving the dead required corpses. Hundreds and hundreds of corpses before Lichtenstein finally saw some semblance of success.

It was during those first initial successes that the mad scientist, who was so obsessed with immortality, met young Mary Wollstonecraft. By day, Edward was a highly likable, although distant and eccentric, professor of the sciences. By night, he would hole himself up in his underground laboratory, beneath the streets of Geneva and far from prying eyes, and spend most, if not all, of his nights with the recent dead of Switzerland. Oh, his laboratory was a filthy place, from what I am to understand. Corpses stacked upon each other, rotting and bloating and stinking. But Edward loved them all. After all, each held the promise of eternal life. What was there not to love?

How do I know such things, you ask? A fair question, since I was born nearly a century after Edward and Mary's fleeting affair. For starters, I have spoken at length with Franklin. After all, my good friend had been one of Edward Lichtenstein's, aka Frankenstein's, greatest successes. Additionally, I had met the man. Yes, Dr. Lichtenstein himself. Not surprisingly, he walks among us today, albeit in a very, very different physical apparatus.

Yes, yes, I'm getting ahead of myself. Thank you for pointing that out, Sam. What would I ever do without you? Yes, I suppose I would be shedding on the furniture. No, I wouldn't be licking myself. May I continue?

Anyway, it took many months of not-so-innocent flirting at the boarding school, flirting from both student and teacher, before things progressed to anything more than a few stolen moments in school hallways, or lingering and meaningless questions after class. Neither was fully prepared—or ready—for the feelings they felt. After all, the good doctor was knee-deep in, well, knees and other body parts. Love wasn't on his mind—reanimating corpses was. Finding a steady supply of the dead was, too. And young Mary was doing her best not to cry herself to sleep each night; after all, never had she been gone so long from her doting father.

She was lonely and not very good at making new friends. She found comfort in Lichtenstein's lingering glances and smiles meant only for her. She was thrilled to have his attention, and wondered if other girls had experienced the same, but dared not ask. Even if it was all in her silly little head, it was still much better than the overwhelming loneliness of the boarding school. Of course, Mary had quite the imagination; indeed, she had already concocted a dozen or more stolen moments in her head, each moment in exceedingly unlikely and dangerous places. Each fantasy gave her a thrill and made her want her captivating teacher just that much more.

Her innocent fantasies were about to very much become a reality, and sixteen-year-old Mary Wollstonecraft's innocence was about to be stolen away from her forever.

***

Although the age difference would pose a problem, Mary, in those days, would have been considered of age to be courted. Edward himself was a bachelor at age thirty. An unlikely romance, to be sure, which was why they kept it private throughout her six months at the academy in Ramsgate. Indeed, the good doctor most certainly would have lost his position had his superiors discovered his dalliance with a student.

Yes, Sam, *dalliance* is still a word. And, yes, people like me still use it. Yes, old people like me. No, I've never considered the fact that I might be older than the hills. Or dirt. Now, can I continue? Thank you.

Now, where was I? Oh, yes...

It behooved the young lovers to keep their affair quiet, which they succeeded in doing so. It was in her fourth month at boarding school that Mary and Victor Lichtenstein took their relationship to a whole new level. At her suggestion—which delighted the doctor to no end—she had suggested they meet that night in a nearby graveyard overlooking the city of Geneva... a graveyard the good doctor knew all too well. It was there, under clear skies and a full moon—yes, all details that Lichtenstein supplied to Franklin—that they kissed for the first time, and expressed their love for each other. It was a tender—and proper—moment for them both. That they both enjoyed the solitude of graveyards seemed to bode well for their future. Or so Lichtenstein hoped.

The next few weeks were a blur of continued classroom flirtations, not-so-happenstance encounters in hallways, and late-night rendezvous, usually in the seclusion of the local graveyard. Lichtenstein, feeling love for the first time ever, pushed aside his own work. His own terribly important work.

Never had he felt such a connection with anyone, and so with the school year coming to a close and young Mary returning home for the summer, he made a very bold move to keep her with him. He planned to ask for her hand in marriage. After all, he was from a good family, with much land and holdings. He was not so terrible to look at, and he had a quick and inventive mind. Just how inventive, young Mary had no idea. At least, not yet.

The pressure was on the young doctor. He knew that his experiments fell far below the accepted norm of the times. Or any times. But he also knew he was close to something big, something unheard of, something this world had not yet seen... the reanimation of a corpse. And not just the reanimation, but the creation of life itself.

Of course, Lichtenstein had never heard of the dark masters. Nor did he know of lost souls actively seeking human hosts. He especially did not know that his experiments were of great interest to those trapped—or banished—on the other side. That in fact, some of his very inspiration had come from these same dark masters, whispering madness into his ears as he slept. He understood none of this. Indeed, he only knew that he was driven to see his experiments through to the end. And he worked passionately, obsessively, sleeping little, if at all, supplementing his income by teaching during the day, and working often straight through the night.

That is, until he met Mary Wollstonecraft. Now, his life had taken on even greater meaning—and more complications, too. What would his beloved think of his experiments? What would she think of him? Would it be possible to convince her of their importance, his importance, that he was truly on the cutting edge of science, and creation itself? Indeed, that he was stepping into the role of God himself?

It was with much trepidation and anxiety that on the eve of her departure, as both of them had expressed their love and their desire to be with each other forever, that he had postponed his marriage proposal in light of showing the would-be novelist his laboratory, located in his apartment basement, nearly thirty feet under the street. The building had been a hotel in an earlier incarnation, and had, at one time, held a vast collection of wine bottles. The cellars in this place were particularly extensive, which was why the good doctor had chosen it. A perfect place to play God.

It was after a particularly moving moment in the cemetery, overlooking the lamplight of Geneva, alone together in the world, each aware that this might very well be their last night together, that Lichtenstein decided to take her down into his basement. He had to show her this side of him. He had to get her to believe in him, in his experiments, in his vision for life itself. He needed her on his side. He saw that now. He saw the benefit of a talented and inspiring woman in his corner. Already his experiments had taken on a fresh angle, which is a weird way to describe the rotting cadavers that lined the old wine cellar.

Perhaps it was too much to ask of a sixteen-year-old girl who was far beyond her years in wisdom and intellect, a sixteen-year-old girl who had a penchant for words—and for the macabre. But his hopes of marrying young Mary, of her being

The Bride of Lichtenstein—yes, that just came to me—was dashed the moment she set eyes upon his laboratory; in particular, the bodies stacked over ice, the sawing tools and stitching implements, and his surprisingly advanced array of electrical conduits, all of which harnessed the lightning strikes above. Brilliant, really, and far ahead of his time.

Yes, Lichtenstein might have been receiving promptings from the "other side," usually through dreams, he confessed later. Either way, Edward Lichtenstein was genius enough to build it all.

How long young Mary stayed around the laboratory, it's hard to know. Surely long enough to absorb the details, of which she would later use to render her famous novel. She eventually fled; screaming, from what I understand, all the way home to her father. She never returned Lichtenstein's letters and refused to see him when he called upon her the next year.

Alone and miserable, with only the dead to keep him company, he eventually quit his position at Ramsgate and poured himself into his work. Remarkably, at nearly the exact time of Mary Shelley's publication of *Frankenstein*, Edward Lichtenstein would revive his first corpse. I always suspected Mary Shelley wrote *Frankenstein* as a healing balm, a way to make sense of what she had seen. No, she never went public with her knowledge, and she never spoke to Lichtenstein again. But her book—her snapshot, really—into Liechtenstein's experiments lives on to this day. And so do

the corpses he revived.
    The many, many corpses he revived.

39.

"And Franklin is such a revival?" I asked.

Kingsley nodded. He had long ago sat back in the client chair as he recounted the tale of the mad doctor Lichtenstein. "He and his many brothers."

"He considers them his brothers?"

"Just one big happy family, Sam."

"Are you being facetious?"

"Maybe. Maybe not. Franklin has many, many brothers, as he calls them. He seems to have fondness for them."

"All of them?"

"Most of them. One or two turned out to be particularly dastardly, particularly evil."

I waited. I heard muffled voices outside Kingsley's door. Nothing too excitable, but I noticed Kingsley cock his head slightly, pause and listen in on the conversation. What was muffled voices to me, was surely clear as day to him.

We are both so freakin weird it hurts.

"You probably have work to do," I said.

"Soon. I am, after all, an ace defense attorney."

"So you say," I said.

He grinned. "And as far as Franklin and his family, most turned out respectable enough. Many are leading normal lives."

"How many, er, offspring—for lack of a better word—did Dr. Lichtenstein create?"

"Ninety-two."

"And all are still alive?"

"Most. After all, they can be destroyed. Most often by fire, but a silver stake in the heart works for them, too, as is the case with most immortals."

I drummed my fingers on Kingsley's oversized desk. I would say he was overcompensating for something, but I knew better. Boy, did I know better.

"Let's back up here. Were Dr. Lichtenstein's experiments a success because he used true science, or because the dark masters found their way into the corpses?"

"I would say a little of both. As you know, there needs to be a transfer of blood. From one immortal to another. Be it vampire or werewolf or, in this case, Lichtenstein's monsters."

"I'm listening."

"After many failed attempts at reanimation, Lichtenstein was called upon by a monster of a different kind; your friend Dracula, in fact. To

Lichtenstein's horror, the Count came bearing gifts. Three corpses, in fact."

"Let me guess: werewolf."

"Good guess, my dear. Three recently killed werewolves, in fact. Turns out, Dracula doesn't much like my kind, as you well know."

Indeed, Dracula had helped me kill an entire werewolf pack just last year, a werewolf pack that would have surely killed me or, in the least, ripped me to shreds. But, yeah, the Count had seemed to kill with reckless abandon, and, I think, no small amount of pleasure.

"Lichtenstein was told, or perhaps even compelled, to use the corpses. To use liberally from the corpses. Something in each of the three killed werewolves needed to be in his reanimated corpses. Something, anything. A heart, lungs, a leg, a foot, fingers, toes. Anything.

"It was only then that Lichtenstein found his first success. It was only then that Lichtenstein raised the dead."

"And these are reanimated werewolves?"

"Not quite, Sam. Although it is the werewolf flesh within them that gives them the spark of life, these are truly a new breed of monster. They are, first off, far stronger than any of us. Yes, Sam, even me."

"Franklin?"

"Especially Franklin. He was one of the most successful of the creatures."

"But he is so... well-spoken."

Kingsley nodded and checked his watch. I could only imagine how disruptive this impromptu meeting had been to his usually hectic days. And to his bottom line.

"Many turned out very well-spoken. Many had no ability of speech whatsoever. Many turned into true monsters that had to be destroyed, lest they wreak havoc upon the world. Some even escaped."

"And each contains the soul of a dark master?"

"Indeed, Sam. I would hesitate to say that most contain a very low-level dark master, with a few exceptions, notably Franklin. The thing that attacked you last night would have been closer to monster than man."

"And you think it is one of Lichtenstein's creations?"

"I don't know for sure. But my best guess is yes."

"Perhaps we should discuss the creature with Franklin," I suggested.

"A good idea."

I'd never had a good heart-to-heart talk with Kingsley's butler before. Truth was, Franklin was a bit of a snob. I didn't relate too well to snobs. Even undead, reanimated snobs.

I said, "I understand that these creations are vessels for dark masters, like you and me. But, unlike you and me, Lichtenstein's monsters didn't have an original soul. Unless I'm missing something here. The souls of the deceased would have been long gone."

"A good point, Sam, which is what makes these creatures different from you and me. However, as you are well aware, departed spirits do, in fact, hang around their dead bodies. You saw it with your husband a few years ago."

He was right. I'd found Danny's spirit hunkered down next to his buried body, deep beneath the Los Angeles River, within a forgotten cavern. His spirit had been confused and unable to move on, for reasons I would never know. I'd always felt like shit that I'd forgotten him down there. That is, until I remembered the bastard had tried to set me up. Anyway, long story short, I'd helped Danny's spirit move on.

"So what are you saying?" I asked Kingsley. "That the original spirit was, in fact, able to return to its deceased body?"

"I didn't say that. Not quite. Liechtenstein's experiments, aided by the werewolf blood sources and body parts, enabled, well, *any* spirit to enter the galvanized corpse."

"Franklin had been someone else entirely?"

"In short, yes. Although, I believe, his is the original head."

Maybe this news should have turned my stomach, but I found myself intrigued. And I don't think it was because of the entity within me. After all, one didn't study criminal justice and not have an interest in the darker side of life.

A thought occurred to me. "Can there be multiple souls?"

Kingsley held my gaze, raised his bushy-ass eyebrows, cocked his head a little toward some raised voices in the hallway beyond, then eased out of the client chair far too easily and swiftly. No one his size should be that fast, that skillful, and that much in control of their bodies. But there it was, right before my eyes, the natural and supernatural blending into one perfectly oiled, if not hairy, machine. He moved around the desk and offered me a hand. I didn't take it, not yet. I generally left when I wanted to leave. Anywhere. Not because one of Kingsley's clients was throwing a hissy fit outside.

Kingsley saw that I wasn't going anywhere and retracted his hand and exhaled and said, "From what I understand, Sam, one of Lichtenstein's monsters can have as many souls as it does different body parts."

"So if one of his monsters was cobbled together with, say, four body parts..."

"It could theoretically have four souls."

"Plus the intrusive dark master," I added.

"Right."

"And how many does Franklin have? Souls, that is?"

"Two. Plus the dark master."

"Does the second soul ever, ah, make an appearance?"

"Often."

I thought back, my mind temporarily blown. But I could find no discrepancies in Franklin's personality. He was always icy, snobby and efficient. I said as much to Kingsley.

"The second spirit will generally make an appearance when the conversation turns to politics."

"Since when do you talk politics with Franklin?"

"He's my most trusted friend, Sam. We talk often and about everything."

"But he calls you Master Kingsley."

"You're going to be an ace detective yet, Sam."

"Don't patronize me. You know what I mean."

Kingsley sighed and resisted an urge to look at his watch again. Good thing, because I just resisted the urge to rip it off his wrist and throw it *through* his office door.

"Although Franklin's spirit is the primary spirit, his secondary spirit, who goes by Spartus, was once a house servant, and prefers to remain so to this day."

"And Franklin?"

"He was a common criminal, Sam. A pick-pocket, I believe."

Mind. Blown. I stared at Kingsley, who was loving this more than he should. Since he couldn't kick me out of his office, he was enjoying blowing my mind far too much.

"Then why isn't Franklin, say, a pickpocket? How did the secondary spirit override the first?"

"They reached an agreement, Sam. If Spartus would mostly remain in the shadows, Franklin would appease him by performing his duties."

Mind not so blown. That made sense. I was

beginning to understand that two competing spirits could, in fact, come to an agreement. I said, "And the dark entity within him?"

"Mostly keeps to the shadows. It seems content to simply exist in this world. At least, for now."

I thought about it, and thought about how Franklin never did seem to be very good at his job. He was often moody and cranky, and this would explain why. I still had one objection, "But he calls you Master Kingsley, for crissake."

"Oh, he's just being facetious, Sam, while still honoring his agreement with Spartus."

"And this man who attacked me at the lake..."

"Sounds very much like one of Lichtenstein's monsters."

"And just how strong is he?"

"Stronger than you and I combined. Maybe even three or four of us."

"Is Franklin that strong, too?"

"Perhaps even more so."

"Even stronger than you in your werewolf form?"

Kingsley grinned, somewhat wolfishly. "Let's call that a wash."

"Can Franklin shape-shift?"

"No. At least, not that I'm aware."

"And the others?"

He shook his head. "I doubt it. Shape-shifting is generally reserved for the higher-level entities. Now, if you'll excuse me, I have a client to meet." Kingsley stepped over to the door and turned the knob.

"Wait. One last question: Can you read minds?"

He gave me a lopsided grin. "Most immortals can, Sam. Even the Lichtenstein monsters. Of course, we all have our own individual talents, usually based on the original talents of the entity within us."

"And is one of your talents influencing people?"

"I have been known to influence a client or two."

"And juries?"

"Mass influencing? Never. At least, not that I'm aware of."

"That's a grayish answer."

"That's me. A gray wolf."

"An oafish wolf, too," I said, and sprang off of the desk and over to the big lug. I hopped up on my tiptoes and wrapped my arms around his neck and gave him a big smooch on his oh-so-soft lips. I broke free before things could get too heated—he was an animal, after all—patted him on his hairy face, and was about to throw open his office door, when he took me by the hand and spun me back around. I was expecting more of the horny wolf man. I was prepared to fight him off me. Instead, I found myself looking up into the concerned amber eyes of a man—and beast—who loved me very much.

"Sam, you can't go out there alone. Not any-more. Not without me. This thing... you are lucky to be alive, Sam. It would have killed you. And then, it would have feasted on you."

"You really know how to ruin a moment."

"Sam, these creatures... these monsters... they're not like you and me. Many have warring spirits within. Many were cutthroats and killers. And many more were absolutely insane. Liechtenstein destroyed the ones he could. Others escaped. Those that remained, he trained and educated and helped."

"Well, I have a job to do," I said. Which was partly true. My job had been to verify the lake monster. Now it had turned into a search for young Luke. Sure, I wasn't getting paid to look for Luke. But I'd made a promise to Raul. And, well, I would be damned if I was going to allow another kid to wash up on shore; at least, if I could help it.

"No," said Kingsley, squeezing my hand. "*We* have a job to do."

"That's corny, but sweet."

He ignored me. "Just promise that you will take me with you the next time you head out."

"I promise," I said, and stood on my tiptoes and kissed his cheeks. His very hairy cheeks.

40.

I had just gotten to my minivan, when my cell rang. A restricted number. These days, it could be any number of officers, detectives and federal agents. I clicked on, told whoever was at the other end that it was their dime, and waited with some excitement for a response.

"Samantha. Detective Oster."

My breath caught in my throat. "Did you find Luke?"

I dreaded the answer, and was instantly relieved when she said, "No. Not yet."

I exhaled. Better he remain missing than finding his half-masticated body washed up on shore.

"My thoughts exactly," said Detective Oster, which was a funny way of putting it, since she had just read my own thoughts. Through the phone. From, like, a hundred miles away.

"Er, right," I said, and put up a shield around my mind. Geez, these days I was just leaking thoughts all over the place, like my old Mustang used to leak power steering fluid everywhere. "So to what do I owe the pleasure, Detective?"

"We might not have found Luke, but we found something. Four somethings, in fact."

I shook my head, knowing what was coming next. I listened as she described the same four men I'd seen. The same four yahoos, all washed up on the south side of the beach, not far from where I'd seen them. All dead, all partially consumed, all missing limbs.

"Any witnesses?"

"A few reported some shouts on the lake. Nothing that raised any alarms. It wasn't until we started receiving a few calls from concerned wives and girlfriends that we conducted a search. We never did find the rowboat."

"Dinghy," I said.

"Come again?"

I told her what I knew. No, I wasn't always so forthright with police. But I liked Detective Oster, and there was nothing here to hide. At least, not yet.

"Yeah, that would be them," she said. "Did you say bow and arrow?"

"I did."

I could almost see the detective shaking her head on her end. "The news is having a field day, and the locals are up in arms. Five deaths in under a week. And to top it off, the biggest damn catfish I'd ever seen washed up this morning, too. Similar wounds, partially consumed. What the hell is going on, Sam?"

"I think you might just have a lake monster, Detective."

"Jesus, I was afraid you would say that. Have you turned up anything?"

I considered what to tell her, and decided that I really didn't have anything to add, at least not yet. Yes, I had seen the four yahoos out on the lake. Yes, I had even seen the catfish in its last moments. Granted, I had seen it in the mind of one of the now-dead yahoos. But none of this would have really shed much light on the investigation, other than to confirm that a reliable witness (me) had seen something black and scaly in the water. And I sure as hell wasn't ready to discuss the Lichtenstein monster. At least, not yet. Still too many questions with too few answers.

I told her I didn't have anything more for her. She held the phone longer than was probably polite, letting me know that her police instincts were aware that I might, just might, know more than I was letting on. I decided to throw her a bone.

"Actually, I have one question, Detective. Who owns the castle by the lake?"

I could almost see her blink on her end. "Why do you ask?"

"Call it professional curiosity."

Now, I could almost see her squinting at me. Finally, she said, "A young guy. Someone pointed him out to me a few months ago."

"What's he look like?"

"Tall, handsome, pale."

That didn't sound like the hulking creature that had attacked me. "Where did you see him?"

"He owns a restaurant in town. Ravioli's. He's there some nights."

"Do you know anything else about him?"

"No. From what I understand, few do. And, quite frankly, fewer care. Had he not purchased the castle, I know the city was thinking of purchasing it and turning it into a tourist attraction. But that was, what, ten years ago."

"And you said he was a young man?"

"I did."

"The desert sun must be good for his skin."

"Maybe. Why do you ask? And if you say 'professional curiosity,' I'll have you arrested for pissing me off."

I grinned and said, "Oh, I have my reasons, Detective," I said, and reached out to her through the phone line, and gave her a mental suggestion to let it go, to trust me, and that I was doing all I could to find the boy. Then I told her, audibly, to have a good day and that I would be in touch. She said nothing, simply clicked off.

I always felt strange when bypassing someone's mental defenses and going straight to their subconscious. It was surely a violation. Doing so invited the demon bitch inside me to grow bolder. I didn't want her to grow bolder. I wanted her to wither and die inside me.

Anyway, I never felt bad withholding info from the police, even from Sherbet. Keeping my cards close to my vest was sometimes best for all involved. It kept my own investigation on course, and kept the key players exactly where they needed to be. I didn't need anyone descending on Raul's home, or even the castle. Not until I had a closer look. And not without Kingsley by my side. I had felt that thing's power. I wasn't much of a match for it. Hell, I hadn't been *any* match to it at all. It had taken Talos to get me out of there safely.

Answers, I thought, as I plugged in my iPhone and started up the minivan. *I need answers.*

These days, everything was an app, even proprietary data bases accessed only by law enforcement, some attorneys, and private investigators. I brought up the app, typed in my passcode, which just so happened to be Fang's old AOL screen name, and plugged in the castle's address. Hard to forget 111 Castle Drive.

A short list of names appeared on the iPhone screen. The castle had had only three owners, the last being Carl Inglebright. I did a search on the name, and didn't get any satisfactory hits. My guess: fake name.

Was Carl the monster? I doubted it. The creature that had attacked me had barely sounded coherent. I had a hard time imagining the monster making a deal for the castle and signing all the necessary paperwork and shaking hands with the real estate agent and arranging for movers and paying his young lawn mower.

No, the thing that attacked me was more of... a guard dog, in a sense. A guard monster. As soon as I'd gotten too close, the damn thing had appeared out of nowhere, pouncing, attacking. Anyone else would have been killed by any number of his punches.

"I know what you are," it had shouted at me, over and over again. Allison had pointed out the thing sounded angry. I thought it had sounded afraid. And, if it was a fellow immortal—albeit created by a mad scientist—he would have seen that I didn't have an aura. He would have known I was different.

So why attack me? Why attack a fellow immortal? What were they hiding? What were they afraid I would find?

I didn't know, but I was going to find out.

41.

After calling Allison and checking up on Tammy for the tenth time that day, I went through my mental checklist of resources:

There was Kingsley, who had been at this immortal game for quite a while, although from the werewolf point of view. His general knowledge was vast, and his information about Lichtenstein had been invaluable.

There was Fang, who had a broad general knowledge of all things vampire. Not much of it was firsthand experience. Most of what he knew had been gleaned through rare texts and a personal obsession. These days, of course, he was gathering his own personal data. Of course, I had him edged out by nearly a decade in that department.

There was Allison, my confidant. Or, rather, my one-time confidant. Now, I was mostly shut out of her mind, so that the entity within me would not be privy to Allison's witchy plans, whatever they were. I knew that Allison and her witch sisters battled some very dark entities on their own, some of which were aligned with the dark masters. I now know that while I sleep, Elizabeth, my own dark entity, finds temporary release. Where she goes or who she meets with, I don't know. But I understand that she herself would forever be privy to my own plans, my own thoughts.

No secrets, I thought.

Of course, she and I were in this together, perhaps for all eternity. If I got rid of her, without the help of, say, the Librarian and his powerful alchemical potions, then I would most likely die, too. I didn't want to die. I enjoyed this life, strange as it was. I enjoyed watching my kids grow older. I enjoyed my friends, and I even enjoyed my job. I liked helping people find answers, especially answers to tough questions. So I wasn't exactly conspiring to remove the entity within me.

Moving on. There was Sherbet, who had one of the sharpest investigative minds I'd come across. And now that he'd been introduced to all things supernatural, he was a great guy to bounce ideas off of, whether he liked it or not.

There was my angel, Ishmael, who rarely made an appearance these days. I suspected Ishmael, whether he wanted to let on or not, was still bound by some ethereal code of conduct. He wasn't too forthcoming with information, either, which was just as well. He might know things I didn't really want the answers to. Or not. Hard to say. Still, he would come if I called him. I rarely did.

There was Talos, my dragon alter ego, who seemed wise in all things. His knowledge was often universal and metaphysical in nature. Except, I needed answers directly related to the strange happenings at Lake Elsinore.

There was now Dracula whom, I suspected, might be a profound source of information. After all, he had tallied up over five hundred years as the walking dead. He had the perspective of history. Hell, he *was* history. Living history. But I hadn't yet formed that kind of connection with him.

Then there was, of course, the Librarian, Archibald Maximus, who was my sort of catch-all go-to person for all things vampiric, supernatural and historical. A man I trusted with my life—hell, with my son's life, too. A man who had given much to me, and had never once asked for anything in return.

To understand the strange happenings in Lake Elsinore, I thought my choice was obvious.

***

Which was why I found myself at Jacky's gym.

No matter how crazy things got, and no matter how busy one seemed, there was always time to unload on a punching bag, all while your trainer urged you to keep your hands up. Up, up, up.

Oh, I kept them up, and as Jacky held onto the bag for dear life, absorbing my onslaught of punches, I did my best to keep the lake monster out of my mind, as well as Lichtenstein and his own monsters and, especially, Tammy's impending accident.

It was just me and the bag and sweat and Jacky barking orders and the sound of boxers working out with their own trainers.

I did this until Jacky finally raised the white flag, so to speak, begging for a break. I didn't let him off immediately and instead, unloaded a flurry of punches that surely knocked the Irish out of him.

And after he stumbled away, punch drunk and rubbing his neck and muttering in something that sounded like ancient Gaelic, I tried to feel bad as he disappeared into the men's shower. He would be fine. He was old, yes, but he was tough as nails. And I thought he secretly liked taking my punishment.

I grinned and grabbed my stuff and headed to my next appointment. Cal State Fullerton.

In particular, the Occult Reading Room.

42.

Months ago, I had discovered a small loading dock behind the Cal State Fullerton library.

This was useful since, being neither student or faculty, I didn't have a parking permit. Nor was I going to shell out $90 for one. Parking in the loading dock was a surefire way to get one's vehicle towed unless one had a cache of magnetized door signs stowed in their minivan. Signs such as "AAA Catering," or "Acme Auto Detailing," or "J&J's Plumbing," or "Mobile Blood Drive." Yes, that last one always made me giggle.

Now, as I parked confidently in the loading section, I admired my latest sign: "Express Espresso Coffee Delivery."

I spotted two students making out in the shadows, and thought that was a pretty good idea. The shadow part, that is. As in, getting out of the sun and into the shadows. Of course, making out is fun, too, with the right guy. Sometimes even the wrong guy.

Anyway, I hopped up onto the loading dock and into the blessed shadows. Yes, I could have lasted a lot longer in the sun, but why do so when I didn't have to? Shade equaled a happy vampire mama. I nodded at the students who were now openly staring at me. I frowned until I caught their thoughts: they had both seen me jump up onto the dock, about six feet straight up. Maybe even higher. I smiled and wiped the memory from their thoughts and commanded them to resume their snogging session. I didn't have to tell them twice.

It was mid-afternoon and the sun was out, and so were approximately ten thousand students, nearly all of whom were on their cell phones. And those who weren't on their cell phones were about to get on their cell phones. I remember when cell phones first became available. Most were used primarily for business. Important business. I remember taking a call on my department-issued cell phone. I remember thinking how important I must have looked. Hell, I remembered feeling important. It was a big day for me. I was an important person, taking an important call, on a staticy flip cell phone the size of a man-purse.

Now, as I hung a right and headed for the main library doors, passing students exiting and staring blankly down at their phones, or talking blankly on their phones, I realized what a dope I must have looked like.

A world of dopes, I thought, and pushed my way into the library.

43.

At the third floor, I exited the elevator, hung a right, and moved along a long corridor with a windowless wall on one side and rows upon rows of research books on the other. The rows extended nearly as far as the eye could see. Even Talos's eyes. I was fairly certain this is where books went to die.

I passed quite a few ghosts. At least a half dozen. Some were fully formed; others were nothing more than globs of multidimensional silly putty. The few that I could make out were moving down aisles with heads bowed, staring at the floor, their feet a good two or three inches off the floor. One sported a bullet wound in his temple. I got the psychic impression this was self-inflicted. Another nearby ghost continuously vomited frothing ecto-plasmic sputum. A drug overdose, surely. Or bad tacos. I suspected these two had died here in the library, or very close to it. A large university with over a half century of history was bound to have a few fatalities... and suicides. And no doubt, murders, too.

I walked past the vomiting ghost and cringed. A puddle of sticky ectoplasm clung to my shoes, then snapped off in a puff. Okay, that was gross.

About halfway down a blank section of wall, a doorway began to form, expanding exponentially the closer I got, like a magic portal into another realm, which it just very well might be.

By the time I reached it, a doorway was waiting for me, complete with a scuffed door that could have used some paint. There was a rectangular window in it that afforded a limited view of the help desk and a hallway beyond. Over the doorway was an etched plastic sign that read: Occult Reading Room. In smaller letters that I hadn't noticed before was another line: Maximum Occupancy: At the Discretion of the Librarian.

I giggled at that and looked over my shoulder. I was alone in the corridor. The ghosts had dispersed, too, as ghosts are wont to do. Once inside, I closed the door behind me, and wondered once again what the scene would have looked like from the outside: a woman stepping into a wall, perhaps? Or would they have caught a brief glimpse of the door; indeed, would they have caught a brief, if not forbidden, view of the Occult Reading Room itself?

And just why was it so forbidden? Well, I kind

of knew the answer to that. The books here were hardcore. As in, world altering. Hell, not so long ago, I'd seen something escape from the pages of one such book, something I wouldn't soon forget, if ever. A demon in the form of a dragon, inadvertently let loose by my son.

Although the Librarian had returned it from whence it came, I suspected an aspect of it—a tendril of it, a whiff of it perhaps—had found its way into my son. I hadn't been able to confirm this, mostly because I'd never been able to read my own children's auras. But more than once, I'd seen my son sitting up in bed in the middle of the night, staring at nothing, enough to creep me out and worry me to no end. Other than his late-night staring sessions, I hadn't seen much else to be alarmed about. So for now, I let it go.

Other than loosing demonic dragons into the world, the Occult Reading Room was *the* place for all things dark and evil. As such, Archibald Maximus, the young man who oversaw this room, did just that: he oversaw who had access to these books. He was, in a sense, their custodian. The room itself was enchanted; as in, only those who had a need to find the room could find the room. Whether or not there was a vetting process, I didn't know. Whether or not Max turned some seekers away, I didn't know that either. And those he did turn away... did they go willingly, or put up a fight?

So many questions, I thought, as I rang the bell at the help counter. The small ding echoed in the medium-sized room, half of which was filled with tomes and diaries and grimoires and parchments and scrolls and tablets, books bound with leather and sheepskin and human skin. They filled the overburdened shelves from floor to ceiling, in row after row. Granted, not quite as long as rows in the library at large, but, trust me, there were more than enough books here to summon Lord Voldemort many times over. Amazingly, the other half of the room was outfitted with reading chairs, lamps and tables.

"Your mind is busy, Samantha Moon," said a voice from down the hallway. To where the hallway led, I did not know.

"Wouldn't yours be, too," I asked the Librarian, "if you were me?"

"Perhaps," he said, appearing from the shadows, eyes gleaming bright, and coming around the simple help desk. He clasped me warmly on the shoulder. Not quite a hug, but warmer than a handshake. He nodded, or actually, bowed. A small gesture, but it looked good on him. "But I would shield my thoughts more often than not. You never know what's lurking in the shadows."

"Like an alchemist who can read minds?"

"Or a vampire mama who can read minds, too."

Hearing him say 'vampire mama' made me snort. "Well, shielding my thoughts is a drag," I said. "Besides, other vampires can't read my mind."

"Vampires aren't your only concern. Others have developed the skill, too." He smiled. "And shielding your thoughts is work, but it's worth it in the end."

"Fine. So is there a way to permanently shield my thoughts?"

The Librarian thought about that. "There is a way to summon a semi-permanent wall, but it involves some darker magic."

"And you know this, how?"

"I believe my mother might have invented the spell."

"Then I need only to ask her."

"In short, yes."

"But asking her requires me to summon her in turn."

"It would, Sam. And it would also mean something else."

"She would want to bargain with me."

Maximus nodded gravely. "I imagine so. People like my mother do not give willingly, if ever. And when they do, they always benefit. Always. Remember that."

"Oh, I will. Which is why she is stuffed as far down as I can keep her. Life is easier that way."

"I imagine so," he said.

I detected a very odd tone to his voice. Sadness? Regret?

"Perhaps a little bit of both, Sam," added Max, picking up on my thoughts a little too easily. "She was, after all, once my mother."

We were both silent, and I honestly didn't know what to say to the guy. That he'd had the world's most dysfunctional childhood, I didn't doubt. At what point she had quit being his mother and had taken on the role of Queen Bitch of Darkness, I didn't know. Max had hinted at seeing terrible things—strange rituals, torture, human and animal sacrifices, and, I suspected, all manner of things that go bump in the night, including real demons and God knows what else these self-proclaimed highly evolved dark masters had summoned from, I imagined, Hell itself.

An air conditioning unit clicked on inside the room, and I wondered who the hell had installed an AC unit in the Occult Reading Room. Max grinned, still following my thoughts. "It hasn't always been the Occult Reading Room, Sam. It was once a special collections room for the university."

"So you hijacked it?"

"You could say that."

"And put some sort of spell on it."

"You could say that, too."

He held my gaze, and I knew our connection was strong, and even though I couldn't see a lick into his mind, I knew he was in mine now, probing deeply, I suspected. I supposed I could have told him to stop or thrown up one of my better walls or, well, kicked his loving ass. But I liked the Alchemist. A lot. Had things been different and Mad Max had been, say, a little less serious, I could have seen myself having a drink with him, or more. But I let that thought slip by, knowing that he had undoubtedly seen it.

But the Alchemist had to know that he was kind of my hero, too. Not only had he saved Anthony from a life of vampirism, his advice in all things had saved my ass time and again. That his mother had been a dark master, well, was something else entirely. Max's early career as an alchemist had taken a decidedly different course, one in which he had devoted his life to fighting the very darkness his mother represented. Fighting and, I suspected, winning. Indeed, Max had been instrumental in sealing his mother—and others like her—away. Removing them from the earth plane into something called The Void. I don't usually use words like "earth plane," but Max did. And he knew more about this stuff than anyone did. Even if he did only look twenty-two. Someday, I would ask him how he and others had defeated the dark masters.

"Yes, a very active mind, indeed. And thank you. It's always nice to be called a hero."

I shrugged and would have blushed, except blushing required movement of blood, the pumping of blood. My blood moved like molasses through my veins.

"Very, very active," murmured Max.

I tried to quiet my mind, to give him better access. I trusted him. He was in there for a reason. Soon, I found myself looking deep into his bright blue eyes and I thought there was a small chance we had a moment; that was, until he blinked and cut our connection, and I realized that I was the only dope who'd had a moment. Or two.

"The boy in your thoughts, the boy who is missing..."

"Luke?"

He nodded. "Yes, Luke. I see him there, but he's faint, almost blurry. Is he..."

I nodded, following his drift. "He's a memory of a memory."

"Ah, that explains why I can't connect his name and why he seems so phantasmagorical."

I nodded, impressed. "Phantasmagorical is my new word of the week. Hell, the year."

He smiled politely. Max wasn't as silly as I sometimes thought he was. Or hoped he was. All it took was for me to remember he wasn't a 22-year-old guy, but a 500-year-old man. I mentally walked Max through how I came across the memory of Luke, culled from the mind of Raul, the old Mexican *brujo*. A witch.

"Raul is a good man. He's one of us."

"Not to be rude, but he's old," I said. "And you look so young."

"Not all are alchemists, and not all choose to be immortal, Sam. It takes... great effort to do what I do."

"You mean, to stay young?"

He nodded. "Indeed."

"You don't sacrifice kittens and/or puppies, do you?"

"No. But I do spend a considerable amount of time each day, sometimes hours, in deep meditation, silently reciting powerful and dangerous incantations."

"How dangerous?"

"One mistake would be the end of me."

"Yikes."

"And not just the end of me, Sam. It would banish me to the same plane as the dark masters."

"I want to know more about that plane."

"Another day, Sam. When you are ready."

"Fine," I said, a little miffed. I was a grown-ass woman. Who said I wasn't ready?

"Perhaps I misspoke, Sam. When *I* am ready, might be more accurate."

Okay, feathers officially unruffled. I said, "Well, a few memorized incantations seem a small price to pay to live forever."

"I thought so, too."

I didn't have to be a mind reader to know where he was going with it. "It limits you," I said. "It binds you to your rituals or whatever you call it. Hard to be-bop around the globe when you are forced to spend a few hours a day in what I assume is isolation."

"You assume correctly."

"And you probably have your potions and crap everywhere. All bubbling and frothing."

"Not quite, but close. I do carry a travel bag of, as you say, potions and crap." He nodded and winked.

"And if I had to guess, I would say it all takes place back there," I said, pointing down the dark hallway.

"A good guess," said the Librarian, this time offering me a grin. Then he smiled sadly and looked away. "It's not easy being us."

"Being sexy? I agree."

He grinned again. "You and I and others like us defy natural laws. In doing so, there's a price to pay, so to speak. With you, it's the routine consumption of blood. With me, it's spending hours in solitude each day, without fail."

"And if you did fail?"

"I think you know the answer to that."

I did, yes. Death and banishment. "I can see why you hang around this dusty old place. You need peace and quiet."

"Oh, I'm only here for a few hours a day, Sam. Often, I can be found elsewhere."

"I sense you are segueing into something."

"Your intuition is as strong as ever, Sam. Indeed, I also run a school of sorts."

"And what, pray tell, is a 'school of sorts'?"

"Myself and a few others like me teach the ways of alchemy."

"My God, so Hogwarts is real?"

He smiled. "Close, but not quite. It is a school, yes, and we do teach the children a wide variety of subjects. But that's where the similarities end. The kids we teach go on to become what we call Light Warriors."

I'd heard the term before. "Are we really having this conversation?"

"We are, Sam. In a secret room here at Cal State

Fullerton, surrounded by enough books to summon Voldemort back many times over."

"Geez, you're good."

"I've had a lot of practice."

"Fine," I said. "So what, exactly, is a Light Warrior?"

"We give balance to the world of darkness, Sam."

"I take it I'm no Light Warrior."

"I'm sorry, but no."

"I'm trying not to take offense."

"Then let me put it this way: I consider you an ally."

I shrugged, but I was still kind of butt-hurt. "That's good enough, I suppose."

"Remember, Sam, you are a vessel for the darkest of them all."

"I get it, I get it. Okay, so who selects the children?"

"We don't select them. They are born into this business, so to speak."

"What do you mean born...?" But my voice trailed off as I thought back to the memory of Luke's aura, as seen by Raul, and just recently by Maximus; in particular, the beautiful silver serpent.

"Exactly, Sam. The boy, Luke, is marked."

"Marked for what?"

"In his case, I fear, death. Had we gotten to him first, it might have been a different story."

"I really, really don't understand." And I was also feeling really, really sick to my stomach.

"Luke, as you might have guessed, is from Hermes Trismegistus's bloodline. As am I. As are you. As are all alchemists or potential alchemists. You, of course, were destined to be on a different path. A witchy path."

"And you know this how?"

"A little angel told me."

"Ishmael?"

Max nodded. "You have lived many lives, Samantha Moon. In each, you have gravitated toward the earth arts."

"Witchcraft."

He nodded. "Yes. This incarnation was to be different. In this current and, I regret to say, *last* incarnation, you were once again born into the great alchemist's bloodline."

"I wasn't always before?"

He shook his head. "Occasionally, but your witchy talents were not quite ready yet, you could say. Your birth in this current and last incarnation is what truly interested the dark masters. Now, for the first time, they had a powerful witch born into an alchemical bloodline, and they were veritably licking their lips."

"So you're saying I didn't have a prayer."

"You had all the protection we could give you, Sam."

"We?"

"Myself and others."

"Other Light Warriors?"

He nodded. "And your guardian angel. His

betrayal, you could say, came as quite a shock to myself and my fellow warriors."

My angel had done it out of love, he claimed. He had done it so that he would be released from his service to me. Until now, I had not known the depth of his betrayal. The bastard had really set me up.

"Yes, Sam. It is true. Had I not put all my trust in him, you would, quite possibly, be one of us today."

"Or a witch."

"Or both."

I nodded. "Like Raul."

"Indeed. He is both *brujo* and a Light Warrior."

Max waited until most of this sank in. And, of course, he would know the moment it all sank in since the cute little bastard was right there inside my head with me. A moment or two later, he went on: "All those in the Hermetic bloodline boast the silver marker, available for all to see. At least all those with eyes to see. It is, unfortunately, our calling card."

"But I can't see your aura."

"Indeed. Most immortals can't see each other's auras. Or read each other's minds. I suspect it's for self-preservation. Most of the dark masters were scheming against each other. Most have a built-in shield, so to speak. The moment I became an alchemical master, my own aura disappeared from the eyes of other immortals."

"You hid it."

"In a way, yes. Truth is, when one reaches the immortal status, there is no longer soul leakage."

"That sounds terrible."

"But accurate. When one becomes an immortal, one's soul is forever sealed in one's earthly vessel."

"Wait for it..." I said, and then mimicked my head exploding.

He laughed, perhaps for the first time. Damn, it was a nice laugh. I said, "But you can read my mind. I can't read yours or Kingsley's or any other immortals' mind."

"My ability to read minds is a gift, if you want to call it that, from my mother, who was and perhaps still is, the world's greatest mind reader."

"Sweet mama, that explains a lot."

"It does."

"Okay, let's put a pin in that," I said.

"Consider it pinned."

I nodded. "So those born with the Hermetic mark are, well, marked. By both good *and* evil forces?"

"Indeed."

"So that would mean my own parents—"

"Your mother, to be exact. And, yes, she was protected by one of us, too."

I gasped. "The cross she wears..." I don't often see my mother, but she's out there, living her mundane life in Las Vegas. Anyway, I had seen the same cross in every picture. I mean, in *every freakin' picture*, from ages five and up.

"Yes, Sam. One of my own talismans. It renders

the silver serpent invisible. And, yes, she's been wearing it ever since our first meeting when she was, I want to say, five years old."

"So you saved her life."

"Perhaps."

"Was she a witch, too?"

He shook his head. "No. And neither was she an ideal candidate for alchemy school."

I snorted. And then I laughed. Hard. Right there in the Occult Reading Room. The thought of my nagging but sweet mother, working secretly as a Light Warrior was just, well, too unreal. And too damn funny. Wait until Mary Lou heard this one.

"Wait, my sister. Her opal ring—"

The Librarian nodded. "Another talisman."

"Jesus, you've been here with us, all along."

"Yes, Sam."

"And my daughter?"

"I have not approached your daughter. We figure she is well protected by you, at present. As is your son."

And as he spoke those words, he held my gaze, perhaps longer than he had intended to... or exactly as long as he had intended to. But the meaning was damn clear to me.

"Oh no," I said. "You can't have him. Not yet, anyway."

"We don't want him now, Sam, but Anthony would make a very, very fine Light Warrior."

I protested some more, shaking my head and mostly mumbling to myself, but I couldn't deny the obvious: yeah, my son would, undoubtedly, make the best Light Warrior ever.

"Can we change the subject?" I asked.

"To whatever you want, Sam."

"Fine. Okay. Let me catch my breath. You know, so to speak."

"So to speak," he repeated, nodding.

"Okay, so if I was marked by the baddies from an early age, why did they wait so long to turn me?"

"I imagine they waited for you to reach peak age."

"Peak age?"

"The age my mother would have wanted to be alive again. An age when you were fully mature, and naturally at your strongest. Her own supernatural propensities would only make you stronger."

I found myself pacing the small area in front of the help desk. As I did so, I ignored the hissing from the books, the beckoning calls. There was something else pulling at me, something from my unconscious mind that was itching to rise to the surface. As I paced, Max continued, "Unfortunately, the young ones are an obvious target for the dark masters, too. Many do not make it to our schools. Many do not make it to their teens. Most perish, murdered, and often slowly."

Now, I was really sick. "What do you mean, slowly?"

"Their blood is highly valued, Sam. The children are drained, usually of every drop. The blood of Hermes Trismegistus can increase a vampire's power considerably, and often for quite a long time after."

"Then why drain them slowly? Why kill them at all?" My words were coming in short gasps. The thing that had lain hidden just below my subconscious was creeping up, as the pieces were falling into place.

"Because most vampires are afraid of them. Afraid of what they will become. Afraid that other Light Warriors will come searching for them, and we have, when possible. Better to do away with them as soon as possible. That is, after capturing all their magically-enriched blood."

I pressed my cold palm against my cold forehead. I continued pacing, continued ignoring the increasingly urgent hissing from behind me.

"Why do your books call to me?" I said irritably.

"They call to *her*, Sam."

I nodded. I should have known that.

"It is a rare day that I allow, pardon me, someone of your kind into this room. The books, and the demons sealed within, are many... and they are understandably excited."

I shook my head, ran my fingers through my hair. More pacing. My mind went back to Luke. "You say they are drained slowly. How slowly?"

"The process, from what we understand, usually takes a week or more."

Which might explain why Johnny had shown up seven days after his disappearance, drained of all blood. Of course, he had also been partially consumed by, from all appearances, a lake monster. He could have bled out through his many gaping wounds... or he could have been bled out before.

Jesus. I continued pacing.

"Yes, the first boy," said Max, clearly followed my train of thought. "His connection to Hermes was not as strong, the silver serpent merely a thread; indeed, he might not have made a very good alchemist, but a vampire wouldn't have cared. To a vampire, the boy would still have been a prize. And two such boys in the same small city, almost unheard of."

"And why didn't you get to them first?" I said, turning on the Librarian, who was watching me closely from behind the desk.

"We were unaware of them, Sam. Some children slip through the system, so to speak. Those we find, we protect."

"Do all go to your school?"

"Only those who have the most promise."

"And the others?"

"We do what we can to protect them. Often for the rest of their lives. We give them talismans to conceal their true natures. We watch over them often. Of course, if your son or daughter chooses to join us, they won't need such protection. They will be safe with us. Indeed, someday they will be providing the protection for others."

"And continuing the fight."

He bowed slightly, not taking his eyes off me.

"The battle has been won, Sam. We see ourselves only as guardians."

"They're just kids."

"Of course. Some enter our school at young ages. Some when they are nearing adulthood. We tailor their education and training for their needs and goals."

"Or *your* needs and goals."

He nodded once. "Maybe a little of both."

I resumed pacing. I could not wrap my brain around my kids going away to some secret school for alchemy training. I paused, hands on hips, took some deep breaths. "So more than likely—at this very minute—Luke is being drained dry by a vampire who knows what he is."

"A vampire... or something else."

"*Grrreat.* And Luke has been missing for four days."

"He has, at best, a few days left, depending how quickly the draining process is. The body can only withstand so much loss of blood. You have some idea where he is, I see."

"Some idea."

"Will you be needing some assistance?"

I shook my head. "No," I said. "I have my own one-wolf army."

44.

I was at home in my office, sitting with Allison.

The door was closed and she had a shield of silence around us. At least, that's what I called it. The silence, of course, only pertained to telepathy. Anyone with ears to hear could have overheard our conversation. Hence, the closed door. Most important, Tammy was in her room, watching TV. It was Friday afternoon. I'd just returned from my meetings with Kingsley and the Librarian, and, it was safe to say, my world had been rocked by the information revealed to me. By both of them. I had relayed such information to Allison, because she was my bestie, even if she herself was still closed off to me, which, in hindsight, wasn't so terrible. In fact, I rather enjoyed not slipping in and out of someone else's thoughts. Other people's thoughts were messy and often infused with depression, sadness, hopelessness, or, in the case of most men, perversion bordering on the criminal.

"So now we're dealing with Frankensteins, too?" she said.

"I'm afraid so. But, to be politically correct, Frankenstein was the mad scientist who created the monster. Hence, Frankenstein's monster. Or, in this case, Lichtenstein's monsters."

"Fine, whatever, and when did you start using the word 'hence'?"

I shrugged. "I hang out with a lot of really old people."

She shook her head. Yes, she could still dip into my thoughts. It just wasn't a two-way street, which was fine with me, for now. She said, "And there's, like, ninety of these things out there?"

"Something like that."

"And Franklin is one?"

"He is, yes."

"And just when I thought my world couldn't get any more rocked."

I knew the feeling. We were both drinking steaming hot breve lattes with cream, because breve lattes have no equal. Anthony was at the gym, boxing his heart out and, I suspected, bonding with old Jacky in ways that were both sweet and profound, ways I didn't need to be part of, but heartily approved. My sister would pick him up for me. My sister knew that tonight was going to be a busy night for me.

"Are you sure you don't want my help, Sam? I

mean, this thing is off the charts strong, according to Kingsley."

"Where there's a will," I said.

"Kingsley's got quite the will," she said, nodding, although that hadn't been entirely what I was talking about. She smiled, and her eyes might have swum a little dreamily. My witch friend, to this day, still had a healthy crush on my boyfriend. Hard not to—that is, if you liked the powerful, hulking, muscle-bound, hairy types. And, apparently, a lot of women did.

"Besides," I added, "tonight might be the night."

She knew what I meant: the night of my daughter's impending fatal accident. Just thinking those words and seeing the images all over again, was just too damn terrible to deal with. No mother should ever, ever have to see what I have seen.

The truth was, it should have been me who watched over my daughter. Except that I knew Allison was perfectly, wonderfully, powerfully capable of helping, especially with the help of her witchy friends (who, from what I understood, would be swinging by tonight to help out, and, yes, one of them was a ghost, and, yes, my life is really damn weird). Besides, she and I had a plan. And if all worked out well, I would be there to protect my daughter. But first...

First, I had to find Luke.

Regarding Tammy, we had already decided that the dream needed to play out, once and for all, and that my daughter needed to be saved, perhaps even at the last minute. I knew she could be saved, of course. I had saved someone else in a similar situation. Of course, the person I had saved hadn't been my daughter, and I hadn't had an emotional connection. And this all just sucked the big one, but what could I do? There was a missing kid being bled dry by a bastard in Lake Elsinore—undoubtedly, a vampire who was now hopped up on powerful, magical, hermetic blood, all guarded by the biggest, baddest, son-of-a-bitch I'd ever seen. Perhaps many such creatures. All while dreams of my daughter's impending death were growing more and more detailed.

"We will watch her, Sam. Closely."

"This needs to play out," I said. "I'm sure of it. If not tonight, it will be another night or another night. Or another."

"We can't stop it too soon, I get it."

She nodded, sipping her coffee. My friend, a part-time personal trainer and full-time psychic telephone operator, was looking her age these days. No, she wasn't immortal. Most witches weren't. I had known her now for a few years, getting closer to her each year, and I had watched her life blossom into the legendary. She, along with her two witchy sisters—who formed a powerful triad—had had some wicked close calls recently. Emphasis on wicked. She was forging her own path, a very magical path. One that I knew would lead her on to many adventures, and many more close calls.

"Hopefully, not too many close calls," she said.

"Close calls suck."

"Just be careful out there," I said.

"You, too, Sam Moon."

I smiled and finished my coffee and got up. I went around the desk and gave her the biggest hug I could without breaking her scapula. And then, I headed out of the office and to my daughter's bedroom.

45.

I poked my head into her room.

"Hi, sweetie."

She looked up from her phone and might have smiled. Her room, I noticed, was a pigsty. *Choose your battles*, I told myself, knowing full well that my daughter was in my head, even as I came into her room.

"Mind if I come in?" I asked.

"You're already in."

"Funny how that works. Mind if I sit next to you?"

"Kinda."

"Scootch over."

"Grrr."

"Did you just growl at me?"

"Mom, I'm talking to someone."

"No, you're texting with someone. You see, the

beauty of texting is that it's not instant." I snatched her phone in a blink of an eye and tossed it onto her pillow.

"Hey—"

"And I'm your mom and we're going to talk."

"You suck," she said.

"Don't I know it."

"I'm not talking about blood, Mom," she said, picking up my playful meaning. "You suck at being a mom."

"I'm not going to lie, that kinda hurt."

She shrugged, folded her arms under her chest, and looked away. My daughter was fourteen and developing slowly, which was fine by me. I had developed slowly, too, which seemed to keep the boys away. For a bit.

"But I also know how fourteen-year-old girls are, and I know someday, you are going to regret saying that to me. And someday, you are going to come up from behind me and surprise me with the mother of all hugs and tell me from the bottom of your heart that you are sorry for saying such mean things to me. You will probably also tell me that I'm the best mother in the world, and that you are lucky to have me. So my future self says thank you, sweetie. That means a lot to me."

"Are you quite done?"

"Not by a mile."

"Grrreat."

"Don't roll your r's at me."

"You're impossible."

"I'm improbable, you mean."

"Mom, are you trying to be irritating?"

"I irritate you when I'm not trying, so I might as well do it right. To do it for realz, as they say. And that's with a 'z', I might add."

"This isn't happening, and you can't keep me locked up in here all night, Mom. That's not, you know, cool."

"And since when have I ever been cool? Actually, don't answer that."

And, shocker of all shockers, that elicited a grin from her and the smallest of giggles.

"You don't think I'm very cool, huh?" I asked.

"Nope."

"But I can fly."

She shrugged. "Not really. Talos can fly. You just sort of, you know, remote control him."

"But I can beat up most men."

"So can Rhonda Rousey."

"But I don't, you know, age."

"Neither does Tom Cruise."

Tom Cruise a vampire? Stranger things had happened. "So I really am a dork to you?"

"Of course, Mom. All moms are dorks, except for Angelina Jolie. Now *she's* cool."

"Oh, brother. Who were you texting?"

"A friend."

"Which friend?"

She shrugged. "Just a friend."

"I hereby ban you from shrugging ever again."

Tammy shook her head, rolled her eyes, and

shrugged. "You can't stop me from rolling my shoulders, Mom. And you can't stop me from having friends, either."

I knew where she was going with that. And she knew that I knew where she was going with that. "Those visions are real, Tammy. They are not dreams, and they are not made up. They do not exist for me to punish you or ground you or keep you locked up in this house."

"Or in Kingsley's cell," she added.

"I'm sorry about that, baby. Kingsley and I were just thinking out loud. You have to understand how desperate I am to keep you safe."

"I know, Mommy," she said, and, I'll admit, I will never, ever get tired of hearing her call me Mommy. "I mean Mom."

"Too late," I said. "You said it!"

I got the teenage trifecta: sigh, eye roll and head shake.

"I heard you and Aunt Allie talking. I understand."

"You understand what? And since when have you heard Aunt Allie and I talking?"

She giggled. "Her shield isn't as strong as she thinks it is."

Now I sighed and shook my head. Jesus, just how powerful was my daughter? I took her hand and she let me. I held it tight, and she let me do that, too. "You understand what, baby?"

"I understand that I have to see this through. The accident."

I took in some air. "And these friends of yours?"

"I met them inside the movies the other day. They're Sophia's cousins."

"And they drive?"

She nodded.

"Are they the ones I see in the vision?"

She nodded again.

"They're going to pick you up tonight, aren't they?"

"Nothing is planned for sure," she said, looking at me, her eyes wet and searching my face, "but I am beginning to think that they will. I'm scared."

I was about to say she didn't have to go with them, but that would go directly against what Allie and I had been discussing, and now with Tammy, too. I could tear out the engine of the car and lock the cousins away, too. But I knew that, at some point in time, she would get in a car with them. Whether tonight or another night. It was going to happen. It was seemingly pre-ordained. Or pre-destined. The question was: how much did the dream have to play out before I was allowed to step in? My only other experience with this was the girl at the bus stop. I had saved her right before the bus had crashed, in true superhero fashion. But had the girl gone on to suffer a fatal bus accident, say, a week from then? I didn't know. I hadn't known her name, and I hadn't followed up. I suspected, though, that the majority of the dream, as I saw it, had to play out. The pieces of the puzzle had to come together, to be, once and for all, disbanded. It did no use to disband them too soon, for there were still mysterious forces at work bringing them together.

"You're making my head hurt, Mommy—Mom."

"I'm sorry, and I heard that. You still don't have to go with them, baby."

"I think I do."

"Allison will be nearby. She will have some friends with her, too. They will help her."

"And you will be looking for the boy the bad man is hurting?"

"Yes. But I will be with you, in an instant, no matter what."

She nodded. She knew, better than anyone, the extent of my new powers. After all, she could relive my memories at will. Indeed, very little was hidden from her probing mind. I was, in a sense, an open book to her.

"You promise you will save me, Mommy?"

Her question broke me up more than I was expecting. "Of course, baby."

"But you need to find the missing boy, too."

"I do."

"They are bleeding him to death."

"I think so, yes."

She nodded and looked down and didn't seem to know what to do with her hands, so I returned her phone to them, and they clasped around it comfortingly. I then clasped my own hands around her comfortingly, too. She lay her head on my shoulder, and I felt her shuddering every few seconds. With fear, I suspected. Cold fear. She didn't want to die tonight. I didn't bother fighting my tears.

"This sucks, Mom," my daughter said after a while.

"I know. But look at the bright side."

"What bright side?"

"You're not going to die tonight, baby."

"You swear?"

"I swear."

46.

We were at a restaurant in Lake Elsinore called Ravioli's, the same restaurant where Detective Oster had spotted the present-day owner of the castle.

Admittedly, I wasn't very hungry and was way too anxious to eat anything, but Kingsley had convinced me that there wasn't much we could do until the sun went down, anyway. He'd gotten off work early to make the trek out to Elsinore with me. Good man, considering the thousands he'd given up. Then again, I liked to think time with me was priceless. At least to the man who loves me.

Unlike vampires and their constant need for blood, Kingsley was a testament that twenty-nine days out of thirty, werewolves ate just like regular folk. Boy, did they. In Kingsley's case, four regular folk.

Anyway, I was sitting at what had to be Lake Elsinore's nicest restaurant, surrounded by good people talking idly, as if this was just another fine evening, as if a teenage girl wasn't about to get into a fatal car accident, and as if a local boy wasn't presently being bled dry for his magical, alchemical blood.

"We should go," I said again.

"The food's not here, Sam. We barely got our drinks. Trust me. We should be here. I have a good feeling about it."

"Good feeling, why?"

"We're being watched."

I nodded. My own inner alarm was tingling mildly. No direct danger, but something was brewing in the background.

"Fine," I said. Then added, because I am such a peach, "This has to be the worst date night ever."

"It's not a date night. For you, it's a work night. Besides, I haven't eaten all day. So think of this as a refueling station."

"Then why are you all dressed up?"

"Because I'm not an animal... most of the time."

"Fine. Whatever. Maybe I can get them to hurry —"

He reached his big paw across the table and took my hand. I almost pulled it away, but I let him think he was comforting me. "Relax, Sam. I'm no good hungry, and you're no good until the sun goes down."

"The boy could be dead by the time you're done

slurping up your linguine."

"Ravioli," he corrected. You don't order linguine in a place called Ravioli's. Anyway, we don't know where the boy is yet. We don't know who has him or why—and whether he's been harmed or not. We need answers first and a cool head."

"He's being harmed. He's being drained."

"That might be the case, but we are still not at full power here, Sam."

"And raviolis will put you at full power?"

"My kind needs food. And lots of it. Trust me, I am far weaker when hungry."

"Fine, whatever."

"Hey, what the devil are you doing? I know that face."

"Nothing."

"Out with it, Sam."

"I just lit a small fire under our waiter's ass to get him moving."

"He's already moving, Sam. It's a busy night."

"And I might have told him to give us priority."

"Sam..."

"It's called compromising, you big goofball."

"Fine. I promise, we'll get to the boy, if we can. And we'll save him, if possible."

"Not if we're sitting here waiting for your molten lava cake."

"Tell you what, I'll skip dessert tonight. See? We both can compromise."

And before I could say something snarky and

undoubtedly mean, our salads came. I didn't want salad. I wanted the boy to be safe. I wanted my daughter to be saved, too. I wanted to punish whoever would hurt a little boy. I wanted to punish my daughter, too, for sneaking out late at night and almost getting herself killed. Of course, that hadn't yet happened. And there was hardly any sneaking being done at this point. But she would have sneaked, had I not warned her.

"Relax, Sam. What's on your mind?"

I shrugged. "What isn't on my mind is the question."

"Didn't you say your daughter's future accident didn't happen until much later at night?"

I nodded and picked up my fork. Allison had helped me scan my dream last night, noting anything I might have missed—it was nice, after all, to have a friend who could read your mind—and she had spotted the time at a nearby bank, displayed in a digital marquee. I had missed it. Indeed, the details of the time were new. After all, with each night, each new dream, details of the accident were growing sharper, more poignant. More real.

The salad was good, dammit, although I still wasn't very hungry. After two or three listless bites, I saw the puppy dog look in Kingsley's eyes and gave him the nod that all men wait for. Yes, he could have my food. And, of course, I didn't have to tell him twice. In a blink, my bowl was gone from in front of me and plopped down in front of him, and he was working it hard with his fork, which looked tiny in his ogre-like hand.

As I watched him eat—or inhale—I knew the big oaf was right. I sure as hell was no match against whatever it was that had pummeled me into Sam Moon pulp. And whatever condition the boy was in would certainly not get much worse waiting, say, two hours. And my daughter's accident—or future accident—didn't seem to be scheduled until around midnight. And whoever had scheduled her impending death could kiss my vampire ass.

If push came to shove, I would be at my daughter's side in an instant. Yes, I had come to care about the boy, even if his own mother didn't. No boy should be left alone, to bleed out in a monster's dungeon, or wherever he was. Besides, the boy wasn't alone, was he? He had Raul, who cared for him deeply. And, I think, he would have the Librarian, too, now that Max knew of the boy's existence.

But first, we had to find him, and get him out alive.

That was my job.

I'd learned from Max earlier in the day that the Hermetic mark—that is, the silver cord interlaced in the aura in all those descended from Hermes Trismegistus—did not act as a homing signal; meaning, there was no way for anyone to actually zero in on the boy. The mark had to be seen with the eyes, by those who knew what to look for. In fact, a person could go their whole life without knowing he or she was descended from Hermes.

That was, if they were fortunate enough to never cross paths with a vampire. Or something similar.

Anyway, it was unfortunate for the two boys that a monster of some sort had moved into the old castle. A monster who had hired the boys to, of all things, mow the estate's massive lawn. A monster who, undoubtedly, had licked his chops when he saw the gleaming silver cords in one of their auras. Perhaps the beast's hunger had gotten the best of him. Perhaps he had seen an opportunity to grow stronger than ever before, and had pounced on the boys. I'd only recently learned that Johnny—the first missing boy and the boy who had washed up dead—sometimes helped his friend Luke cut grass.

The waiter swung by with our meals: three orders of ravioli for Kingsley and one normal-sized order of linguine for me. Yes, I'd ordered linguine in a place called Ravioli's. Hey, I'm not a rebel vampire mama for nothing. The waiter, I noticed was moving with an inspired pep to his step.

Back in the day, I found it morally reprehensible to control others, to bypass their free will. Now, not so much. This change in me had nothing to do with Elizabeth, I think. I told myself that it was because I knew, deep down, I wasn't hurting anyone. The control wore off quickly. Indeed, the human mind eventually bypassed such control. Except in the case with Russell, my sexy boxer ex-boyfriend. His connection to me ran deep, thanks mostly to the introduction of sex into our relationship. Without my knowing it, the man had become bound to me, perhaps for life. His own will and ego had been buried deep under heavy layers of compulsion, so deep as to never be free again. Until I'd released him. Now, I knew, I could never have sex with another mortal; unless, of course, I wanted a love slave.

That should have sounded horrible. But, in this moment, it didn't. Okay, now that had been Elizabeth. The freaky, kinky bitch.

Kingsley said, around a cavernous mouthful of ravioli, "Have you considered the fact that your drive to save the boy tonight comes back to the fact that he is, however distantly, related to you?"

I blinked. Hard. I hadn't thought of it that way.

Kingsley continued. "Perhaps you are compelled—perhaps even supernaturally—to help one of your own."

I thought of that, even while I chewed the linguine, even while Kingsley wolfed down his raviolis, even while my inner alarm began to chime a little louder. Yes, indeed. We were being watched.

I was about halfway through my meal—and losing interest in it rapidly, when the chef himself came out of the kitchen and approached our table. And as he approached, I noticed the limp. And the scar at his wrist. And the fact that he had no discernible aura.

"And how was your dinner, mademoiselle?" he asked, speaking in a sing-song French accent. His name tag read, 'Pierre.' Pierre was not a big man. And, if I was a betting gal, I would say he wasn't a man at all. A *living* man, that is.

"I've had better." I wasn't sure why I had chosen this confrontational route. In the least, I was a bit blindsided by seeing what I assumed to be one of Lichtenstein's monsters here at the restaurant, let alone as the head chef. No, he wasn't the same brute who'd done his best to wipe me off the planet, but the coincidence of seeing him here wasn't lost on me. Especially considering the owner of the castle also owned Ravioli's. Ultimately, it was never a bad idea to poke the enemy. Poking produced results. Often quickly.

He studied me, showing no indication that he'd taken offense. Then again, maybe subtle facial cues were beyond him; after all, he had, at some point, been exhumed from the grave. He turned to Kingsley. "And how about you, monsieur?"

"Hated it."

There's a reason why I love the big guy, and this was it. The dude had my back, no matter what, even if he wasn't entirely sure what my back was up to.

Chef Lurch looked down at Kingsley's two finished plates, veritably licked clean. "Perhaps, monsieur might enjoy the third plate?"

"We'll see. But I'm not very hopeful."

"Perhaps my training at some of the finest culinary schools in France has been a waste of time."

"You said it," he said. "Not me."

He nodded and, I noticed, glanced to his right. I

glanced, too. Damned if the *maître d'* wasn't also a
fellow monster. I'd missed it the first time around,
but now, I saw it. The big guy seemed awkward in
his clothing. No discernible scars, but not all of the
monsters would have scars, would they?

"As they say here in America," said Chef Freak,
"you can't please everyone all of the time."

"I would say you're oh-for-two, buddy," said
Kingsley. "So you haven't pleased anyone yet, at
least here at this table."

"Perhaps monsieur would prefer rotting flesh?
And mademoiselle a goblet of blood."

"Now you're talking," I said. My inner alarm
was humming nicely now. Something was either
about to go down, or there was an impending swarm
of bees coming up Main Street.

"You're here for a reason," said Kingsley. "Out
with it."

The man-thing before us, which did not appear
to breathe and which emanated a palpable stench—
yes, the sickly sweet odor of death—nodded.
"Master Lichtenstein requests the pleasure of your
company at his hilltop castle residence. He will
send a boat for you at seven."

47.

We were in one of Roy Azul's lakeside cabins.

The cabin was nicer than I'd expected, and bigger, too.

Then again, I suspected we wouldn't be in the cabin for long. At least, not tonight. I didn't have to be psychic to know that I might have a very, very long night ahead of me. Still, it was good to have a base of operations, so to speak, and this was it.

"What time is it?" I asked.

Kingsley was laid out on the bed, his belly noticeably rounder, but that could have been my imagination. He glanced at his Rolex. Yeah, I didn't know they made them that big either. "Six-forty-five," he said, and slipped his hands back behind his big, shaggy head. Somewhere under all that hair was an obliterated cabin pillow presently wondering what the hell it had done in a past life to deserve this.

I paced in front of the bed. I caught a glimpse inside the adjoining bathroom, where the house-cleaning service had made the most adorable elephant out of the extra towels. Despite myself, despite my worry and confusion and frustration, I had to smile each time I saw that dopey elephant.

"What the hell is going on?" I finally asked, out of pure frustration.

Orange County's most famous defense attorney didn't bother to open an eye. "Your guess is as good as mine."

"Is Lichtenstein here, in Lake Elsinore?"

"The presence of three of his monsters seems to suggest so."

"With two of them working at the same restaurant."

"Maybe more, if he owns the place. According to Franklin, Lichtenstein had gone out of his way to educate his monsters, to make them presentable. He really believed he was creating a new race. He wanted to present them in a favorable light."

"Is Lichtenstein a vampire? Or is he a monster, too? Did he somehow use his own mad science on himself?"

"I would say anything is possible."

I made a very noncommittal comment, bordering on rude, and continued pacing. This time I didn't smile at the cute-ass elephant. After a few moments of this, I stopped by Kingsley's side and slapped his meaty thigh. He was now wearing loose-fitting work dungarees. The fly was unbuttoned. Kingsley always unbuttoned his fly. I thought it was my open invitation.

"Ouch!" he yelped.

"Will you get up, you big buffoon?"

He accommodated me by opening one eye, then winking at me. I growled, sounding a lot like my daughter.

"I thought I was the only one who growled," he said, rousing himself into a sitting position.

"Is he really picking us up by boat?"

"Someone is."

"And we're just going to let him?"

"I don't see why not. There's no easier way into the castle than to be escorted in. You said he has a private dock."

The castle did. It was a dock that stretched straight out from the cliff, where a small outboard boat was often tied up. I'd seen it on my many fly-bys. Perhaps strangest of all was that the chef had known where we were staying. We'd only checked in an hour or so before heading to dinner.

"How did he know we were staying at the cabins?"

"I don't know," said Kingsley. "But Lichten-stein might have eyes and ears everywhere. No pun intended."

I thought about that. Thought about it hard. Then got up and peeked out the curtain. Nothing was out there, but my warning bell pinged once. Just once. There was someone out there. I waited, holding my breath, although I didn't have to. Old habit. I waited, waited. Kingsley was about to say something and I promptly shushed the crap out of him. He lay back on the bed, butt-hurt.

And there it was. Across a sort of courtyard between the cabins, was a man pulling a garden hose from a shed. Maintenance, no doubt. He looked my way once, paused, then looked away, and resumed rolling up the hose. More importantly: no aura.

"There's another one."

"Another what?"

"Lichtenstein's monster." I paused. "I remember now. Ivan, my client's groundskeeper, is probably one of them. No aura. He's the one who likely tipped off Lichtenstein that we were here."

In a blink, Kingsley was off the bed and next to me, moving fast enough to make me gasp in surprise. I should be used to all this supernatural stuff, but I just wasn't. Not yet. Someone as big as Kingsley should not be able to move that fast. Yet, here he was, by my side in a blink, looking out the curtain, using his own brand of perfectly wonderful night vision.

"Yup, that would be one of them."

"What's going?" I asked.

"I think," said Kingsley, dropping the curtain, "that Edward Lichtenstein might have taken over Lake Elsinore."

"But why?"

"I don't know," he said. "But I have a feeling

we're going to find out." He pointed off to the right. "The boat's here."

48.

After helping me into the small skiff, Kingsley followed behind, sinking the small skiff another foot or two into the water. I think the lake's overall waterline might have crept up an inch or two.

Sitting at the outboard motor wasn't a living man. He was dead and probably cold, and at one time in his distant past, he'd probably spent some time buried six feet under. Probably parts of him were from other bodies, too, and perhaps that was how Lichtenstein helped keep his monsters immortal: replacing body parts when necessary. Hands, arms, hearts, you name it. The thought should have repulsed me, but I was oddly interested in the process. And so was the demon bitch inside me. I had literally felt her perk up inside my head, watching all of this unfold, undoubtedly interested.

For his part, Kingsley took all of this in stride. Of course, he'd been living with such a monster for years. Still, motoring across Lake Elsinore in the dark of night, with only a small lantern swinging on the skiff's prow to guide us, and one of Lichtenstein's freaks at the helm, had to be one of the creepiest experiences of my life.

Wind beat our clothing, mussed our hair. Small waves slapped the hull. Water spray sprinkled our faces. The motor seemed obnoxiously loud, seemingly the only sound in the world. Cars moved around the lake, their headlights occasionally flashing our direction. Still, the only noise I could hear was the incessant throb of the outboard.

Kingsley sat behind me, one hand on my lower back. Occasionally, his own long hair blew over my shoulder and into my face and mouth. I spit it out. The man-thing at the helm said nothing, nor did he do anything other than guide us, invariably, over the mostly calm surface of Southern California's largest natural lake. Before us, out of the gloom and only lit sporadically, was the massive, hulking, walled castle that sat above the lake, upon a small cliff. It looked out of place and out of this world. Its domed pavilion was silhouetted against the mostly starless sky. Brighter lights lit the exterior walls of the structure, but the castle itself was dark, brooding, foreboding. Then again, I'd had my face beat in there just a few days ago. I might be a little biased.

As we approached, the wind picked up some more, and the slapping waves hit with more regularity and force. I knew a rare fall storm was coming tonight. I just didn't know it would hit so quickly.

The lantern swung wildly, its yellow light catching the foaming crests of the black lake water. The rain came quickly. At first, I didn't distinguish it from the spray of waves bursting over the hull, but soon, the drops grew in size and came with more regularity. By the time the narrow dock materialized out of the mist, we were in a full-blown rainstorm.

Our skiff captain cut the engine and drifted in next to the first pylon. He tossed a rope expertly around a bolted anchor and pulled us in. He stepped easily out of the vessel and first helped me out, and then, Kingsley.

Once we were on the floating dock, which rose and fell and creaked and jostled, the man-thing unhooked one of the lanterns. He then led us along the rocking dock, through the driving rain, and toward the black castle that rose above us.

Ominously, I might add. Again.

***

The dock segued into a sandy beach, as if this weren't the middle of the desert. Our host, who still hadn't uttered a word, and who didn't even have the good decency to turn his head away from the driving rain, stomped through the dampening sand and straight for, well, the cliff face.

I looked at Kingsley. He looked at me, shrugged, and stomped right behind our guide. Both, I noted, completely lacked an aura. I lacked one, too, which was a damn shame. I was willing to bet my aura had, at one time, been bright and fairly cheery.

Although I didn't stomp, I followed along, ducking my head away from the rain, and wondering what the hell I'd gotten myself into.

***

It was an elevator.

Although I can see easily into the night, I wasn't entirely prepared for an elevator door opened at the base of the cliff. Neither was Kingsley. In fact, after the man-thing had pressed something in the cliff, and the door hissed open, Kingsley jumped. Straight into Lichtenstein's mute monster. The monster only grunted and brushed Kingsley off and stepped into the dimly lit elevator.

Kingsley, once again composed, motioned toward the open elevator. "Ladies first and all that."

"How chivalrous," I said. "And cowardly, too."

I headed inside and he followed behind, grinning from ear to ear. You would have thought that the big ogre was heading up to the penthouse suite at the Luxor in Vegas.

The elevator itself wasn't very big. In fact, I was fairly certain Kingsley and the monster were rubbing shoulders. Yeah, awkward and silent and weird. This "monster" was of average size and build. Not like the thing that had beaten me into vampire mush. Certainly not all of Lichtenstein's creations were going to be hulking. Undoubtedly, he took the bodies as they came, and mixed and matched parts as he saw fit.

Meanwhile, the elevator creaked and rumbled up through the sandstone cliff. The structure was ancient and probably not very well kept, either. I saw no inspection stickers or safety certificates. I tried reminding myself that I was an intrepid vampire mama who laughed in the face of death. Then again, getting stuck in an elevator in the middle of a forgotten cliff, with two monsters—a werewolf and a Frankenstein, no less—was anything but funny. Especially when one of the monsters—I'm looking at you, Kingsley—took up more than half of the elevator.

Not a word was spoken. The silence, if possible, only seemed to deepen as the rickety cage climbed up, up—perhaps twenty-feet or more. The mushroomy smell also seemed to deepen, too, or enrichen. It was the smell of death, of course. And it was coming off the dude at the other end of the elevator. The dude who didn't seem to care that he smelled like wide-open ass. Then again, he didn't seem to care about anything, let alone small talk.

Probably for the best. I remembered the thing screaming at me that night, his voice barely intelligible. I really, really didn't want to hear that voice again.

And then, mercifully, the elevator dinged open. Yes, *dinged*.

The man-thing waited, and so did Kingsley. I didn't need to be told twice. I stepped out of the elevator and into the castle's courtyard.

49.

The courtyard belonged in another time and place. Certainly not here in present-day Lake Elsinore.

High stone walls surrounded us, all lined with small windows flickering with candlelight. Before us, cobblestone paths, interspersed with thick grass, wound through perfectly trimmed hedges and gardens of flowers. Along the base of the inner walls were stone walkways, complete with inter-spersed walkways. This could have been a Scottish castle. Or a monastery high in the Himalayas. The people milling about could have been monks deep in silent worship or prayer, or on their way to meditations. But we were in the deserts of Southern California, and the people moving through this courtyard weren't people at all. They were Lichtenstein's monsters. Every last one of them.

"They look like zombies," I whispered to Kingsley. I didn't have to whisper loud. The big guy had pretty good hearing.

And it was true, too. For every Lichtenstein monster who walked normally, two others lurched or limped or lumbered. I counted nine total. Most seemed to wander aimlessly, although some moved purposefully through hallways and under archways, disappearing into the various entryways deeper inside the castle.

We followed our guide, who ambled smoothly enough, and seemed to be of one body—which, I think, would be preferable. I gave Lichtenstein credit for creating what he created. It couldn't have been easy re-building a human being—or giving life to the dead. I knew the dark masters had helped him at some point. Still, the man was devoted to his craft. As evidenced by the walking dead around me.

Some of the hedges, I saw, actually formed a central labyrinth. We passed the opening to one, and I spied a Lichtenstein monster seemingly stuck in one corner, his face pressed into the dense brush, his feet walking, walking. I wondered how long the poor bastard had been stuck there.

We followed a cobblestone path past a small pond where, you guessed it, I spied a man-thing just emerging out of the water. Rather than going around the pond, the creature had walked *through* it. He didn't seem to care. Hey, if he didn't care, I didn't care. I watched him cut across the grass, his shoulder knocking into a small tree. I found myself holding Kingsley's hand, tightly. I might be a bit of a badass myself, but this—well, this was just too damned freaky.

It was at that moment my cell phone vibrated. I keep said cell phone in my front pocket—never understood people who kept it in their back pockets —and saw immediately that it was a text from Allison.

Tam Tam is on the move.

My heart wanted to skip a beat, but it didn't, couldn't. Instead, I instantly felt sick to my stomach. My fingers flew over the keyboard.

Stay close, keep me updated.

Will do, babes, came her response.

We crossed the courtyard and up some stone steps, where we were led along an exterior tunnel. Archways dotted the tunnel every ten feet or so. I didn't see the point of such archways, but I guessed rich people had to spend their money somehow.

Lurch opened a heavy-looking double door and stepped aside. I let Kingsley go in first and then followed behind. Our escort continued down a darkened hallway, and we followed like the idiots we were. A vampire, a werewolf, and Frankenstein —all together in one creepy castle at the edge of a lake with a real live lake monster. Where were Abbott and Costello when you needed them?

That there were ghosts flitting through walls and drifting languidly down the corridor was a given. I knew Kingsley could see them, too, because we both stepped out of the way of one such specter who appeared up out of the floor and just stood there, staring at us. I quickly noticed a trend.

"Most of the spirits are men," I whispered to Kingsley.

"I was just thinking the same thing," he whispered back, although his whisper might have sounded more like a guttural growl.

"You just said that because I did," I said. "Admit it."

He grinned and pretended to whistle. Once again, I wished I could slip inside his thick skull and see what the devil was going on there. But, alas, his thoughts were closed off to me.

We passed many doors, some with light flickering under the heavy wooden doors. In some I heard speaking. In others I heard screaming. In still others, I heard moaning and weeping. Some a combination of all of the above. Kingsley could undoubtedly hear more of what was going behind the closed doors than me. Then again, I'd heard enough. I didn't want to know what was going on. I didn't like this place. Not at all. Not one fucking bit.

We came to another door, set into another arch. If I never saw another arch again, that would be great. Our fearless and mute guide turned the lever, pushed it open, and what I saw inside was enough for even the demoness within me to squeal.

It was, I was certain, the laboratory from hell.

50.

The lab resembled a morgue; that is, if a morgue was in the monster-making business.

I counted no less than fourteen corpses stacked around the room. All men. All pale and stiff. Some had fabulous wounds: missing limbs, missing sections of skulls, concaved chests. There had been, I recalled, a mining accident not too long ago, and not too far from here, either. An underground explosion at a clay and shale mine that had resulted in a tunnel collapsing, with nine miners being killed. Rescue efforts took days. Big news. Some of these fourteen corpses showed signs of an explosion, while many had been clearly crushed. The remaining bodies had no discernible markings. Correction, the closest body to me, lying face up on a metal table, had a smallish bullet wound directly over his heart.

Some of the dead were stacked ingloriously upon each other, arms hanging to their sides, looking miserable even in death. Most notable was what I didn't see: the boy, Luke, was nowhere to be found, which, I think, was a good thing, considering that this room seemed reserved for the dead.

The recessed center of the room, accessed by a four-step descent, featured only a single, metal table. Upon the table was a dead man. Standing next to the table was a living man wearing a surgeon's magnifying goggles and holding a scalpel. Oh, and he was also holding a severed hand, which he casually dropped into a metal bin. As he did so, he looked up at us, smiling, his big fish eyes bright behind the goggles.

"Am I really seeing this?" I asked Kingsley.

"I'm afraid so."

I really wanted to freak out, knowing to do so was the proper reaction. But the more I saw of the bodies, the wounds, the cutting instruments, the splatters and pools of blood everywhere, the more interested I became. So very interested...

By all counts, I should run screaming from the room. But there I stood in the doorway, transfixed. My stomach, curse it to hell, growled.

"Jesus, Sam, was that you?" whispered Kingsley.

"Don't judge me, mister. I've seen what you eat when the moon is full."

"That will be all, Rufus, thank you," said the man in the goggles. He carefully set aside his scalpel, pulled free his gloves and pushed up his goggles which, admittedly, made him look less like a homicidal maniac.

Our ferryman guide—apparently named Rufus —nodded once and exited, and never once, from the boat ride to the elevator ride to here, looked our way or acknowledged us. The door shut quietly behind him, leaving us alone with the mad scientist.

"Samantha Moon and Kingsley Fulcrum, welcome to my house of horrors. Or, perhaps, my castle of corpses." He chuckled at this, speaking in a surprisingly strong French accent.

I nearly said "domicile of the dead," but held my tongue, reminding myself this was no time for my sometimes adorable wit.

He made his way up the steps and greeted us with firm handshakes. He did not sport an aura, always a sure sign of strangeness. His hand, I noted, was warm. I would kill to be warm again.

He bowed slightly. "Victor Lichtenstein, at your service."

Lichtenstein was not very tall, which ruled out werewolves, who tend to creep up in size over the decades and centuries. He did, however, look like a reject from *The Big Bang Theory*. Nerdy, off-putting, awkward. He said to Kingsley, "Franklin is one of my better creations."

"He doesn't take kindly to being called a creation."

"Which is exactly why he is such a success. Most of these brutes you see lumbering through this castle, or wailing in their cells, are incapable of caring what they are or why they are here."

"You're creating more."

Lichtenstein chuckled. It was the chuckle of a proud and modest father. And, perhaps, that of someone who had completely lost his mind, too. Hard to say for sure, as the bastard presented himself fairly well. "I'm always tinkering, looking for better and better ways to bring my children into the world."

"Children?"

"Do not scoff, Mr. Fulcrum. Some of us hunger for companionship."

"And some of us make friends and get married or join online chat groups."

He might have glanced my way. "And for some of us, none of those are easy. Some of us suffer tragic, overwhelming shyness. And some of us have loved and lost, and have decided to never love again."

"You are speaking of Mary Shelley," said Kingsley.

"Mary Wollstonecraft to me, but yes. I loved her and she betrayed me."

"*Frankenstein.*"

"An atrocious book, and wildly inaccurate. Fiction at its best. She had, after all, seen but a glimpse of my experiments." He took in some air, which seemed to be his first breath since joining us. "But where are my manners? Would either of you care for a nightcap?"

I looked at Kingsley. He looked at me. Of one thing I was certain: we had obviously seen too much here in Castle Lichtenstein. I doubted the good doctor had any intention of allowing us to leave.

So, hell, I might as well enjoy a stiff drink.

51.

We were in a smallish room.

A massive tapestry hung before us. The tapestry looked old enough to belong in a real castle. The scene woven into it was that of a fox hunt, with dozens of hunting dogs, horsemen, and one solo fox legging it out. I hoped the little guy made it.

The sitting room wasn't quite a library, but almost. A number of books filled some shelves on one side. Most of the books were, predictably, ancient-looking, but I did spot one or two Stephen Kings and Michael Crichtons. No surprise there.

A lush carpet was underfoot, so deep and comfortable that I nearly removed my sneakers. What I would give to run my toes through it. *Big picture, Sam.* We sat in high-back chairs made of the softest velvet I'd ever had the pleasure to rub up against. Each of us had a glass of wine, a French syrah and the deepest red I'd ever seen. I enjoyed the crap out of it. A dry wine, I tasted hints of blackberry and maybe even cherry. That it also looked like blood was something I was trying to ignore.

"You were hired to find a lake monster, am I correct, Ms. Moon?" asked the doctor. This was the first time Lichtenstein had addressed me.

I blinked and set the glass down on a claw-foot side table. There was no coaster, just a richly embroidered doily. "I was, yes."

"And how is your investigation proceeding?"

"It's ongoing," I said.

"Any leads?" he asked.

"There appears to be something there."

"I imagine so. That poor boy. Those fishermen. Terrible."

"I'm surprised I didn't see the fishermen in your laboratory," I said.

"Oh, they were far too gone to be of any use to me, although I suppose I could have parted them out."

"Jesus," said Kingsley, shaking his head and taking a healthy chug from his wine.

"It is a dark business, Mr. Fulcrum, I agree. But a rewarding one, nonetheless."

"Rewarding, how?"

Lichtenstein stared blankly at Kingsley. "I create life, Mr. Fulcrum. What could be more rewarding than that?"

"You create monsters."

"Say that to Franklin. Say that to my other successful creations. You met one such creation at Ravioli's. Pierre is a world-class chef, and I couldn't be more proud of him. For every ten simpletons I create, there is one monumental success."

"And what do you do with the, ah, simpletons?" I asked, rather enjoying my own wine. It had a hearty, earthy, slightly metallic taste.

"You see them here, on the grounds. I have use for them, obviously. Some are strong as oxen. And I apologize, Ms. Moon, that you had to experience that firsthand. Gunther is house security who patrols our grounds."

I realized Gunther was the one who had beaten me so badly.

"What if I had been, I dunno, someone lost and needing directions?" I asked.

"I sincerely doubt someone lost and needing directions would have scaled a fifteen-foot high fence. But, to answer your question, Gunther is trained to look for auras, or the lack thereof. He is trained to snuff out any supernatural threats." He didn't say it, but I suspected I knew of which threats he meant: alchemists. He continued, "I'm pleased to see that you've made a full recovery from the ordeal."

If anything, he seemed more pleased that his bodyguard monster had performed his job astonishingly well, even if it meant giving me the beating of a lifetime. Ten lifetimes. Lichtenstein finished the last of his wine and asked if we'd like another round. Kingsley seemed all too happy to do so. My boyfriend seemed to be enjoying himself entirely too much. Last I checked, this wasn't a social visit. There was a kid missing, possibly dying, and the big oaf was drinking our host under the table. Suddenly irritated, I declined another glass. Truth was, the wine was upsetting my stomach a little.

"Is the wine not to your liking, Ms. Moon?"

"I've had enough, thank you."

Kingsley sat forward, almost spilling his recently-topped glass. "So how many of your creatures work in town?"

"Many of them, Mr. Fulcrum. I own many shops and restaurants, many of which provide working opportunities for my children."

"But why?"

"Why not? Those who are capable of working need to be stimulated. Many of them have been with me from the beginning and have learned valuable trades."

Kingsley studied the doctor for a moment, eyes narrowing. He wasn't quite buying the explanation. Neither was I.

I said, "Who invited us to visit tonight?"

"I did, of course. Some of my more competent creations are quite adept with modern technology. I was called immediately when two of the soulless entered the restaurant. A quick description was sufficient to know who, exactly, was at my estab-lishment. You can imagine my pleasure and delight.

I thought it only fitting to invite the two of you over for a nightcap."

Absolutely none of this was making sense, and to top it off, my stomach was gurgling with, I assumed, anxiety. Although that would be a first for me.

"And they all live here?" I asked.

"Of course. They are my children, Ms. Moon. Do your children not live with you? Now, a small handful have left the fold. And I miss each tremendously." He let his words hang in the air. He didn't look at Kingsley; then again, he didn't have to.

"There is such a thing as free will, doctor," said Kingsley. "Franklin made his choice."

Lichtenstein nodded at that, pondered it, and said, "There is also such a thing as gratefulness. My other children are grateful, so much so that they..." He let his voice trail off.

I deduced the direction he was going, and so did Kingsley. "That they worship you," said Kingsley, who didn't bother disguising his contempt. Kingsley and the not-so-good-doctor seemed to have some history, and I let it play out. Why should I intrude? Besides, it wasn't every day that one got to see a real-live werewolf and, for all intents and purposes, the real Dr. Frankenstein, work out their grievances.

"Perhaps some see me as..."—he tried to look humble—"... a sort of god, yes."

"And do you remind them that you are only a

lonely scientist looking to make friends. Emphasis on *make*."

"Oh, I am looking to make much more than friends, Mr. Fulcrum." The doctor reached over and refilled his glass of wine. "I'm looking to create a whole new race. Emphasis on *create*."

Kingsley rolled his eyes. Perhaps a little drunkenly.

"Yes, I might sound crazy, Mr. Fulcrum. I might even sound like the world's loneliest man. But I have been given the keys to the kingdom, so to speak. I have been given the ability to create life where there was none before."

"And you would be their god."

"Is that so bad? My children have a natural affinity to me. I haven't quite understood that. It is a rare offspring who leaves the fold completely."

A sudden thought occurred to me. "You use your own blood to help galvanize them back to life."

"Of course, Ms. Moon. My blood and another. All combined under the right conditions, with the right science, with the right intent."

"Intent?" I asked.

"A powerful intent can move mountains, Ms. Moon. In this case, help spring forth life."

Coming from anyone else, this would have sounded like quackery at its best, but I had seen his monsters. I had seen their apparent loyalty as well. What else would explain the compound filled with freaks? Indeed, Dr. Lichtenstein was clearly onto something. Whether he was onto something worth-while or not, I didn't know.

"Why here?" asked Kingsley. "Why in Lake Elsinore?"

"Why not? It's a fairly quiet town. Most people keep to themselves. Most people stay away from the castle, too. Those who don't, get run off." He glanced at me. *Or beaten to a bloody pulp*, his glance seemed to say. He continued: "We'll pick up shop someday, when the time is right. For now, we have our space, and I am very, very at home here in this modern-day castle. Fitting, if you ask me."

"Cliché, if you ask me," said Kingsley.

"Perhaps, but this home gives me pleasure, and so do my children, and so do all my future children. Speaking of which, I have something of Franklin's that I've been meaning to return to him. Something I am sure he would appreciate having."

I was wondering what the devil it might be. An arm? A foot? Photos from his past? Maybe information on the family he'd left behind?

Kingsley arched a caterpillar-like eyebrow. "Very well. I'm sure he would appreciate it."

"Well, it's something I've been meaning to give him, something I know he would want, even if he doesn't remember. Perhaps it's better that I show you? And you can decide."

"Very well," said Kingsley, and as he said those words, my inner alarm, which had been pinging mildly this entire time, picked up its tempo.

I grabbed my wolf's hand. "Maybe I should go

with you."

Lichtenstein laughed heartily at that. "There's no one here interested in your werewolf boyfriend, Ms. Moon. I assure you, he will be back in no time. Please, stay seated. We will return."

And with that, Kingsley leaned down, kissed me on the cheek, promised he would be okay, and then left with Dr. Lichtenstein.

I was alone in the sitting room, and not liking it. Not one bit.

J.R. RAIN

52.

I paced the small sitting room.

And the more I paced, the weaker I felt. And not just weak, but my stomach hurt like hell, too. That was new. Oh, and something else that was new: the beginning of a headache. A doozy of a headache, too.

Meanwhile, my inner alarm was growing in volume, but not obnoxiously so, not like it had when I found myself on the wrong end of a monster mash. No, these warning bells were meant to just get my attention, to let me know that no good would come from being here for very much longer. But, if I knew my alarm correctly—and I think I did— there was no imminent danger to me... yet.

So what had set off the alarm? Any number of things. The potentiality for harm was everywhere. I was, after all, surrounded by a sea of Lichtenstein monsters, undead humans housing the lost souls of the lowest of the low dark masters. Perhaps 'master' was being too generous. The walking husks that I had seen barely exhibited life, let alone intelligence. And thinking about all this only seemed to make my head hurt more.

I continued pacing, wondering where Kingsley had been taken, wondering why my inner alarm had picked up, and wondering why I felt so damn... weak.

I nearly paused and sat down, but I continued pacing, alternately running my hands through my thick hair and holding my upset stomach. I tried the sitting room door, and found it locked. Generally, locked doors take about as much time to open as an unlocked door. But, as I turned the handle, this lock felt heavy, impenetrable, eternal.

Silver, I thought, releasing my hand, which now burned. The handle was made of silver. Probably not the locking mechanism itself, but the handle sure was.

I told myself I could just sit and wait and relax and try to feel better. Yeah, let's do that. Let's sit and relax and maybe the pain will subside, a pain that had now spread to my arms and legs and chest. I sat, breathed, held my head and stomach, and anything else I could hold.

I felt drugged. I also felt as if I had been run over by a truck. A thought that left me feeling panicked all over again. After all, how could I save Tammy, feeling like this? How could I save anyone, let alone myself, feeling like this?

I shot up out of the chair. I stumbled over to the door and gripped the handle and turned with all my strength, even while my hands burned and smoked and hissed. Nothing much moved. No cracking of tumblers, or breaking of the doorjamb itself.

From behind the door, I heard footsteps.

A single set of footsteps, that is.

I released the damnable lever and stepped back, hands burning. I gasped, breathing hard, and waited for the door to open...

* * *

Dr. Lichtenstein was alone.

"Where's... where's Kingsley?" I gasped. I suddenly needed to sit. I stumbled back into a straight-back chair, holding my chest.

"I see the colloidal silver is taking effect. Good. Shame you didn't drink more of the wine, Ms. Moon. Let's just hope you ingested enough to play nicely."

Sold in many health food stores, I knew the stuff. It was meant to aid health by ingesting traces of silver. Or, perhaps, it was meant to stop vampires. "Where's... Kingsley?"

"Oh, he's not very far at all. Lucky for us, he drank more than his fair share. Much, much more. He didn't put up much of a resistance at all." The doctor chuckled and swept through the sitting room and over to the hanging tapestry.

"You, you drank it, too," I gasped.

"I did. I am immortal, like you and your werewolf friend. So are all my children. But, alas, we are neither vampire nor wolfman. Nor are we alchemists, although we are closest to the latter."

"The boy... Luke..." I gasped. "Is he alive?"

"Really, Ms. Moon. Does it matter? The life of one boy? I suppose there might be some life in him, but I suspect we are reaching the point of no return. He is worth more alive than dead, but the alchemists have a way of zeroing in on their own. Better to get what I can from him, then dispose of him."

"Monster..."

"I prefer... harvester, Samantha Moon. Is the farmer a monster for leaching nutrients from the soil? I don't think so. And this boy in particular is so very rich in nutrients, Sam. The richest. A powerful young man, really."

"The dark masters... are... using... you..." I gasped.

"I see you know your history, Ms. Moon. Yes, the so-called dark masters—although I am not beholden to anyone—provided me with the final clue. The final piece of the puzzle, if you will. A man, in fact, who claimed to be the dragon prince himself, Dracula. And, yes, they thought they could use me, to help bring back their own into this world. But little did they know the power of my mind. The control I have over every neuron and synapse. Indeed, even now I can feel one of their dark entities within me, trying to escape. But I won't allow it. And neither will my children; at least, those who are advanced enough to understand. I train each in the power of the mind. In truth, it is I who use the dark masters. Use them to create my children... and to live forever. While they reside only in shadows."

I tried to sit up, but was too weak to even do that. My God, I'd only had a half a glass. Kingsley had, what, two glasses? Maybe three? A whole bottle?

"And you?" I asked, feeling a throbbing pain in seemingly every part of my body. "What are you?"

"I am like my creations, Samantha Moon. Like them, I have died, only to be reborn again. There is a reason I miss Franklin so."

"He brought you back to life?"

"Of course, Ms. Moon. I drank arsenic and died. I was dead for two whole days before Franklin brought me back to life, using all my techniques to perfection."

"You killed yourself?"

"It had to be done to be reborn, Sam. Ah, death is a beautiful thing. I saw things that I will never forget. But I knew I must return to Franklin, that I must lead my children forward into a brave new world."

"You... you gave up eternity for this?"

"I would give up eternity a thousand times over for this, Sam. We are creating a new world, after all."

"God... complex," I gasped.

He grinned, and nodded. "Is having one so bad, Sam? It takes a rare creator to forge a new species, does it not?"

"Where's Luke?"

"Being a particularly rich source of Hermetic blood, he's being carefully attended to. The other boy, not so much. His blood was weak, diluted, impure, although delicious."

"You... drink blood?"

"No, Sam. Although I can, and sometimes will. But, like your werewolf boyfriend, I and my children need to consume flesh, albeit twice a month, during full moons and new moons. Animals work nicely, and we have a small farm out back, full of chickens and sheep and other morsels. Only rarely do we feed upon people."

I imagined a long dining hall full of Lichtenstein's monsters, all feasting on raw meat. I shook my head, sickened all over again, and tried to sit up. As I did so, I noted some of my strength had returned. Indeed, some of the pain in my stomach had receded, too. The headache seemed to be fading, as well. The colloidal silver was, mercifully, wearing off, albeit slowly. I continued to play it up.

"Where... where is Kingsley?"

"Yes, Kingsley. He and I have a little history, Ms. Moon. After all, he went out of his way to steal away Franklin, my favorite creation. My most successful creation."

"Seems to me like Franklin... left... on... his... own," I said, and told myself to tone it down a tad.

"He did. But he had help, too. Most of my creations are incapable of surviving on their own. Even Franklin would need some help, at least initially. Food, shelter. Perhaps a job. Perhaps even legal paperwork. Kingsley provided all of that for him and more."

"You should be... happy that one of your creations"—It was all I could do to not say monsters—"struck out on his own. You should be proud." I needed to keep him talking. I needed more information. I needed to regain my strength. I needed to find the boy, find Kingsley, and then we needed to get the hell out of here and save Tammy...

All in a night's work. I glanced at my watch. It was nearly nine. Three more hours...

"Perhaps I should be proud, Samantha. But I do not see it that way. I see it as betrayal. I see it as abandonment. I see it as worshiping a false god."

It was all I could do to not roll my eyes.

"Mock me if you want, Sam, but my creations have a tendency to be beholden to their creator—"

And then, I suddenly got it. "And Franklin brought you back from the dead. He is, in essence, *your* creator."

He smiled sadly. "Now you see the source of my distress, Sam. I am his creator, and he is mine."

"Then why did he leave?"

"He was always a particularly free spirit. He had probably been so in his first life, too. His bond with me had always felt shaky, even from the very beginning."

"And now he's gone and bonded with Kingsley," I said.

Lichtenstein's eyes flashed. "Yes."

"Which is why you hate Kingsley."

"More than anything, Samantha Moon. More than anything on this fucking Earth."

"Is it why you moved here?"

"I knew someday I would have my time in the sun. I did not know when that someday would arrive. I did not, in fact, expect to see the two of you enter my restaurant tonight. I knew you were in town, yes. In particular, I knew a vampire was in town. My children are everywhere, you see. They are my eyes and ears. Nothing surprises me in this town, my town. Yes, I knew you were here, and I knew your association with Kingsley, too. And, yes, I have been keeping tabs on the bastard werewolf for quite some time. Ever since he stole my Franklin."

I sat forward, but that effort nearly caused me to vomit, a reminder that I was still not at full strength. I suddenly had a very, very bad feeling about all of this. Even worse than a few minutes ago, now that I knew the depths of the doctor's hatred.

"Where's Kingsley?"

Lichtenstein grinned—maniacally, I might add. "Better I show you."

And with that, he stepped over and, like a shower curtain, yanked aside the heavy tapestry. Behind it was a floor-to-ceiling window. I blinked, confused. That is, until Lichtenstein flipped a switch near the glass.

"See for yourself, Samantha Moon."

I stood on still wobbly legs and headed over to the glass. Turned out it was actually a window that looked down into what could only be called an arena. A dirt arena, like a miniature bullfighting ring. And there, hunched over on all fours and vomiting violently, was my Kingsley. Sweat poured from his forehead and glistened off his forearms. He ducked his head away from the light, blinking. He'd been sitting there in the dark this entire time. Admittedly—and I hated myself for thinking this— he looked like a big, wet, shaggy, miserable dog.

"Your Kingsley is full of the colloidal silver, Ms. Moon. Look at him there, so sick and helpless. The silver should stop him from shape-shifting— just as it should stop you from shape-shifting, too. Yes, I know of your pet dragon."

He would, of course, have known about Talos. After all, I'd transformed to escape his brute. "Why is he in there?"

"Like God, I love all my children. But also like God, I will strike down those who fail me... and recycle the best of them, always hoping to create a better man, a better servant, a better worshiper."

I wasn't entirely sure he had this God-complex business pegged, but the key here was that he believed it. Every word. I turned and looked at the man who stared down through the glass window, a man who gave crazy a whole new meaning, a man who just might have lost his mind not just decades ago, but whole centuries ago. A man who was too smart for his own good, too driven for his own good, too talented for his own good, too lonely for his own good. Combine all of that, and this was what you get: a castle full of lurching monsters, and a creator who demanded to be worshiped. A creator who loved his creations. A creator who punished them, too.

Lichtenstein pressed his hand flat against the glass. "And Kingsley's been a very bad creation, Ms. Moon. Very, very bad."

53.

As Kingsley continued vomiting—I think he was well into the dry-heave stage at this point—a panel near him slid open.

He didn't notice at first, but I sure as hell did. And it was what stepped out of the panel that made my own mouth go dry. The biggest of Lichtenstein's creations stepped out of what appeared to be a monster-sized cubbyhole. It occurred to me that this creature was always there, always waiting to be summoned. That it, in fact, lived in that cubbyhole.

Jesus.

"What is that thing?" I asked.

"That *thing*, Ms. Moon, is my most powerful of creations. He represents the best, the strongest, the most agile and obedient of all my children. Nigel is the punisher. Nigel is the executioner, too. Nigel is all the things I have done right, and none of the things I have done wrong."

"Ah, fuck," I said, and pounded the glass. Except Kingsley was still hunched over, still dry-heaving. Probably dizzy as hell, too. He didn't look up, even as I continued pounding, half-expecting the glass to shatter under the force of my blows. That is, until a hand seized my right wrist.

"Don't make me subdue you, Ms. Moon."

I was about to tell him he could fuck off when I saw that someone else had taken hold of my hand, someone who'd entered the room quietly. Someone with undeniable strength. I turned, slowly, and looked up into a nightmare. It was the same terrible security guard—Gunther, I believe he was called—who had beaten me to within an inch of my eternal life. I might have squeaked. Then I nodded to Lichtenstein, who, in turn, nodded to Gunther, who, in turn, begrudgingly released my wrist. I got the impression that Gunther would have preferred to continue the beating he'd started a few days ago. With one eye on Gunther, I turned my attention to the events unfolding in the arena.

Mercifully, Kingsley had, by now, spotted Lichtenstein's gladiator, inexplicably called Nigel. The hairy beast I called my boyfriend had found his feet and was presently swaying. He looked like he might topple over at any minute.

"This is hardly a fair fight," I said, moving closer to the glass and now thoroughly ignoring Gunther behind me.

"Who said life was fair, Ms. Moon?"

Lichtenstein grinned and eased himself down into one of the straight back chairs, which swiveled to face the glass. He motioned for me to do the same, and I did, slowly. Jesus, the bastard had made watching his animals tear each other to pieces a recreational sport. I glanced back one last time at Gunther, who stood close enough behind me to reach out and snap my neck.

I took in some air. The silver was wearing off. I was shaking less. Feeling stronger. Now, I looked out through the glass, and down into the arena, where the games were about to begin.

***

The monster was butt-naked.

Even from here I could see its many scars and stitchings. To say that Nigel looked like a rag doll on steroids wouldn't quite be accurate. It looked like a walking, stalking, hulking quilt in human form. It had no genitals. No nipples. Its skin along its torso looked newer somehow, like it had been recently replaced, which lent credence to my theory that Lichtenstein was constantly rebuilding these beasts.

Kingsley didn't look like he was in any condition to get in any good shots, let alone survive. Or shape-shift, which was probably his only chance at survival. I had a very, very bad feeling that I was about to watch my boyfriend get torn limb from limb, and there wasn't a damn thing I could do about it. And I happened to love each and every limb.

I was feeling better, stronger, but I didn't let on, for obvious reasons. Lichtenstein, safe in the knowledge that his hulking security stood watch behind me, leaned forward with obvious glee. The light from the arena below reflected off his pale face, the whites of his eyes, and even his teeth as he grinned.

Below, Kingsley took a shaky step backward. The creature before him was terrible to behold. It had a tiny slit for a mouth, and a strange, misshapen nose that, I swear to God, looked to have been attached sideways. His straggly hair grew only from the right side of his head.

My human side wanted to scream, to run, to hide, to call the Avengers; indeed, what I was seeing was straight out of a comic book, or a horror movie. The demon bitch inside was fascinated by all of it. She had long since stirred. Next to me, I somehow caught the smallest movement from Dr. Lichtenstein: A minor head nod. Down through the window and into the arena, I noted the creature return the same head nod, and charge forward on huge, powerful legs that must have taken Lichtenstein years to find.

The movement startled my boyfriend, who managed only to raise his hands and wobble some more, before the giant in front of him lashed out with a backhand that connected across Kingsley's face, and sent the big lug spinning sideways. I could hear nothing, but I might have *felt* the impact from the blow, all the way up here.

Oh, Kingsley, I thought.

I really, really didn't want to watch my boyfriend get killed before my eyes. Not so for Doctor Strange next to me. He was now sitting on the edge of his chair, a wicked gleam in his eyes, eyes that had seen far too much horror for my taste. Even for the taste of the demon bitch inside me, too.

And that was saying something.

Kingsley didn't so much recover as stop stumbling. And just as he did so, the monster was on him again, swinging another backhand that rocketed out faster than, I was certain, anything Kingsley had ever experienced before. My boyfriend, the biggest, hairiest, strongest thing I had ever seen, was lifted off the ground by that last punch.

The monster, whether directed by Lichtenstein or not, charged the wounded werewolf, and drove a knee into Kingsley's chest, and, if I had to guess, no doubt breaking a few of my boyfriend's ribs in the process. Kingsley fell to his back and the monster leaped upon him, unsealing a ferocious barrage of inhumanly, supernaturally, ungodly powerful blows.

"Stop him!" I shouted.

"Oh, but I can't, Samantha Moon. My son fights only to the death."

I tried to stand but was forced back into my chair by a hand that wouldn't give me an inch.

Lichtenstein looked from me to Gunther, then back down into the arena, where Kingsley had managed to roll out from under the hulking beast, and find his feet. A credit to his will to live. Perhaps adrenaline was moving the silver through him, but clearly not fast enough. He still looked punch-drunk, was clearly hurt, and was now favoring one side.

"Please, you have to stop this."

But Lichtenstein ignored me, and Gunther only applied more pressure to my shoulder, forcing me deeper into the chair.

Through the window, I watched the famous defense attorney try to mount his own attack. He lunged at the approaching monster, grabbed for a leg, only to be unceremoniously swatted away. Kingsley hit the ground, rolled, and was rewarded for his efforts by a swift kick to his ribs that kept him rolling.

I was feeling better, stronger, but I knew, even at full strength, I was little match for the brute behind me, let alone for the beast in the arena. Below, Kingsley had managed to catch one of the kicking feet. He held it, twisted. The creature roared through the slit in its mouth, although I couldn't hear a sound. Lichtenstein frowned, and I thought there might be hope yet, until the creature pounced on Kingsley, and I saw only flailing limbs and punching hands.

Lichtenstein nodded his approval, and as I thought desperately for a way to help the big oaf, I heard a commotion through the closed door behind us. A commotion that only seemed to be getting louder... and, for the moment, had gone unnoticed by Lichtenstein and his henchman.

And just as Kingsley managed to roll away from a flurry of flying fists, the door into the sitting room —or viewing room—burst open. We all turned in unison to see Franklin standing there, breathing hard, a long and bloody knife in one hand.

54.

Lichtenstein was on his feet. The brute holding me released his grip. I was up and out of my chair as quickly as I could move. Granted, not as fast as I wanted to, but I was pleased to feel my strength returning.

"Kingsley drank silver—" I began after dashing over to the butler's side. Never had I been happier to see the big, gangly, irritable servant.

"I know," said Franklin, cutting me off.

"Of course he knows," said Lichtenstein. "He's bonded with Kingsley. He knows all of his master's moods, his happiness and his pains. Franklin would be highly aware that his *new* master is in grave danger. Like a homing pigeon, Franklin would know just where to find him, too." The doctor completely ignored the one-sided battle that raged on in the arena below, a battle that, undoubtedly, would not end well for Kingsley. "And make no mistake, your new master is in the gravest of dangers."

I hadn't known Franklin could drive, and I hadn't known he was in the area either. Kingsley and I had driven here together. Maybe the creepy butler had taken an Uber ride. I didn't know.

"Stop him." Franklin motioned with the bloody knife toward the big window.

Lichtenstein, who stood before us and mostly blocked the big window, shook his head. I think the bastard just wanted to be a dick. He wanted to be cool. He wanted to show that he was in control, but I saw otherwise. I saw a man who was thunderously hurt, a man who felt betrayed beyond words. A man who seemed very much in love with the awkward-looking butler standing next to me.

Not in love, I realized. He was bonded, perhaps permanently. Franklin had been bonded too, but the bond hadn't held, and seemed to have easily trans-ferred to Kingsley. Not so much for Lichtenstein, who seemed to have it bad for the gangly butler.

Lichtenstein said, "Indeed. No doubt, Franklin perked up as soon as Kingsley began to feel the first pangs of silver coursing through him."

I looked at the butler. "But Yorba Linda is..." I shook my head. "More than an hour away."

Now the butt-hurt doctor found some humor in the situation, and it was, of course, at my expense. "So says the dragon lady."

I blinked, shot a glance at Franklin. "You can

shift?"

Franklin hadn't taken his eyes off Gunther, continuing to hold the long knife between them and us. Yes, us. I was squarely on the side of Franklin.

"Oh?" said Lichtenstein. "You are unaware of Franklin's many gifts? There is a reason why I consider him one of my greatest achievements—"

"I am not an achievement," said Franklin. "I am a man."

"You *were* a man. Now you are something far, far greater." Lichtenstein looked from him to me. "Franklin is a fellow shape-shifter, Samantha. Tell her, Franklin. Tell her what you can do. Tell her about the many gifts I have bestowed upon you. Gifts you scorn."

"We'll talk another time, Sam. Now is not—"

"Now is the perfect time to discuss all that I have given you, Franklin. Now is the perfect time to discuss your lack of appreciation for all that you are, thanks to me."

Franklin suddenly gritted his teeth, looking truly pained, and I realized that he was, vicariously, experiencing Kingsley's own suffering.

"You feel his pain, don't you, Franklin? Good. Good. I was hoping you would. What I didn't expect was to see the pain on your face. Good. Good. Now, maybe you can understand the pain you have caused—"

"Enough!" shouted Franklin. Gone was all trace of his tantalizingly mysterious European accent. "Sam, I do not change into anything. I can run quickly, so fast that I am often a blur to those around me."

"The Wind, I used to call him," said Lichtenstein proudly. "He ran like the wind, and I was so pleased. Never had we seen that tendency before. That particular trait. Yes, some of us can transform. Not all, Ms. Moon. One needs to be particularly evolved. And my Franklin was one such —"

Franklin gasped and stumbled, as if someone had suckered punch him. "Call him back," said Franklin, standing once again, the sword held surprisingly steady.

Lichtenstein glanced out the window and down into the arena, where from my vantage point I could see some movement but no details. "I'm afraid it's too late, my boy. You know how Nigel is once he gets the taste of blood. Like you, there's no stopping him."

Too late??

I was about to act, but Franklin beat me to it. He cried mightily and leaped forward, swinging the sword. I watched it plunge deep into the neck of Gunther. The guardsman didn't blink or react. And he continued not blinking or reacting, even as his head rolled off his wide shoulders.

I was too stunned to notice Lichtenstein escaping through a side panel, but I saw the panel swing shut.

"Forget him, Sam," gasped Franklin. "Can you teleport us down into the arena?"

55.

I told him I didn't know, and just as the words came tumbling out of my mouth, Franklin grunted and doubled over. I shot a desperate glance down into the arena...

The beast, Nigel, stepped away from Kingsley, who had dropped to his knees, holding his stomach. At one point, the creature had retrieved a sword, I didn't know when, but he held one in his hand now. Blood poured through Kingsley's fingers. The creature circled Kingsley, and I suspected I knew what was next.

I happened to like my boyfriend's head right where it belonged, thank you very much.

"Please, Sam," grunted Franklin, clearly suffering. How great his pain was in comparison to Kingsley's, I didn't know.

I forced myself to calm down—damn hard to do

with Gunther's own severed head staring up at me. I turned away, breathed, and summoned the single flame... or tried to. Only a flickering of light appeared in my thoughts. I tried again, and managed the same result, a formless flicker. No flame, not really. It was the colloidal silver still in me, making the flame nearly impossible to form.

I opened my eyes in time to see Kingsley reach feebly for the bastard's leg, but miss. Blood poured from his broken nose and bloodied mouth, pumped from his stomach and over his hands. The sword, I realized had traces of silver in it. The wound wasn't healing.

"Sam, please..." grunted Franklin.

Again I tried, and again nothing. On my fifth or sixth attempt, I was able to form the flame, but it winked out almost as quickly as it appeared. Shit, shit, shit. I opened my eyes one more time, and saw Nigel standing behind Kingsley. He lowered the weapon, taking aim like a golfer before a big swing.

"Sam..." moaned Franklin.

I summoned the flame again, held it, lost it. Tried again. Held it longer, lost it again. Tried again, held it... held it... and saw within it the dusty arena... my target landing place.

I didn't waste another second. My hand shot out, grabbed Franklin's wrist, and we vanished.

56.

Only to reappear in the arena.

I'd learned the technique on a special flight to the moon. Yes, the moon. It is a wondrous, jolting, life-altering thing to be in one place... and then find oneself in another. I see my destination first in the flame... and then I am there, in a blink. These days, the sensation of "jumping" is less and less jolting, but the experience was obviously new to Franklin. He stumbled to his knees and landed on his hands, his long knife skittering out of his grip. He shook his head like a wet dog and looked up... but I was already moving on wobbly legs. I tripped, caught myself on the palms of my hands, and, like a cornered hellcat, hurled myself at the thing called Nigel. In particular, at his cleaving sword arm.

I caught his wrist as my momentum carried me up and around the brute, much like a stripper circling a brass pole. Except, in this case, the pole was a thickly muscular arm that might as well have been dipped in cement. My prying fingers found no success. Sword and hand might as well have been glued together.

The thing called Nigel shook me loose, and I went tumbling head over rear, skidding to a stop in the dirt. Most of the skidding had been done on my face. As I snapped my head around, blood from my wounded chin flung to one side—

The sword blade came slashing down to Kingsley's exposed neck. But that was as far as it got... *toward* the neck. It was met by an explosion of sparks and a steel blade that held firm.

Franklin's own long knife was the only thing separating Kingsley from, well, having his head separated from his shoulders.

"Get him out of here, Sam," grunted Franklin.

I scrabbled over the dirt and grabbed hold of Kingsley's boot. "What about you, Franklin?"

"I... have... some... unfinished... business... here," he grunted, straining. "Hurry!"

I nodded, summoned the single flame.

This time, it came quicker, steadier. Except, for the briefest of moments, I didn't know where to go. As the flame wavered in my thoughts, empty, waiting, I cast my thoughts out around us, pushing beyond the walls of the arena, beyond the ceiling, and even the floor, too.

The floor...

Beneath us was a tunnel, perhaps manmade,

perhaps natural. I didn't know, and I didn't care. But there it was, clear as day. At least, to my inner eyes.

And then, we promptly disappeared. Or jumped. Or teleported.

Whichever way it happened, when I opened my eyes again, we were alone in the darkness of the tunnel, safe.

At least, for now.

57.

I projected my thoughts up, and directly above us, I saw Franklin and Nigel engaging in an old-school grudge match. Swords clashed and punches were thrown. Kicks, too. It looked like a knock-down, drag-out fight that I wanted no part of. Indeed, whatever was going on up there was personal. And what was going on down here, in the tunnel, was personal, too.

"You okay, big guy?" I asked the groaning hulk —or husk—of a man presently kneeling at my feet. The same position he had been in.

"I hurt, Sam."

"Don't be such a wuss."

I thought of the escaping Lichtenstein, and the boy, Luke, who had to be somewhere here in the castle. I needed to move. "You'll be safe down here, I think. Rest up, you big wimp."

"Where you going?"

"I have a boy to save."

I scanned my surroundings. My ability to see beyond me—through walls and fish guts even—was handy as hell, but it only went so far. I gave Kingsley a loving pat on his head—good doggy—and dashed off.

***

I found myself in a storage room, completely abandoned and forgotten. I frowned, hands on hips, knowing there was a young boy in this castle being bled dry.

Running through the castle, searching room by room would take too long. I thought about what I had to do, nodded to myself, and got to work. To jump, I always needed a target place to land, something I had seen before and could clearly imagine. In this case, Lichtenstein's lab of horrors.

I stumbled into a corpse, steadied myself by grabbing a cold shoulder. Once settled, I saw that I was alone. At least, no one living was here. I closed my eyes and scanned my surroundings, up, down and all around. Nothing of note, other than more rooms... and more monsters. No boy or Lichtenstein. So I picked a long hallway, summoned the flame, and jumped.

And appeared in the hallway. I scanned again, searching room by room, or as far as I could mentally see. Nothing. I leaped into the furthest, empty room. Scanned, leaped again. In this way, I popped in and out of rooms throughout the castle. The structure was immense, with many hidden rooms, corridors, and storage rooms. Many bedrooms and a great ballroom. I saw many, many lurching monsters. I also saw many of them lying seemingly comatose on cots and beds. Dozens of them. Precious few of them seemed truly alive. Most, if not all, were abominations, a testament to one man's out-of-control ego. Many of these creatures should be put out of their misery, allowed to rot away as nature intended.

I knew it was his successes that continued to drive Lichtenstein. Franklin was such a success. And there were, no doubt, others. But for every one success, there seemed to be a dozen who turned out mindless zombies.

Few noticed me or gave me much mind. Most sat or lurched or lay. The smell of decay was everywhere.

In and out I jumped. Room after room: back rooms, balconies, living rooms, even the kitchen. Grand rooms, not so grand rooms. I jumped and jumped, growing dizzier and dizzier with each flame I summoned, each new room, I appeared in.

One thing was certain, Lichtenstein was nowhere to be found. And neither was the boy.

In the master bedroom, as I stood next to what I assumed was Lichtenstein's rumpled bed, holding a bedpost to steady myself, I scanned the surrounding closets and hallways, and there, just behind a bookcase was a small, dark, hidden room, a room with a single bed inside. Tubes were attached to an elaborate machine of some sort. Refrigeration, I realized. The blood was going from the warm body of a young boy, straight to a cold-storage unit.

The boy. Luke. I held the image of the secret room, saw it in the flame, and jumped.

***

I stumbled, crashing over the small, occupied bed. I braced myself, gasping. One thing was certain, with each jump I was growing weaker... and hungrier. Indeed, I was only now discovering that I seemed to have only so many jumps in me.

Now, as I steadied myself, I found myself highly aware of the sweet scent of fresh blood. Blood that I knew was special and rich, pure and fresh. Magical blood.

The room was small and completely enclosed. No windows, no obvious doors, no light. No doubt, soundproof. A true torture chamber, of sorts.

Yes, I was hungry, but my heart broke for the little boy who had been forced to lay here, bleeding into a refrigeration-storage system, a boy who, upon checking for a pulse was alive, if barely.

I paced the small room, fighting myself, fighting the demon within, too. I knew I was surrounded by rarefied blood, but was it not also the blood of a distant ancestor, too? Were we not all related to the same ancient alchemist?

We were. The boy, however distant, *was* related to me.

That made him a relative, of sorts.

It did, dammit. It did.

I paced and fought my hunger. I needed to feed. I needed to wash the poison out of me, so to speak. Waves of dizziness washed over me. I quit pacing the small room, to conserve my energy.

Never, never had I been so hungry, so weak, so in obvious need of blood.

Wouldn't the blood go to waste? I reasoned.

Perhaps. But it was the blood of a relative, however distant. But didn't relatives give each other their kidneys? Maybe... but they are given. They are not taken.

I pushed my fingers through my hair—and made a decision.

I reached down to his arm. Gripped the tube leading into the vein just inside his elbow... and pulled.

58.

I knew I wasn't a monster, and I knew I couldn't feed on a boy, even if his own blood would go to waste or be destroyed later.

There had to be another way, and the demon bitch inside me could go straight to hell.

Blood poured free from the hole in his arm, the blood glowed brightly to my eyes. I plugged the hole with a finger, took his hand, and thought of the only place I knew that could help.

And summoned the single flame.

This would be, I knew, my last jump... unless I could find another source of sustenance.

***

It was a room I was familiar with, a room I had spent many agonizing hours in as I had once watched my own son, Anthony, fight for his life... and ultimately, turn into something far stronger than he had ever been before.

Now, as I stumbled forward, it was all I could do to not topple over the boy in my arms. A freestanding machine took the brunt of my shoulder. Luckily, it held firm and I stayed upright.

When I opened my eyes again, I found myself staring into the very startled face of a young girl, sitting up in a hospital bed. She was covered in tubes as well, her head shaved.

"Hi, sweetie," I said, gasping, trying not to faint on top of her.

"Are you an angel?" she asked.

I nodded, sucking air, although that did little to help my cause. I needed much, much more than air. "Something like that. Do you mind if I leave Luke here with you? He needs help really, really bad."

"Sure. I'll take care of him."

I smiled—or tried to—and set the boy as gently as I could next to her.

"Can you hit the nurse's button for me?" I asked.

She nodded eagerly and reached for the nurse call button located directly on the hospital bedrail. I stumbled out of the room, and regained my composure just as I passed a young nurse moving quickly toward the room I had just exited.

***

Gasping and stumbling, I followed the signage all the way to a very different laboratory, one that wasn't designed to raise the dead. At least, so they thought.

At the desk, I commanded the nurse to allow me into the back rooms. She did so, getting up and moving around and opening the door for me. Once through, I saw a male phlebotomist drawing blood from a young man. Both looked up at me.

"Can I help you?" asked the phlebotomist, and not very nicely.

"As a matter of fact, you can."

***

I drank deeply from the test tubes.

Not straight from the tap, so to speak, but nearly. Both men watched me, blank expressions in their eyes. Their mouths might have gone slack, too. Both expressions might have been my fault. After all, they'd been told to forget I was ever there.

I tossed the second empty capsule in a nearby trash can, having knocked it back like shots at a nightclub. I proceeded to do the same with the third and fourth capsule samples lined up on the tray. I ordered a fifth to be drawn. Both men complied. Once finished, I drank from that one, too, relishing the warmth, knowing I was activating the demon bitch inside me. In this moment, as my hunger had nearly spun out of control, I didn't care. A small price to pay, and I would deal with her later.

I ordered one more capsule for good measure, knocked it back, then considered my options. It was still just under two hours before midnight. I had some time before my daughter fulfilled a devilish destiny. I could wait at the intersection where my daughter's destiny would be fulfilled. Or, I could chase down the monster who preyed upon children. There was, after all, some unfinished business at Frankenstein's castle.

It didn't take me long to come to a conclusion. Besides, there had been something nagging at me, something the good doctor had said: *"Franklin is a fellow shape-shifter."*

The implication had been subtle. He could have been talking about Kingsley and me, but I suspected he just might have been including himself in the mix.

Sweet Jesus.

With my strength somewhat replenished—I would have needed perhaps ten more vials to be fully restored—I summoned the single flame.

59.

I found myself once again in the arena.

As far as scenes go, this was a terrible one. Terrible and exciting. There was Nigel's head, stacked neatly on his powerful, if not mismatched body. There was an arm nearby, cleaved clean through just below the elbow. And there was Franklin, squatting down, bracing himself with Nigel's own sword. Both hands gripped the pommel. His head hung down to his chest. I got the impression that the fight had only just ended. Franklin and the monster executioner had, I suspected, been fighting to the death this entire time.

I came over and squatted next to him. Blood dripped from his sword, oozing down the blade, to spill into the dry earth. All immortals bled, I knew. How important that lifeblood was, I didn't know. I doubted I could bleed to death, but I didn't know for sure. How much our blood differed from mortal blood, I didn't know that either. My own blood—thanks to Danny and one of his stupid schemes to control me—had tested normal years ago, whatever that meant.

"He had been like a brother to me, Sam," said Franklin, although he did not look up, his forehead still pressed into his hands, themselves holding the pommel of the sword.

I waited. The room was silent. How many creatures had perished in here?

"We had both been successes, as Lichtenstein would call us. He'd had so many failures. Whereas, my intellect developed rapidly, Nigel's had not. I didn't care. He was, like I said, a brother to me. Although we emerged into these bodies, fully formed, we had a learning process to complete, a maturation process, if you will. To be blunt, we were like children, experimenting with these new bodies, these powerful bodies. Later, Lichtenstein chose one of us to kill for him, and the natural choice had been Nigel, who'd always been a little stronger, and always a little simpler. Nigel didn't complain. He took on the role proudly. Anything to please his creator."

Franklin spit into the earth... a big, bloody wad of the stuff. There might have been a tooth in the mix. He continued: "I grew to hate Lichtenstein. I saw him for the monster he was. How I was able to break my bond with him, I don't know."

"And, later, he became bonded with you," I

said.

Franklin glanced at me. "You know your monster history, Sam."

"I happen to be an ace detective."

"Indeed. Yes, later, Lichtenstein chose me to bring him back from the dead, using his own patented techniques of monster-making, if you will. Once he drank the arsenic, I considered leaving him for dead. But the bond I had with him at the time, although tenuous at best, was enough for me to fulfill his dying request: to bring him back from the dead. I regret that decision now."

"Do you remember who you were?" I asked.

"Before Lichtenstein brought me back from the dead? Sometimes. Scattered memories. Incoherent memories. Only Lichtenstein has managed to retain his old memories of his past life, and even then, I suspect he forgets. Like you, there is another in him, fighting for control."

"You as well?" I asked.

"All of us. But many here are operating at a very base level, not fully functioning. I can hardly imagine a highly evolved dark master showing interest in them."

"I need to find him," I said.

"I know, Sam."

"He can't keep preying on innocent children."

"I know that, too."

"I might have to kill him, Franklin. Will you be okay with that?"

He continued looking at me. "I wouldn't have it

any other way."

"Do you know where I can find him?"

"My guess? He's waiting for you by the lake."

"The lake?"

Franklin held my gaze, and I nodded, finally getting it. Of course, it all made sense.

"Thank you, Franklin. Are you going to be okay?"

"Don't worry about me, Sam. I have work to do here. Work I should have done long ago." He nodded to himself, and a pained look crossed his face. Finally, he glanced at me. "Just be careful. The doctor hasn't managed to stay alive this long for nothing."

For the first time ever, I gave Franklin a hug. He didn't hug me back, although he *leaned* in my direction. Good enough.

I dashed off.

60.

I considered teleporting to the lake, but decided to conserve my energy. Besides, with all my jumping, I now knew the layout of the castle like the back of my hand.

As I ran, I checked my new Apple Watch, which flashed on every time I turned my wrist. Handy when you're running. Not so handy if you're trying to remain hidden from bad guys, say, in the dark. I wondered if the Apple geniuses had thought of *that*. Tonight, I had dressed up for my night out with Kingsley. Granted, once in the hotel room, I had changed to jeans and running shoes. But the cool Apple Watch remained. We would see if I ever saw it again. When shape-shifting to Talos, I tended to lose a lot of clothes and jewelry and watches.

I rounded a curve and spotted the bright light at the far end of the tunnel. At least, bright to my eyes.

The cave entrance. Or, in my case, the exit. At the mouth of the opening, I nearly gasped at the epic view before me: the lake stretched nearly as far as the eye could see, glittering with life, sparkling with energy, undulating with movement.

The cliff itself was a steep drop into the water. Cool night air buffeted me. It was good to be free, good to be out of the stifling tunnel, which had proved to be hotter than I was comfortable with. Boulders surrounded the opening; indeed, the cave would have been nearly impossible to spot from the lake itself.

It didn't take very long for me to pick out the single rowboat in the center of the lake, or the two men in it. My eyesight is spectacular—as clear as it could be, in fact—but at this distance, even I couldn't make out who they were.

But I could guess.

I stripped off my clothes, and, yes, carefully removed my fancy new watch, too. I laid everything over the rocks, easy to spot from the air. Then I stood upon the highest boulder... and prayed like hell I wasn't too weak to shape-shift.

And I kept praying even as I leaped out into the air... and summoned the single flame, inside of which I saw Talos, waiting and watching me. Arms spread out, I arched up and out over the rocks, then began plummeting down. I didn't jump nearly as far out as I had hoped, and I was seconds away from dashing face-first into the outcropping below, when the image of Talos rushed towards me. A nanosecond later, I felt the wind catch in my huge, leathery wings. The membrane snapped taut, and instead of crashing into the boulder, I only grazed them. I flapped once, twice, and gained some altitude.

That was close, Talos. I'm sorry.

Rough night?

You have no idea.

Oh, I have some idea. Once Talos and I were united, he had access to all my thoughts and memories. There was literally nothing hidden from the giant flying beast. *But there is good news, Sam.*

What's that?

I'm as strong as I ever was.

That's very, very good news.

I circled the single rowboat which sat adrift in the center of the lake. Rufus sat at the helm, holding an oar in each hand. His job seemed to be Castle Lichtenstein's official ferryman. The passenger was none other than Lichtenstein himself. Unlike my eyes, Talos's own pierced the darkness at great distance and with supernatural ease. Lichtenstein stood in the small boat. Surely not advisable. I also noted he wasn't wearing a life jacket. Tsk, tsk. Neither man gave off an aura. And, like other immortals, neither sparkled with life. Hell, the buzzing mosquitoes around them gave off more light.

The walking dead, I thought.

Lichtenstein's pale face angled up, following me as I circled the boat. I wasn't sure what to do next, or what to expect next, but what finally did happen didn't surprise me very much.

Not one bit.

Lichtenstein gathered himself... and then leaped into the air. The transformation was instant and explosive. Something dark, slithery and monstrous splashed down into the dark water. If my eyes weren't deceiving me, the creature seemed to be emerging from the air itself, through a rift in time and space, perhaps. I was reminded of a clown car with its dozens of passengers, all emerging from one tiny door. In this case, one fabulously long beast, its rubbery hide gleaming in the moonlight, as it continued to splash down into the water. I noted the thick, undulating muscles rippling along its sleek hide. Finally, its forked, barbed tail came into view, and splashed down last.

There, just beneath the surface, I watched a shadowy, serpentine creature weave deeper and deeper until it nearly disappeared from view. The lake wasn't quite deep enough for it to truly disappear; indeed, I could just make out its long, undulating form moving slowly over the lake bed, dark against the glittering water. Like its human counterpart, the worm-like creature gave off little auric light. If the creature was anything like Talos, then Lichtenstein had full control of it. He was, I suspected, ready for a fight.

It was time to give it to him.

Are you ready, Talos? I asked.

As ready as I ever will be, Sam.

We got this, I thought.

Easy for you to say. You're safe and sound in

my world.

I grinned, hesitated for only a moment, then tucked my leathery wings in and dove down...

Down, down...

Down into the black water...

J.R. RAIN

61.

It occurred to me, as I splashed down into the lake, that should I kill this massive snake-like thing, Lichtenstein himself wouldn't die.

No, I thought, but he would be trapped in whatever world he'd currently teleported to, when he'd switched bodies with the beast.

This is true, came Talos's confirming words.

Is this creature from your world, Talos? I asked, as I oriented underwater.

No, Sam. It is from another.

Have you ever seen anything like it?

I'm afraid not.

I absorbed this information as I flapped Talos's mighty wings just beneath the lake's surface. I'd discovered long ago that Talos made for a most excellent underwater conveyance. His massive wings seemed particularly suited to underwater propulsion. I picked up speed, flapping my wings hard, forcing the water down and behind me. Talos gave me complete control over his massive and beautiful and powerful body. I was determined more so than ever that he would make it home, too.

I admire your determination, Sam. But do not forget: like Lichtenstein, should I perish in this world, you would be forever stuck in mine, as well.

Below me, I could see the massive, serpentine creature moving over the lake floor, a dark silhouette moving against the brighter background that was the lake and its teeming life forms. I had him trapped here in the lake. Or he had me trapped. Either way, now was the time to take him out. Now was the time to end his plundering of the dead, his abominable creations, his God complex, his murdering of innocent children. Now was the time to end it all.

I knew the risks involved tonight. I knew there was a chance I might never return home. That I might never get a chance to save my daughter from the destruction that awaited her at midnight. And should I get Talos killed tonight, I knew that I might find myself trapped in an alien world, forever.

I knew all of this and more, but most importantly, I knew right from wrong. And what Lichtenstein was doing—and what he had been doing throughout the decades and centuries—was wrong on so many levels. Sure, he gave the world Franklin, and I might even someday be friends with the sourpuss butler. But Lichtenstein had also given the world much pain, too.

Too much, I thought. *It ends tonight.*

Apparently, Lichtenstein and his pet worm were thinking the same thing. It quit slithering along the lake bed and turned and faced me.

I paused, hovering, Talos's giant wings undulating in the water. His vision was damn good, but not so much underwater, although still better than mine ever would be. Along the lake floor, thousands of tiny fish pulsated with an inner light, as did the swaying plant life. The giant serpent that was Lichtenstein didn't emit any light.

And then it charged.

I wanted in on the fun, too, although I didn't so much charge as I flapped Talos's mighty wings, hard, surging through the water and straight for the massive, slithering creature.

62.

The force of the collision sent me spinning sideways through the water in a hail of bubbles. As I righted myself, it came at me again, and I swiped Talos's clawed hand and raked it along its underbelly.

Blood poured free from its deep wounds, clouding the lake, and I briefly wondered what alien blood might do to Lake Elsinore's fragile ecosystem —hell, to the whole world—that is, until its whip-like tail lashed out from seemingly nowhere. I hadn't noticed the spikes before, but I sure noticed them now, especially as they dug deep into my right leg.

I felt pain, I think, for the first time ever in Talos's body. God-awful, excruciating pain. The barbs in the tail, I was sure, were poisoned. Even more crazy, I could feel them digging in independently, like fingers.

Sweet Jesus...

Now, a thick, muscular coil wrapped around my upper torso, pinning both wings to me. As I struggled, more coils looped around and around, and now, out of the bubbles and nebula of blood, came the monstrous face with its circular rows of teeth, a face that attached to Talos's shoulder. I screeched as the hundreds of teeth took hold.

We spun together deeper into the lake.

Deeper and deeper...

***

We settled on the lakebed, scattering silver, luminescent fish. Silt and blood exploded up and around us.

The coils constricted, even as the creature's jagged maw dug deeper into my shoulder. It heaved and undulated and drank deeply from Talos in what I imagined were great, bloody, heaping gulps.

I struggled, but the coils might as well have been from steel cables of comparable size. Black-ness encroached on my vision, and for the first time in a long, long time, I felt a strong need to breathe. Talos needed air. Worse, the poison was doing a number on the big guy. I suspected some of his internal organs might be shutting down or slowing down. Not to mention he was losing a lot of blood, thanks to the leech presently attached to his shoulder. I'd done a terrible job at keeping him alive.

Something broke inside of Talos. Perhaps his ribs. Perhaps his great spine, perhaps a wing. I didn't know, but I felt it reverberate through me, and I nearly sucked in a great snoutful of water.

I had one option, and one option only—that is, if I didn't want my magnificent friend to die—and if I didn't want to trap myself in his world forever, wherever the hell that might be.

I summoned the single flame, and saw the lake's nearby shoreline within it...

***

A shocking jolt later, and I was stumbling through weeds and coughing violently. As I coughed, great geysers of fire erupted and burned through the sporadic lake grass.

When I was done coughing, I sucked in a lot of air and winced. That is, if the great, hulking Talos could even wince. I doubted he had a very expressive face, but then again, what did I know? But, yeah, definitely a broken rib or two.

Or three, Sam.

I'm sorry, Talos. That was all my fault.

I'm not arguing. Okay, I'm ready.

Ready for what?

I think you know what.

But your ribs, the poison...

I'll deal with all that later. Go get the bastard, Sam.

I wanted to grin, but we were in too much pain to do so. I sensed this had gotten personal for Talos, and I didn't blame him. A heinous giant worm had tried to crush the life out of him, poison him, and feed from him, all in one felled swoop.

I stretched out Talos's massive wings and leaped as high as I could, all too aware that the poisoned barbs had taken effect. We were clearly weaker than before. Not to mention, I had no idea just how much blood the giant sucker had drained from the old boy.

I dipped and dropped and sagged on my ascent, but soon righted myself and angled over the lake. There. A long, dark form streaking just under the lake's surface, pushing a domed wall of water before it. It swam at a remarkable rate, more reminiscent of a torpedo than anything else. At this rate, it wouldn't take long for Lichtenstein to reach the far end of the lake.

Check that. It wouldn't take Lichtenstein long to reach the solitary rowboat bobbing a few dozen feet from shore. Or the man presently sitting in it, a man who had no idea what was bearing down on him.

I dipped my wing down, turned sharply, and dove like a bat out of hell, which I very well might be.

***

The guy in the boat seemed to spot the approaching wall of water for the first time. He stood on wobbly feet and gripped the starboard rail with both hands.

I had to redirect the creature, and the only way I could think of doing it was lowering my good shoulder, tucking in my wings, and slamming as hard as I could into the monstrosity that was Lichtenstein.

I wasn't entirely prepared for the sheer force of the impact. An explosion of light filled my head, and I tumbled head over tail, until I finally sank below the surface. I could only hope that the collision had rocked Lichtenstein's world just as much—or more so. Definitely more so.

I gathered my wits, shaking my head clear, and stood in the shallows of the lake—undoubtedly looking like Godzilla rising from the depths. As the world came back into focus, I saw two things: the first was a brief glimpse of the man in the boat, paddling furiously in the opposite direction. Smart move. The second was a black maw full of the sharpest damn teeth I'd ever seen bearing down on me. So much for rocking Lichtenstein's world.

I didn't dive down. I didn't fly away.

Hell, I didn't even think.

Instead, I waited.

A wall of roiling, black water preceded the approaching creature. Bubbling froth filled the space between its dagger-like teeth. A nightmare was approaching me, bearing down on me, ready to launch itself at me, and still, I stood my ground in the shallow water.

Standing my ground was dumb. Talos had been drained of blood, crushed and poisoned. By all rights, I should take to the air, and safely transition back to my vampire self, and release Talos to his own world where, I hoped, he could heal.

And here I stood, water dripping from my great, leathery wings, watching a watery landslide of teeth and hate approach, a creature that was clearly at an advantage in the water.

Ready, Talos?

As ready as I'll ever be.

I'm not entirely sure I remember how—

You'll remember, Sam.

I nodded, and steadied myself... and took as deep a breath as Talos's damaged ribs would allow. And then, I took some more air. I nearly gasped, nearly lost the air. I steadied myself, calmed myself.

And when Lichtenstein's worm launched itself out of the water and directly at me, I let loose with a magnificent blast of superheated fire that surprised even me. It vomited from my mouth in a continuous eruption. How my lips didn't burn off, I didn't know.

Turned out, I had a pretty damn good aim. The fire raced out and up, arcing slightly, and directly into the black, toothy cavern that was Lichtenstein's face. The creature pulled up, screeching. A wave of water splashed over me, but the blasting fire sliced through the water, turning it into instant steam. In this case, fire trumped water. Especially when the fire was dragon fire.

The monstrous worm had caught fire from the inside and was now combusting from within. It writhed and splashed down in the water, and still, I blasted it with one continuous, vomitous conflagration of apocalyptic hellfire. I continued even as the creature began to glow from within. And still, I blasted it until it was finally entirely consumed in flames.

I shut my mouth and the fire winked out of existence. I half-expected my own lips to be on fire, or my tongue or inner cheeks... but nothing. Perhaps a little warmth, but nothing more.

Yeah, I thought. Magical.

I was, however, out of breath and still sick from the poison. As I sucked in some air, filling Talos's massive lungs and alternately gasping from the pain in his ribs, I watched the last of the burning lamprey smolder on the lake surface, I wondered what science would make of the charred remains? And would the alien organic matter pose a threat to the lake? To humans? To our world at large?

Sirens wailed nearby. Further way, cars had stopped along the lake's edge. The smell of cooked flesh filled the air. A not entirely unpleasant smell.

How are you feeling, Talos?

The poison is leaving my system.

I have a car accident to stop.

I know, Sam.

You up for one more jump?

I'm up for anything.

I smiled and hoped so. I didn't know the time,

but my guess was that it was too close to midnight for my liking. With flashing lights pulling up to the lake, I summoned the flame and within it, I saw the image of the intersection in my dreams—in particular, the airspace above the intersection—and I promptly disappeared.

To hell with the burning alien remains.

63.

I appeared high enough in the sky to avoid telephone wires and trees and low-flying drones. I really didn't want to think what could happen if I materialized on top of something. Or inside something. I suspected it wouldn't be good.

You suspect correctly, Sam.

Figured as much. So how you doing, big fella?

Stronger, but not out of the woods yet.

And here I am putting you through the wringer.

I've been put through worse.

There, down on the street corner below, next to the busy intersection, was the very same bank I had seen a dozen times in my dreams, the same bank that had, over the past few days, come into striking clarity. So much so that I had finally seen the time on its marquee, exactly midnight.

The exact same time it was displaying now.

I nearly dove down out of the sky—that is, until I noticed two things: one, my daughter's car—that is, the one I had seen in my dreams—was nowhere to be seen; and, two, the time on the bank's marquee was flashing: 12:00... 12:00... 12:00.

Broken, I thought. *The damn clock was broken.*

My heart sank and I nearly let out a squeal, or whatever the equivalent was coming from Talos's lips. As I circled, feeling seriously sick to my stomach (or Talos's stomach), I could also surmise that the intersection was clearly not the scene of a recent and horrific crash. There was no evidence of fresh gas and oil spilled over the roadway, or fresh skid marks—a concept I knew Anthony would giggle at (and maybe me, too, under different circumstances). Anyway, there was no evidence anywhere that four young high schoolers had recently lost their lives.

It hadn't happened yet. I was sure of it.

Hope swelled in me.

I needed to land somewhere, to clear my head, to catch my breath, so to speak. Maybe the bank. Maybe that nearby Starbucks over there. Mostly, I needed this long, crazy-ass night to come to an end.

But not without my daughter, I thought. Not without her safely in my arms, preferably curled up on the couch, sharing some rocky road ice cream... and most likely, bawling our eyes out.

I chose a dimly lit Chick-fil-A, which appeared to be closed for the night. Now, I didn't know the time, but I knew it had to be fairly close to midnight.

A helluva night, I thought. And it still wasn't over.

I settled in, adjusting Talos's massive claws at the edge of the tiled roof. Unlike New York, Vegas, and Hollywood, no one walked in Rancho Cucamonga at night. The city itself was vast and sprawling—one of the few places in Southern California that allowed drivers to legally drive 50-55 on their streets. Their long-ass streets. Rancho also sported one of the greatest views in Southern California: of the magnificent Mount Baldy, the highest point in Southern California at 10,000 feet. The city itself climbed as high up the mountain's slope as it could before the roads petered out into restricted farmland and blocked government land. Additionally, Rancho Cucamonga and its sister-in-crime city, the nearby Ontario, boasted the most shopping centers of any city, in any state, in any country, on any continent, on any planet. Ever.

Perhaps I exaggerated.

Or not.

The two massive shopping malls—Ontario Mills and Victoria Gardens—spilled out into the surrounding streets like a college championship riot, expanding out into the city in ever-widening gyre. The malls themselves acted as hubs, and the many, many, *many* shopping centers were the spokes. So many restaurants, so many Lazy Dog and B.J.'s Cafes, so many Best Buys and Kohl's. And Starbucks. My God, the sheer number of Starbucks.

And here, I perched on one of its busiest spokes. Victoria Gardens was behind me and a Chick-fil-A was beneath me. A Starbucks, a USBank, a local pizza place, three or four hotels, a Lowe's, a Sonic, a sushi place, another pizza place... and about two dozen more shopping centers within eyesight. Granted, I sat high on a roof—and Talos could see all the way to China—but you get the point.

And there was the intersection itself, of course. As in, the intersection of my dreams, the crossroads where I'd been watching a big rig run a red light and kill my daughter dozens of times, over and over. Haven and Fourth Street.

I took in some air, and noted that Talos's ribs didn't quite hurt as much with the inhalation.

You're healing, I thought.

You noticed. Sitting here is doing me some good.

That's a relief. Not more than twenty minutes earlier I had been lying on a lake bed, with a giant alien monster wrapped tightly around me, doing its damnedest to squeeze the life out of me. Or out of Talos.

Had I really toasted alive the very man behind the Frankenstein mythos?

You did. And quite thoroughly too.

He was going to kill us.

Of that, I have no doubt.

Where was he now? I wondered. Stranded in some far away, forgotten world? I didn't know, and I didn't want to know. Depressingly, his fate could have easily been my fate tonight.

I shuddered and tucked in Talos's wings a little tighter, and huddled there in the shadows, high upon the Chick-fil-A, as the minutes and hours rolled by...

***

I wasn't asleep, but I was in a sort of suspended hibernation: aware of my surroundings, but also, deeply contained within myself. I knew Talos had spent the time healing, and I was happy he'd had these quiet moments. Truthfully, I was happy, too. I needed to shut my brain off from all the craziness. Enough already.

Additionally, it was nice to relax in someone else's body, without slipping into my usually deep, dark, dead sleep. The experience was enlightening, and much appreciated—but something had awakened me out of it. As I blinked and turned my head this way and that, emerging back into Talos's body, I saw what had alerted me:

The familiar big rig, chugging down Haven Avenue—and going far, far, far too fast. The bastard. I turned my head and saw the oh-so-familiar Honda Accord, going nearly as fast. The Accord had the green light. It also had my daughter.

And there she was, too, in the front seat. And there, much further down the road and speeding like a madwoman in the same direction, was Allison's banged-up Camry. My daughter and her friends had somehow managed to lose my witchy friend. Now, Allison was doing all she could to shorten the distance. But she was going to be too late.

Of course, she would be too late, and of course, they had somehow ditched my friend. The accident was happening, as it happened, every night in my dreams for the past few weeks.

Like hell it is, I thought. *You ready, Talos?*

Oh, yeah.

I spread his giant wings—and leaped from the Chick-fil-A.

64.

The streets were mostly clear.

There was a single car waiting at the red light, in the outside lane. The big rig was coming up fast in the inside lane. Had this been business as usual, the big rig would be slowing down about now for the light. Except this wasn't business as usual, and, as I came swooping down along the intersection, I could see the driver's head lolled to one side. He was, I realized, either asleep or dead from, say, a heart attack.

Had I been particularly adept at jumping, perhaps I could have jumped into the cab of the speeding truck and wrested the steering wheel out of the passed-out driver's hands. Except I didn't know how to steer one of those damn things. And when I jumped as a giant dragon bat, I re-appeared as a giant dragon bat.

I considered my options, as I'd been considering them since the dream first occurred to me. A runaway big rig was going to end badly for someone, maybe a lot of someones.

But not my daughter. Not on this night.

My only conclusion, as the two vehicles inevitably converged upon the intersection, was to tackle one problem at a time.

And so I gained altitude and banked to port, coming up along Fourth Street, and behind the Honda Accord. At least, I would have expected her to somehow convince her friends to leave her behind at, say, an all-night Denny's. But there she was, in the front seat, plain as day. I doubted she could read Talos's mind, but then again, her remarkable abilities just might transcend alien species.

But here we all were. Dancing with fate.

Just how strong are you, Talos?

I guess we're going to find out, came his words, *if you're thinking what I think you're thinking.*

You would know better than most.

I flapped my wings hard, once, twice, and rocketed down—

***

I came up behind the speeding Honda, adjusted my wings this way and that until I was lined up over the roof. Had there been a sunroof, the passengers would have gotten quite the surprise.

As the big rig and the Accord converged upon the intersection, I reached out with Talos's massive claws... and broke through the driver's side and passenger's side windows. Screams from within. I even heard Tammy screaming. Talons curled through the now-broken glass, I gripped the roof's sheet metal, and now, I was lifting and flapping my wings as hard as I could, even while the speeding, out-of-control big rig bore down upon us from the right.

We were airborne, but I didn't have time or space or strength to gain the altitude necessary for the truck to pass safely underneath. So I did the next best thing.

I increased my speed, flapping faster and faster, and just as the truck roared behind me, clipping my own tail, we cleared the intersection.

***

A few hundred feet away, once I slowed down, I eased the car down along the side of the road. With the kids inside still screaming, I leaped up into the air, flapped my wings hard, gained some altitude, and turned back toward the runaway rig.

***

I banked to port, and raced down Haven, behind the speeding big rig.

The road curved ahead, just enough so that

something—say a hurtling out-of-control big rig—would careen off the road and directly into whatever was in front of it.

And, in this case—big surprise—it was a Starbucks.

Hell, I would have been surprised if it *wasn't* a Starbucks. I flapped hard, doing my best to catch up with the rig, itself going close to eighty miles an hour, maybe faster. I could just see the driver slumped against the window, his face pressed against the glass. Out cold or dead. He'd better hope he was dead, by the time I was done with him.

The good news: it was late and the Starbucks looked closed. The bad news: there was still a small crew inside. Through a side window, I could see one of them wiping down tables.

My options were rapidly running out—hell, I barely had time to catch up to the hurtling death trap, let alone formulate any kind of workable plan —I did the only thing I could think of.

I dropped down onto the rig's cab and pulled off the roof. It tore away surprisingly easily, especially when you're a hulking, twenty-foot monster with claws that could make a velociraptor envious.

Now, with the metal roof peeled free like a sardine can, I bid Talos adieu and summoned the single flame...

The transformation was instant, as it always was, and I went from straddling the roof cabin, to dropping down inside, naked as the day I was born. I pulled the slumped driver aside, leaped over him and jammed my bare foot down as hard as I could on the brake, certain I was going to smash the whole contraption down through the floorboards.

And now, the truck was slewing sideways, threatening to roll. I held the wheel firm and somehow righted the son-of-a-bitch. I rode the brake hard for the next few seconds as tree saplings were obliterated before my eyes.

Finally, finally, the whole damn thing came to a shuddering, skidding, screeching halt, just a foot or two away from the Starbucks side wall, which sported plenty of glass and now two frightened workers. With luck, Starbucks would be open in the morning, right on schedule. You're welcome, world.

Next to me, the driver moaned. He was alive. My guess, judging by the dark spot in his aura over his chest, he'd had a heart attack. There was a lightweight windbreaker on the passenger's seat that looked like it might have been a 2X. I grabbed it, slipped it on, and leaped straight out of the roof. Before I landed, I had already donned the windbreaker, which fit me like a short dress.

The Starbucks employees had eased out of the coffee shop like two frightened kittens. I smiled and suggested they forget me. I didn't see any security cameras, and so I dashed off to check on my daughter.

65.

I gave my daughter's friends the collective false memory that they'd suffered the damage in a drive-thru accident. And because all the kids were high in the car—including my daughter—I let the driver believe he'd also knocked over a golden arch.

I next removed the memory that my daughter had been in the car at all. And because these new friends of hers were punks, I was tempted to remove the memory of their friendship altogether, except I didn't want to overstep my boundaries. And my daughter would still remember, of course, and it would be terrible, I suppose, if her friends had forgotten her.

"Yes, it would be terrible," said Tammy on the bus bench next to me. Allison had dashed off to the local Taco Bell for some drinks and food... and to also give me time alone with Tammy.

"You get no vote in the matter," I said to her. "Zero. And I will work out any moral complexities on my own, thank you very much."

I'd had the driver and his two friends—all older than Tammy, I might add—pull his car into a Jack-in-the-Box parking lot and call his parents, since he was still too high to drive. And while I was at it, I implanted within them all to never drink and drive again—or get high and drive again. For the rest of their lives. Period.

"Was that last part necessary, Mom?"

"It was, yes."

"But you can't control people."

"I can when they nearly kill my daughter."

"It wasn't Derek's fault. You know that better than anyone."

"You're high. You were all high—"

Tammy lay her hand on my wrist—her very warm hand. "I know you're uncomfortable with this, Mom. I can see it and feel and hear it, like, oozing out of you. I can also see that you experimented with... marijuana... when you were eighteen. I get it. I'm young. But I'm also not like you, or like anyone. I'm old beyond my years."

"Are you now?"

"I am, whether you like it or not."

"Well, if I hadn't swooped in tonight, you would have died at the ripe old age of fourteen."

She opened her mouth to rebuff that, but had nothing.

I went on, "Yes, you can read minds. Yes, you

have information available to you that few will ever have or dream of having. That does not mean you have lived enough years on this planet to make good choices."

"But the accident wouldn't have been our fault —"

"Was it a smart decision to let Derek drive high tonight?"

"I can hardly control him—he's seventeen!"

"And aren't you a little young to have friends who are two and three years older?"

"I like them. They like me."

"Or do they like you because you, somehow, always know the right thing to say to them? Or, somehow, you just so happen to like exactly what they like, too? Or you, somehow, just happen to know what's funny to them, or what they're thinking?"

She shrugged, looked out the window. There were a half-dozen Ontario and Rancho Cucamonga police cruisers with flashing lights, parked willy-nilly around the big rig. An ambulance had come just a few minutes earlier. They had just extracted the driver carefully. From what I could gather, he seemed to have made it.

I said, "We don't need show off to win friends. We are pretty awesome in our own right, don't you think?"

"Well, I am," she said, looking at me sideways. "You're kind of a dork."

"An awesome dork," I said.

"That's an oxymoron."

"Hey," I said, "who are you calling an ox?"

"And who are you calling a moron?" she finished, an old joke, and we giggled and sat back on the bus bench.

After a few minutes, I said, "Do you think it might be a good idea to have friends more your age?"

"Maybe."

"Growing up fast isn't all it's cracked up to be," I said. "What's the rush? You'll be a grownup your whole life. Why not have fun with kids your own age, and do fun things?"

"Really?' she asked. "Roller skating?"

"I did," I said, knowing she had picked up my errant thought. "It's good, clean fun. Nothing wrong with roller skating and laughing and drinking a Coke and learning new skating tricks."

"You are such a nerd."

"Nerds are fun, too."

She smiled and looked back at the still-steaming big rig. "How are they going to explain the roof being ripped off?"

"They'll assume it was a tree or something."

"And you really jumped in there and stopped the truck?"

"I did."

"Maybe I should call you Super Nerd."

"Call me anything you want, baby."

"Mom?"

"Yeah, sweetie?"

"Why do you love us so much?"

"Because it's the law," I said.

She giggled and I pulled her in close, and we sat like that until Allison returned with some food. My kid, after all, had the munchies. I did, too.

Except, of course, I was high on life.

***

I called to tell my client, Roy Azul, the truth— the whole truth, so help me God—about everything creepy that lurked under the surface of Lake Elsinore. I unloaded on poor Roy every gory, frightening detail. He was amazed and shocked, elated and chagrined. And then, I made a reservation for my family to have a little vacation there, at half the usual price, which was the barter we'd agreed upon when he'd hired me to find evidence of the creature in the lake.

After he took my credit card and I had my reservation confirmation number, I only felt a little guilty when I removed Roy's memory of having ever met me or hired me. Then, a little sadly, I also took away his memory of the monster's fleeting shadow that he'd seen in Lake Elsinore.

When I arrived with my kids at Lake Elsinore for a much-needed getaway, we would be guests like any other guests of his fine establishment. And our lake vacation would be monster-free. *Except for me.*

66.

It was a week later, and I was in the Occult Reading Room.

I'd swung by with a few questions, but the Librarian said he had a surprise for me. He asked me to wait, which was what I was doing now, waiting and ignoring the slithery, oily whisperings from the darkest of the books.

During the past seven days, my daughter and I had, miracle of miracles, grown closer. After all, she wasn't scheduled to like me again until, officially, five years from now, when she was nineteen and in college and missing her mom.

This was, I knew, unprecedented. After all, the ages of thirteen to nineteen were, officially, the dark ages. As in, parents were in the dark when it came to their teenagers.

Truthfully, I thought I'd lost her there for a

while. The drinking, the smoking, and now the drugs. The older friends. Her snotty, piss-poor attitude. Yes, I saw a lot of myself in her. At least, at that age. I hadn't exactly been a peach either. And, yes, I understood that kids—hell, everyone—had some rebellion in them. After all, who wants to be told what to do? Especially when you're a fourteen-year-old mind reader who thinks she knows more than everyone else.

Of course, that had been before she'd gotten the fear of God put into her. I suspected she previously hadn't taken my prophetic dreams very seriously. She had hinted as much. I think it didn't get real until she saw the runaway truck coming for her. Nothing like a near-death experience to bring a mama and daughter together, especially when said mama had saved the day. In fact, there might even be a chance she now thought I was cool.

Okay, now I was pushing it.

Lichtenstein. Franklin had taken it upon himself to rid the castle of the most simple of the creatures —those with little, if any, reasoning faculties. How he'd gotten rid of them, I didn't really want to know, but I was led to understand that a bonfire in the central court had been put liberally to use.

With that said, there remained about six Lichtenstein monsters who had been fairly advanced. All six now resided with Kingsley, and all were working for him in some capacity, especially Chef, as Kingsley now called Pierre. Apparently, the monsters had all taken to the big hairy oaf. Which was one reason I'd stayed away this week. I'd seen enough of Lichtenstein's creations for a lifetime, thank you very much. With all this free labor and the adoring love of his subjects, I was beginning to think Kingsley's own mansion in the Yorba Linda foothills was beginning to look suspiciously like the castle out at Lake Elsinore.

Speaking of which, Raul the *brujo* had taken it upon himself to burn the remains of the giant lake monster. I friended him on Facebook and thanked him in the messenger app for helping save my ass. He hadn't responded yet. Maybe old *brujos* from a long and powerful magical lineage didn't know how to use Facebook Messenger?

There were a few long-distance grainy images of what might have been a giant dragon fighting a giant earthworm circulating the internet. Then again, it could have been one giant blotch fighting another giant blotch, with bursts of fire here and there. Most people thought these images were photoshopped. God bless the cynics of the world. They kept people like me safely in the shadows.

There was the small matter of the intersection camera's footage in Rancho Cucamonga. Luckily, I thought ahead, made a few inquiries, and, miracle of miracles, the digital footage had mysteriously been deleted. Probably for the best. I was fairly certain the world wasn't ready to see a giant vampire bat swoop in and carry off a car full of teenagers.

Somewhere out there, trapped in a distant world,

was a man named Edward Lichtenstein. He was immortal, which meant he would be trapped there for a very, very long time. Did he deserve it? I dunno, but he sure as hell deserved something. How many young alchemists had he killed for their magical blood I didn't know, but I suspected many, if not dozens.

Yeah, he could just rot out there, wherever *there* was.

Meanwhile, I heard footsteps approaching from the shadowy hallway behind the Alchemist's help desk. Two sets of footsteps, in fact. I looked up, already smiling.

With Maximus Archibald was, of course, little Luke.

67.

Luke didn't know me, and he seemed shyer than I'd expected. Then again, he'd spent the last seven days in a hospital having a blood transfusion and recovering from his ordeal. I wondered if such a transfusion would dilute his own magical blood.

"It doesn't work that way, Sam," said the master alchemist, reading my thoughts, exactly like the weirdo he was.

"Of course not," I said. "How silly of me to think such nonsense."

"Not silly, Sam. And certainly not nonsense. Much of what we do here—you and I, and others like us—is done without precedent. Meaning, nothing like us has ever existed in the history of the world. Everything is new. Everything is strange. Everything is open to us. Everything is evolving and expanding and taking on a life of its own. It is all we can do, sometimes, to keep up with this expansion. So I am often learning, side by side with you, even if I might have a few years of experience on you. In this case, I happen to know that the, ah, *life force* in young Luke can never be diluted. Indeed, if anything, it is stronger than ever."

I appreciated that he used words like "life force" around the boy. No reason to freak the kid out more than we had to.

"Take a look for yourself, Sam."

There it was. And the more I looked, the more it formed before me. The silver dragon. It wove slowly through Luke's own brilliant aura. A few years ago, I had seen the exact opposite: a black serpentine creature weaving through the cursed Thurman family for generations.

Now, the silver dragon slithered purposefully, confidently, and continuously. Always moving, always weaving, always undulating. It could have been a sea snake gliding over the ocean floor, around coral and through drifting seaweed. The ghostly serpent's face was often blurred, but sometimes, it coalesced into something frightening and beautiful. Sometimes, I saw a snout and teeth, and a sort of trailing, wispy, Fu-Man-Chu goatee. Once, it even seemed to pause and regard me, before continuing on, moving under his armpit and back around his shoulder, its graceful, thick, tubular body following behind, glowing, undulating.

"What am I seeing?" I asked.

"It is his mark, Sam. It is his bloodline. Your

bloodline, too."

Luke watched us idly, but seemed more interested in the reading room itself, no doubt in the books that contained various levels of evil. In fact, I picked up his thought: he wanted desperately to take down a book on a high shelf that was calling out to him.

"Okay, fine. But I thought I couldn't see my relatives' auras."

"Only your immediate family, Sam. Your kids, sister, parents. The rules can fluctuate, but it generally holds to that."

True. I had seen my son's aura years ago, back when he was dying.

Meanwhile, the Alchemist smiled and asked the boy to take a seat away from us—and, I noted, far away from the darker books. Luke looked at me, looked at Max, then nodded and slipped away, taking with him his magnificent aura and the silver dragon.

"Who makes these rules?"

"The Puppet Master."

"Who the hell is the—"

I saw he was joking and slapped his arm.

He smiled shyly and said, "Remember, many of us are learning as we go. And, yes, sometimes rules can change when there's strong enough intent. Nothing, I have discovered, is set in stone."

A new thought occurred to me. "Does Anthony have an aura?"

"He does. His aura is particularly brilliant,

but..."

"But what?"

"Yes." Max suddenly looked away, drummed his fingers on the wooden help desk. "But your son also harbors something dark that I have not been able to put my finger on."

"The demon in the book," I said. "From last year."

"I'm afraid so, Sam. Something attached to him. Something in this very room, as you recall. Something I do not yet understand."

I'd suspected this. Sometimes, I spotted my son sitting up in bed, at night, staring at nothing. It didn't happen often. Indeed, it happened infrequently enough that I was able to mostly forget that he acted so strangely.

"We'll keep an eye on it. And so will someone else." He paused and let his words hang in the air. The more they hung, the more I knew who he was talking about.

"Ishmael..."

"Yes, your one-time guardian angel."

I might have snorted.

"Don't knock him, Sam. Ishmael has done an admirable job of keeping your son safe, in ways you don't fully appreciate or understand."

"Fine, so he's a saint."

"Hardly, but he is trying to right his wrongs."

"Well, he can just keep righting them for all eternity."

"He just might." The alchemist paused. "Sam,

there's a reason why the dark masters are targeting your son, and why Ishmael works so diligently to protect him."

I nodded, suddenly sickened. "My son carries the mark, the silver serpent."

"Indeed, Sam. With his great strength and powerful bloodline, there is no greater threat to the dark masters. Sam, your son could be the greatest of us all, which is why he has a very big target on his back."

"Are you trying to make me vomit?"

"I'm trying to get you to understand. Anthony Moon is safe enough now. Ishmael looks out for him, and so do you. So do Kingsley and Allison. And me, of course. For now, your son is insulated enough. But when he is a man, he will be mostly on his own. Although Ishmael will never be too far away. But he is only one angel."

"What are you saying?" I asked. I literally had to hold my stomach. Vampire or not, I was feeling like I might heave my earlier lunch.

"As you know, I run an academy for young alchemists. We take them at all ages, although many are in their late teens. They come to us from around the globe. Often, they are orphans. Often, they have endured great turmoil. All are targets for the dark masters. We train them to become all they can be."

"Like the Army."

"Like the Light Warriors they are, Sam."

"And what do these Light Warriors do?" I asked.

"We keep the balance of light and dark. When necessary, we will engage the dark masters directly —"

"You mean vampires."

"And werewolves, and other creatures they choose to return as."

"Like Lichtenstein's monsters?"

"Those and others that defy classification. Powerful others, and they walk—and swim— among you."

"Great."

"We are preparing for what might be the next great battle, although we hope to maintain the peace.."

"Similar to the battle five hundred years ago?"

"Yes, Sam."

"When you guys first banished the dark masters?"

"Correct."

I drummed my long, pointed nails on the help desk, inadvertently pecking holes into the wood. *Oops.* I quit drumming.

"And Luke?" I asked.

"He will be enrolling in our school."

"And it's definitely not Hogwarts?"

"Sadly, no. But it's quite a place, nonetheless. There, his education will continue, with an eye toward the real history of our world, and his place in it. He will be taught alchemy. He will be taught self-defense and mastery in all weapons. He will be shown the hidden mysteries of this world, too.

Some of the greatest secrets will be bestowed upon him. All in due time, of course. We have made all the necessary legal arrangements."

I nodded. "You are adopting him?"

"So to speak. As far as Anthony—"

"What about Anthony?"

"We want him to join us, Sam. Sooner, rather than later."

A range of thoughts and conflicting emotions gripped me, from 'hell, no' to 'maybe it's for the best,' to fear to sadness to anger to missing him already. Finally, I said, "I will need to think about that. FYI, I am leaning toward probably not."

"It could save his life."

I took in some worthless air, let it out. "And where is this school?"

"That information is confidential, Sam. The entity within you could use the intel against us. Surely you understand."

"I understand that you're proposing to take my son away from me to God knows where."

"I know where, and it's perfectly safe and pleasant. Most students have the time of their lives there."

I looked over at Luke, and he looked at me, too. I smiled at him, and he smiled back for the first time. Then, he surprised the hell out of me by getting up and running over and hugging me tightly around the waist. His thoughts and emotions poured out of him. I felt his appreciation for being saved, and his excitement for his new life. He was going to miss his mother, but not the mean men who came to see her. He missed his friend, Johnny, and he wanted to make Max proud. He didn't know me, but he knew I had saved him, and he didn't want to stop hugging me, even as he cried like a girl. *His thoughts, not mine.*

I didn't want him to stop either, and I hugged him back tightly, and let my own tears flow.

Just like a girl.

68.

I'd recently watched *The Martian* with Kingsley. He watched it for the riveting tale of survival. I watched it for entirely different reasons.

As a commercial, of sorts. A commercial that just so happened to star Matt Damon as the pitchman. Hell of a yummy pitchman.

By the end of the harrowing movie, I'd made a decision. A decision I kept to myself. After all, Kingsley tended to worry when I ventured to other planets.

Now, with the latest picture of the Mars Rover firmly planted in my thoughts, I sat comfortably on my living room couch. The kids were asleep. Kingsley was asleep, too. It was a little past two in the morning.

I'm really doing this, I thought.

I really was.

With legs crossed, I rested my hands on my knees. I took in some air, held it, held it some more, and then let it go because I was tired of holding it.

Then, I summoned the single flame.

***

I felt the wind first, and the intense cold. I smelled the ancient dust, not so foreign from our own... but lacking *something*. Something organic, perhaps.

I opened my eyes, and found myself high upon an untouched cliff. The rock beneath me was flat and windblown and blasted smooth over the eons. It was also a richer red than I was expecting.

I didn't bother breathing, although I did inhale some of the scents, some of the dust, some of Mars itself.

The wind was icy and strong. I rocked gently on my perch.

And as the updrafts and crosswinds continued to rock me, and as the smell of something ancient and forgotten permeated my nostrils, I smiled and settled in for the night.

It's good to be me.

The End

About the Author:

J.R. Rain is an ex-private investigator who now writes full-time. He lives in a small house on a small island with his small dog, Sadie. Please visit him at www.jrrain.com.

CPSIA information can be obtained
at www.ICGtesting.com
Printed in the USA
BVHW041205230220
573073BV00013B/303